ALSO BY DANIEL LOGAN

The First Migration
Sense of Wonder Press, 2005

THE LOST PORTAL

THE LOST PORTAL

BY
DANIEL LOGAN

Sense of Wonder Press
JAMES A. ROCK & COMPANY, PUBLISHERS
FLORENCE • SOUTH CAROLINA

The Lost Portal by Daniel Logan

SENSE OF WONDER PRESS
is an imprint of JAMES A. ROCK & CO., PUBLISHERS

The Lost Portal copyright ©2011 by Daniel Logan

Cover Photograph ©2011 by Connie Logan
Cover Design ©2011 by Daniel Logan

Special contents of this edition copyright ©2011
by James A. Rock & Co., Publishers

The cover photo was taken near Sedona, Arizona at the Palatki Ruins in the
Coconino National Forest. It shows a pictograph made by the Sinagua, pre-historic
Native Americans who lived in Arizona more than a thousand years ago.
The Sinagua, whose name translates to "without water," thrived in an arid
land by using check dams and irrigation ditches to water their crops.

Epigraph: "Introduction: A Semidesert with a Desert Heart," from *Cadillac Desert,*
revised and updated by Marc P. Reisner, copyright ©1986, 1993 by Marc P. Reisner.
Used by permission of Viking Penguin, a division of Penguin Group (USA) Inc.

Address comments and inquiries to:
SENSE OF WONDER PRESS
James A. Rock & Company, Publishers
900 South Irby Street, #500
Florence, South Carolina 29501
E-mail:
jrock@rockpublishing.com   lrock@rockpublishing.com
Internet URL: www.rockpublishing.com

ISBN: 978-1-59663-833-4
Library of Congress Control Number: 2010926407
Printed in the United States of America
First Edition: 2011

To Connie

with all my love

—always

ACKNOWLEDGMENTS

Thanks to my wife, Connie, for her beautiful cover photography and for tolerating numerous houseguests during the time I spent writing the story (all the characters in the novel who lived with us for more than a year!). Her thoughts and encouragement were instrumental in the culmination of this work.

My appreciation goes to Rhea Parshall, Robert Shauver and fellow author Suzanne Bailer Smith, *Laughter: A Woman's Best Defense*, for their comments and suggestions on the initial drafts of the manuscript. Thanks, too, to the members of the Noble Writers Group and others in the writing community for their support.

Once again, thanks to my copyeditor, Heidi Newman, whose professional work improved mine.

Finally, I am honored that you have chosen this book to read. I look forward to hearing from you. You may contact me through my website: www.thefirstmigration.com or Connie at: www.conniesphotodesigns.com.

Enjoy!

In the East, to "waste" water is to consume it needlessly or excessively. In the West, to waste water is <u>not</u> to consume it—to let it flow unimpeded and undiverted down rivers.

—*Cadillac Desert* by Marc Reisner

… Nor any drop to drink.

The Rime of the Ancient Mariner
—Samuel Taylor Coleridge

PROLOGUE

People with varying viewpoints were united in awe of the demolition of the Glen Canyon Dam scheduled to take place within the hour. The white concrete dam stood in stark contrast to the red rock canyon walls, like an abandoned drive-in theater screen spoiling the pristine countryside surrounding it. Some in the gathering crowd saw the man-made icon as an obscenity, a middle finger raised to all humanity, responsible for defiling a majestic wilderness, while others marveled at the enormous power it had once generated by controlling the raging and chaotic Colorado River. Still others remembered the boating and recreational opportunities created by the immense Lake Powell it used to hold back.

A half-mile downstream, bleachers were erected at the canyon's edge on each side of the river—now merely a dry wash filled with outcroppings of sage and juniper. A few lucky people with coveted green badges suspended from lanyards around their necks were scrambling to gain the best seats in the V.I.P. section.

I hope they're not lost. Dwy Stewart scanned the growing crowd with concern, trying to spot his parents, Darren and Tracey, who were uncharacteristically late.

The sun, at its highest point in a cloudless, cobalt-blue sky, bathed Dwy and the other onlookers in its oppressive heat. Vendors hawked bottled water, sunscreen and straw hats, working the growing crowd by yipping their wares like overgrown prairie dogs calling out alarms to their colony.

Catching sight of his parents, Dwy stood and waved. Once they saw him, he ran down the steps of the bleachers to greet them. When he neared, he saw his mom had been crying, but she smiled and hugged him, not letting on that anything was wrong. He shook his dad's hand and escorted them to their seats in the president's box. His mom surprised him by sitting on his left, instead of next to his dad, who remained on his right. Always before, his mom and dad would have been seated next to each other. *They've been arguing.* Dwy could sense the strain between them.

Dwy stood and scanned the sky to the southwest, searching for a white-topped helicopter. Checking his watch, he frowned.

"He's going to have to hurry," he said.

"It won't start without him. I promise," Tracey replied. "And anyway, it'll give us a chance to catch up on some things until he gets here."

Dwy smiled. Always the optimist, his mom found the good in anything. "You look great, Mom," he said, ignoring her puffy eyes. "You're incredible. At your age you still turn men's heads. I saw several guys staring at you on the way up."

Tracey laughed. "Some of the old ones maybe, but the only man I worry about is your dad."

Turning toward Dwy, his dad said, "You know, Dwy, your mom isn't old ..."

The whup-whup-whup of a helicopter rotor interrupted Dwy's response.

"… that's him. President Earlman!" Dwy shouted and pointed to the approaching craft.

They watched the Marine helicopter fly over and descend in a graceful curve to a landing pad behind the speaker's platform. Surrounded by Secret Service agents, the former president, out of office for two terms, strode from the helicopter to the podium. Dressed in a chambray shirt and khaki pants, he ignored isolated catcalls and boos and lost no time in beginning his address. A resident of the eastern United States, his mere presence made the more antagonistic westerners in the crowd bristle with anger. He chose his words with care to avoid further provocation.

"It is my duty today to carry out the executive order of President Mitchell. This symbolic action is intended to begin the healing of our wounded nation, before the scars become permanent. President Mitchell asks that environmentalists and industrialists, East and West, Government and Citizens, begin to work together to resolve the conflict that is turning us one against another. By eliminating this symbol of the issue that separates us, let's pledge to work toward the resolution of our differences."

President Earlman paused. Sweeping one outstretched hand toward the dam, he raised the other and pointed to the sky. Media helicopters circled at a safe altitude overhead, like giant, noisy gnats competing with each other for the best view. People took cell phones from their ears and aimed them toward the dam in anticipation, ready to record the sights and sounds to come. Shutters on still cameras clattered as photographers attempted to capture the very first dramatic image. President Earlman abruptly dropped his upraised hand as the signal to begin.

Bursts of light raced up the seams in the face of the dam. Seconds later, due to the lag caused by the distance, sharp staccato explosions could be heard. The echoes ricocheted from the canyon walls until the individual sounds were lost in a cacophony of noise. Quiet reigned for a moment as wisps of smoke from the detonations drifted away.

The first major blast caused shrieks from members of the crowd. Individuals flinched but continued to watch the awesome spectacle. Then a second concussion shook the very earth beneath the bleachers. A third and a fourth followed. Giant chunks of red sandstone at the dam's junctures with the canyon walls were blasted outward and fell in huge arcs to the riverbed below. Five—six—seven—and eight. Still the dam stood, but its connection to the walls had been compromised.

"Get ready," Dwy yelled. "Cover your ears. The bunker busters are next."

Separated by precise intervals, a succession of massive explosions blew apart the dam's face. Each shock wave hit the spectators with a blast of hot air. Then, in slow motion, the dam began to fall in upon itself, becoming obscured by a rising cloud of concrete dust. An enormous, terrifying rumble coursed down the canyon and reverberated off its walls.

But no rush of water came from behind the dam. No flooding torrent cascaded over the rubble. As the powder from the debris dispersed, a clearing image of a blue sky could be seen behind the opening. After being blocked by the Glen Canyon Dam for more than 50 years, a desert breeze swept unimpeded through the rift, carrying the remnants of the gray cloud away with it.

Finally, silence returned.

CHAPTER ONE

SKEETER

"Hold on. Give me a little time, and I'll find it," Darren Stewart, director of NASA's Project TIME, pleaded with the caller on the other end of the line. Shuffling through the prints scattered across his desk, knocking some to the floor, Darren searched for the drawing he needed to answer the question posed by his boss. Cradling the phone between his ear and shoulder, he became agitated about misplacing a diagram that had been right in front of him a minute before. "Let me call you back in a bit," he said and hung up, knocking over his cup of coffee as he did so. It spilled into the prints, ran over the desktop and splashed into his lap. He bolted to a standing position, cursing his own clumsiness and trying in vain to blot the stain from the soaked prints.

"Dr. Stewart?" his secretary asked, peeking into the doorway to see what all the commotion was about. "There's someone here to see you. Says he doesn't have an appointment." Then, noticing the spill, "Oh, what a mess! Let me get you something to clean that up."

Sandy turned from the door and rushed toward the kitchenette.

"Who is it, Sandy?" Darren asked, yelling after her.

"Jim Myers. Says you know of him," Sandy said, returning with a batch of napkins.

"Know *of him*? What does he mean by that? I don't *know* a Jim Myers." Darren took the napkins and tried to soak up the coffee.

"No, he says the two of you have never met, but it's important that he talk to you," Sandy said. Then, staring at his pants with a frown, she continued. "You know, flight attendants recommend you use club soda on spills like that. I think there might be some sparkling water in the fridge."

Darren's shoulders slumped. He stared at the mess on his desk and the stains on his clothes.

His jeans reeked of the burnt amber smell of coffee. *I sure won't impress any visitor right now, but what the hell, it's not my nickel.* "Okay, Sandy. Show him in. Bring me the sparkling water as soon as he leaves."

In a minute, Jim Myers stood before Darren, trying not to show he noticed Darren's predicament. He sported a full, but neatly trimmed, beard and wore rugged clothes, not unlike those a construction foreman would choose. A big man, he had a friendly smile.

"Dr. Stewart, it is an honor," he said, extending his hand.

Darren shook the visitor's hand, noting his rough palms were callused and his grip was strong, like many of the farmers who were Darren's neighbors when he grew up in the Midwest.

"Do I know you?" Darren asked.

The visitor smiled and shook his head. "Not 'Jim Myers', but you may remember me as 'Skeeter.' Skeeter Johnson. It's been more than 15 years, though."

Darren's mind searched to find a memory. Nothing at first, then a fragment came. "Skeeter? You're the guy ... uh, the snow cat driver in the Antarctic who pulled the base commander out of the Anomaly after he lost his sister? You're *that* Skeeter?"

The man laughed. "How many other Skeeters do you know?"

Darren motioned for him to take a seat. "But didn't they put you in protective custody out of a concern you'd leak some of the details?"

"That they did. In case anyone ever tries to convince you otherwise, protective custody isn't some cakewalk where you're given free room and board—it's prison. It's solitary confinement. And it cost me my family, my sobriety, even my career. That's why I'm here today."

"You lost your family?"

"Oh, they were allowed to visit, but I couldn't tell them anything. I knew if I did, they'd be put in the program, too. My two girls couldn't understand why I was in jail, and my wife couldn't handle it, either. Their visits became less frequent until one day, they stopped altogether. I tried to put things back together after I got out, but they had moved on."

"Your sobriety, too?"

"Dr. Stewart, what I saw in the Anomaly shook me. That and the loss of my team members. I struggled to keep it all in perspective, but it changed my life. I knew something big was going down. Then to be locked up for more than four years with no outside contact, no way to know what had transpired, I ended up guzzling anything with alcohol in it after they released me from the program. Before you have to ask, that's what busted my career."

"Well, you look good now."

"I've been through hell, Dr. Stewart, but I'm on the way back. The trouble is, with no identity prior to rehab and A.A., I can't get a decent job. When I heard about your work, I figured it was an area I knew something about. That's why I'm here. I need your help."

"Didn't the government provide you assistance with getting a new start?"

"Yeah, they gave me a new name, an address and a driver's license. That's it. I've never felt so humiliated as when I walked out of that place. No family, no job—not even a place to stay or a car to drive. The only clothes I owned were the ones on my back, and those were government issue. Yes, I saved someone's life, but in so doing, I lost mine."

Darren faced a dilemma. He sympathized with the man standing before him, but it would be a big risk to accept his story without corroboration. He stood and looked out the window at the NASA research complex, now being decommissioned.

"Tell me your qualifications," he said.

"I'm an atmospheric scientist. Top of my class at Texas A&M— but of course, they'll have no record of me. And a sub-major in geology. I'm real good at rocks," Skeeter grinned. "Sorry, that kind of slipped out. But you won't find my geology background anywhere, either."

"That expertise won't help much. Anything else?"

"Well, I've got a lot of experience in heavy equipment—snow cats … dozers … haulers. Stuff like that. I know how to start a diesel engine when it's 50 degrees below zero."

Darren studied the man's face, reaching a decision. He knew he'd have to square things with his construction superintendent. "Okay, Skeeter. You show up back here at my office at 6:30 Monday morning. You bring me some proof you are who you say you are, and we'll talk about a job. But for now, you'll have to excuse me. I have to make my rounds. See you Monday."

"Thanks, Dr. Stewart."

"Good luck to you, Skeeter."

Darren watched him go. Sandy arrived with the sparkling water and a washcloth. He wetted the cloth and began dabbing his pants, not sure whether he was making things better or worse. Finally, he gave up. He told Sandy to order background checks on both a Jim Myers and a Skeeter Johnson. "Start with Texas A&M and search the roster of U.S. geophysical team members in the

Antarctic, too. Use all the personnel security databases we have and go wherever they lead you. It's important. Put everything you've found on my desk before work Monday morning. I'm going to go check on things before I leave."

"I'll do it. Be sure and call your boss back before you go."

"Damn it! I forgot all about him. Thanks, Sandy."

* * *

Darren drove from his office to the hub of the construction activity. He could see huge cranes operating in most of the sectors of the 30-mile-diameter project. He shook his head. The cranes weren't being used to build anything, they were dismantling the facility instead, piece by piece—at least everything above ground. The underground sections were to be mothballed and sealed to prevent vandals from entering. Soon, that portion of the White Sands Missile Range would once again become a barren desert. The arc of the ring closest to his office, Sector 1, was being turned into a museum. Visitors would be able to see and wonder at the complexity of the system that had allowed humans to travel in time—if only on one occasion.

Adjacent to that sector, a magnificent building had been erected to display the machine that had made the huge time facility obsolete. Its upswept, abstract roof resembled a white sand dune. Visible through the museum's enormous and unbroken glass facade was a mammoth time-travel ship. The craft had been brought forward from a period more than 200 million years ago and left to the United States as an expression of gratitude by the Pangaeans, the ancient humans who were indebted to Darren and his team for saving their lives. *Seems like yesterday*, Darren mused. But it had been 15 years, the same 15 years Skeeter mentioned. And, in an eerie parallel of sorts, Darren had lost his family, too. His son Dwy now lived in Sedona and operated a flight tour business. He and Dwy, with little in common, found it difficult to relate to each other, even though they both tried. And Darren's wife, Tracey, well … she was now living in D.C.

"Darren, it's about time you showed up for work," Spence said, interrupting Darren's introspective mood. "How are we going to get this museum built if you don't check on us?"

Darren knew that Spence's lighthearted jab was directed at his hands-on leadership, a trait that usually served him well but could also create problems with his staff. Spence had worked for Darren a long time. Because of that experience, Darren chose Spence to be the project leader for the museum. Still, the two knocked heads over their differences now and then.

"Spence, I'm going to have some new help for you Monday."

"Don't need any help."

"I know, but I've got my reasons. He'll make you a good hand, probably a foreman after you get to know him. Of course, if he doesn't measure up, you can let him go."

"Okay, Darren, as long as I get to make that call, I'll take him."

"Fair enough. Still think you're on schedule?"

"It'll be ready on time. Don't worry about that."

"Fine, I'm going home now. See you Monday."

"See you."

Darren drove out of the complex toward his home on the outskirts of Alamogordo. Once he turned into his driveway, his dog—named for the project's central component, the VME, or "Vimmy"—barreled from the back yard to greet him, panting and tail wagging. Vimmy became obsessed with the coffee stain on Darren's pants, sniffing and snorting the area until Darren pushed his nose away. Then, as always, Vimmy ran to the other side of the car and anxiously whined for Tracey to get out, to no avail. Darren walked around the car, patted the dog on the head and said, "I miss her, too, Vimmy." He opened the door and walked into an empty house, his footsteps echoing in the silence.

CHAPTER TWO

DWY

Dwy Stewart banked the Turbo Cessna and lined it up with the main runway at Sedona. Once over the trees, he cut the power and slipped the plane to a greaser of a landing. After taxiing to the Flight Tours building, he shut the engine down. He jumped out and grabbed a portable step from the storage compartment. Placing it on the concrete beneath the plane's door, he steeled himself for what he knew would come next. Not only would he have to chat with the passengers, but he would also have to answer a multitude of inane questions. Dwy loved the flying portion of the tours—not the post-flight interactions.

Taking in a deep breath, he opened the door and began to help the people deplane. The first, a middle-aged woman, squeezed his arm as he assisted her. "Thanks, Mr. Stewart. Could I have my picture taken with you in front of the plane?"

"Yes Ma'am, but let me get the others out first."

Next, a man with smoke-stained fingers jumped down and began to light a cigarette.

"Sorry, not here, Sir. You can smoke once you get inside."

The man glared at him, placed the unlit cigarette in his shirt pocket and stomped toward the gate mumbling, "Can't believe I spent four hundred bucks on a hot, bumpy ride over the Navajo desert. Nothing in Monument Valley but goats."

Dwy smiled. *They either love it or despise it. I'll never understand what makes the difference.*

A blonde in boots, a pair of tight jeans and wearing enough turquoise and silver jewelry to fill a display case, reached for his hand. "Thanks for the ride, Hon," she said. "I'll be in the Coyote Lounge by myself this evening in case you'd like a drink."

Dwy shook his head. Women were drawn to him. In his early thirties, Dwy remained a free spirit, and his appearance belied the fact that he was an exceptional pilot. His mid-length wavy hair, when tossed by the breeze, revealed a silver earring. A two-day growth of beard shaded his face. His features favored the good looks of his mother. A tattoo on his left shoulder peeked out from the sleeve of his blue cotton shirt. His sandals would be shunned by most aviators. But his smile made men accept him as an individual—and it absolutely melted women. He removed his sunglasses, smiled and gave this woman his standard answer.

"Sorry Ma'am, my mechanic and I are pulling a safety inspection on this bird tonight."

Once the picture-taking ceased and everyone had departed, Dwy inserted the gust locks to keep the wind from damaging the control surfaces. Then he tied the plane down. That night, in truth, he and his young Hopi mechanic, Aaron Eaglecloud, *were* performing a required inspection on the plane. It had to be ready for another tour in the morning. Completing the inspection overnight would mean long hours, but it was a better option than a drink with a peroxide blonde fighting a losing battle with the aging process.

Dwy walked to the small Flight Tours office, a leftover construction trailer converted into a quasi-permanent facility, plastered with signs and banners advertising the business. Aaron acknowledged his entry, saying with a smile, "Your mom called while you were up. Wants you to call back. She's coming for a visit."

Dwy loved both his parents, but he especially enjoyed being with his mom, Tracey. She accepted him for what he was, unlike his dad who always tried to remake him. He had not seen her for a year or so, not since the Glen Canyon Dam demolition. Dwy still had not been able to accept the separation of his parents and hoped someday they would find a way to reconcile.

In his office, Dwy dialed his mom's number.

"Hello, this is Tracey."

"Hi, Mom."

"Dwy, it always makes my day to hear your voice. How are you?"

"Fine. What's going on?"

"I'm going to be in your part of the world later this month. I'd like to see you and get your thoughts on something. All I can tell you about it now is that it's pretty exciting."

Dwy was used to his mom giving him information in stages. When he was growing up, she was a deputy press secretary for former President Earlman—recently named by President Mitchell to head a task force to address the nation's worsening water shortage. His mom never revealed secrets, but Dwy could always tell when she knew more than she was telling.

"Pretty exciting, eh? I know, uh … you're going to run for president," Dwy teased, half worried that it might be true.

"No, I've seen firsthand what that job does to people. I'll tell you more when I see you."

"Okay, Mom, give me a call when you know your schedule. Maybe by then I can give you some news of my own," Dwy said, enjoying the thought of being able to play his mom's game.

"Your news? Oh, Dwy, you're not going to leave me hanging. Tell me more."

"Can't now, Mom. See you when you get here. Bye."

After a long pause, his Mom answered, "Bye."

CHAPTER THREE

THE ANOMALY

Monday morning at exactly 6:30 a.m., Darren heard a knock at his office door. He set aside the papers Sandy had left for him. They were of no help. As predicted, Skeeter Johnson never existed, and there were scant details about Jim Myers.

"Skeeter?" Darren asked, acknowledging the knock.

"The only," Skeeter replied, walking through the door, dressed in a workman's clothes.

Darren appreciated people who were on time. Noticing that the man had nothing with him other than a lunchbox, Darren worried that he had no documents proving his identity. "Sit," Darren said. "And prove to me you are who you say you are."

Skeeter fidgeted with the handle on his lunch box. Then he leaned forward and stared straight at Darren. "Dr. Stewart," he said, "The only way I can convince you of my identity is to tell you something that you already know."

"What do you mean?"

"Well, I know the details of what happened in the Antarctic that accelerated your whole NASA research program on time travel. All the other eyewitnesses are gone. I'm the only one left. There's no way I could cite this information without being the man I say I am."

"Go on, I'm listening," Darren said.

Skeeter took a deep breath, in obvious discomfort about recounting an experience that had led to so much grief. Then he began, "Taylor and I, uh … we were returning to the base camp in a convoy of snow cats, when …"

Skeeter paused and looked at the floor. Darren knew the torment the man felt.

"When we got lost in a storm and I, uh … we saw this city. Yeah, a big city, if you can believe it. Right there in the middle of Antarctica and there was a large aircraft of some kind flying over us. After a few moments, the storm came back and obscured our visibility. We had no choice but to hole up and wait for rescue. I didn't think at the time we were going to survive, but we did, even though the carbon monoxide almost got us. We both passed out from the leak in the cab."

"Keep going," Darren said, aware of Skeeter's obvious struggle.

"Well, when Taylor and I came to, we were in the base infirmary. They questioned us about what we saw. The doc tried to convince us that we had been hallucinating from the carbon monoxide, but Taylor and I knew we had seen something surreal." Skeeter couldn't help but glance at his watch as he continued, "Our watches proved it."

Darren knew he was hearing classified information—facts that no civilian would be able to acquire. He believed Skeeter.

"Your watches?" Darren asked.

"Yeah, they were both off by the exact same amount of time. We knew that wasn't possible without …"

"Without what?"

"Without something affecting them. A strange force. It didn't dawn on us that we had gone through a time shift when we were in there. At least not until later."

"Then what happened?"

Skeeter shifted his position in the chair. "Do I have to?" he asked.

"A little more, that's all."

"Well, the next day, the base commander ordered Taylor and me to drive him and a convoy of hand-picked team members—including his sister—back to where we got lost. With the GPS, we found it. We drove on in. The temperature got warm, like a summer day. The snow disappeared. Taylor and Lynne, uh … the base commander's sister, were in the first cat. We were right behind them, and they drove through a transparent curtain, a vertical mirage of some kind. Nothin' that looked dangerous, just a haze in the air. The two of them just … uh, they just …"

Skeeter stopped. His eyes were focused on a point far outside the window behind Darren. Skeeter swallowed several times. He leaned forward and whispered, "… just turned into fountains of a crimson, bloody mist." He stopped again, reliving the horrible memory.

"I know it's hard, but Skeeter, I need to have you finish it."

"Well, then I slammed on the brakes, but we still hit whatever it was. The front of our cat vaporized, and Jennings' … uh, the base commander's legs … they … I could tell he was seriously hurt. He was screaming something terrible—not only because of his injuries but from seeing what happened to his sister. I started to pull him out, but he refused to let me. He began pounding on me and reaching for his pistol. I knew he didn't want to live. I got the gun away from him, and then he passed out. After that I managed to drag him through what was left of the door. Thank God the doc was there and got tourniquets on his legs. He saved him."

"You're a brave man, Skeeter. This country owed you recognition for what you did."

"They shut me up, instead. And they put me in prison. That's how they paid me."

Both men sat in silence. Neither knew what to say next. Darren could hear his wall clock ticking, as if to remind him of the role time had played in both their lives since the discovery Skeeter and Taylor had stumbled upon. Darren decided the moment had come for Skeeter to go forward.

"Skeeter, have a cup of coffee with me. I'll bring you up-to-date on what happened since your encounter. After that, Sandy has a few papers for you to sign. Then I'm going to take you to your new boss. You've got the job."

* * *

Darren's Jeep jolted over the rough terrain as he drove Skeeter to meet Spence. The two had little to say during the ride. Darren liked the man, or at least what he knew of him so far—especially his authenticity and straightforward manner of speaking. Darren pulled up in front of the construction trailer and hopped out, calling for Skeeter to follow. Spence came outside to greet them.

"Morning, Darren," he said. "Is this the new guy?"

"Yeah, Spence, this is Skeeter—Skeeter Johnson."

"Skeeter?"

"It's a long story," Skeeter said, stepping forward to shake hands. "I'll tell you over coffee sometime."

"Okay, then Skeeter it is. Darren says you've got heavy equipment experience."

"Some, but nothing in this hot weather," Skeeter replied with a chuckle.

"Do you see that Caterpillar D7 dozer over there?"

"Yep."

Spence took a set of keys from his pocket and tossed them to Skeeter. They jangled as Skeeter caught them in midair with a reflexive grab.

"You take that dozer over to the mound to the right of the museum foundation, and you start spreading the dirt over the concrete that covers the underground works. I want the surface looking like a fairway when you're finished. Don't hit anything, either."

"Okay."

"Hardhat's in the seat. I'll check your work when you're done. If I'm satisfied, I'll assign you to a crew. And don't worry about running out of work. We've got 360 sectors to do—exactly one hundred miles."

Skeeter turned toward Darren.

"Thanks," he said. "I'm indebted to you."

"You may be indebted to him," Spence said, "but your ass is mine until this job's completed. We've got only three months before the grand opening."

"I'm on it."

CHAPTER FOUR

THE FIRE-SHIP

Inside the hangar, halogen lights bathed the aircraft in a blue-white gleam, interrupted only by the shadows of the two men pulling the panels from the engine, wings, and fuselage for the required inspection. The men moved in a deliberate, no-lost-motion manner. The Native American held the FAA license to perform the maintenance and certify the plane's readiness for flight. In a reversal of roles, Dwy, the owner of the company, now performed tasks at the young man's direction to comply with the regulations.

Dwy didn't mind, because he liked the Hopi technician, who grew up on the reservation under the tutelage of his father, a medicine man. Aaron had the spiritual skills of his father but aspired to the field of aviation instead. He left the reservation and became an excellent aircraft mechanic, yet remained faithful to the ancient beliefs. Sometimes his spiritual self surfaced in the most unexpected ways. His family relationships had been strained and nearly broken by his departure. He found himself in a constant struggle to mend them. Yet Aaron's approach to aircraft mainte-

nance was all business. Dwy marveled that Aaron could perform
his work without getting a spot of oil or grease on his long-sleeved
red shirt. His headband kept his black hair neatly out of the way.
When the Hopi would open a drawer in his toolbox, the wrenches
and other tools could be seen arranged in a neat, geometrical pattern so that any missing tool would be obvious—and would not
be left by mistake inside the airplane. As they worked, the two
had an opportunity for a kind of conversation not possible in a
usual business setting.

"Aaron, I've always wanted to know something about you."

"What's that, Boss?"

"How does a Native American raised on a reservation get a
name like Aaron?"

Aaron grunted, and then laughed. "Aaron is only my name,
the name I use when I'm in the Anglo world. I didn't have one of
your names before I left the res. I picked Aaron after seeing a man
named that in a soap opera. I thought Anglos would like it."

"Well then, what about Eaglecloud?"

"Oh, that's not my name, it's who I am."

Dwy didn't understand. He paused in his work and gave Aaron
a quizzical look.

"You see, our identity is defined by some event in our youth,
unique to us. Just after I was born, an eagle flew over me. My
mother saw me smile and reach for the eagle. She said I watched
it soar all the way to the clouds. So she calls me 'Eagle-To-The-
Clouds.' I shorten it a little when I'm in your world."

"Is that where your fascination with aircraft came from—eagles?"

"Yes. When I was a young boy, I saw my first plane. It looked
like a silver eagle to me. Ever since, I've loved planes."

"But you're terrified of flying in one. Why?"

Aaron shrugged his shoulders and glanced to the ground.
"When I grew up, I realized that eagles don't crash—planes do.
I'll work on them, but I only fly on the ones I've certified, and
then only when absolutely necessary for my job."

"Well, the ones you work on better not crash."

"I pray to the spirits that they won't," Aaron said. After a pause, he added, "But the spirits have told me my ancestors came from an aircraft that *did* crash. For some reason, the spirits speak to me about it, but they do not tell my father. He scoffs when I talk about it. He thinks my mind has been poisoned by the Anglos."

Dwy never ceased to be amazed by Aaron's connection to the lore of his culture. His beliefs, though strange when viewed by those outside the Hopi culture, were the core of his being.

"We Hopi believe we are the descendants of the Anasazi, or as we call them, 'Hisatsinom'—the Ancient Revered Ones. We believe our ancestors were once part of a great civilization that lived underground. No disease or wars. One day, they climbed to the surface of the earth through an opening called a 'sipapu.' They did not like living on the surface and tried to return but a coyote had hidden the opening with a stone. With all the stones looking alike in the desert, the opening was lost forever and the Hisatsinom had to learn to live on the surface. It was a hard life."

Dwy dropped a bolt to the floor. With a metallic ping, it bounced back into the air and spun, finally falling back to the concrete and rolling under the plane. On hands and knees, Dwy brushed his fingertips across the floor to find it.

Bolt in hand, he stood. "But what does that story have to do with an aircraft that crashed?"

"I don't know. It's not part of the Hopi culture, but the spirits have told me that the aircraft was a shiny ship that flew on a beam of fire under the stars as they changed positions in the sky. They said my ancestors were all aboard it when it went down. Most survived. I think the fire-ship and the opening from under the ground are somehow tied together."

Darren shook his head.

"Okay, Aaron, I've heard enough of your spirit stuff for a while. We need to get on and finish this plane. Otherwise, we'll be here all night."

Aaron didn't stop. "It's near here, somewhere."

"What?"

"The fire-ship. But it's lost. Probably forever."

* * *

Darren waited in his Jeep for Skeeter at the end of the work shift, attending to some work on his laptop as dusk approached. An hour later, he saw Skeeter walk through the construction gate. Darren waved him over for a ride back to the office. Even after a long day wrestling with the dozer, Skeeter looked fresh and alert.

"Get in. I'll give you a lift to your car," Darren said.

"Thanks."

"You still got some energy left? I'll show you something before you leave."

"Let's do it."

Darren drove to the entrance of the museum. He unlocked the main door and the two men stepped inside, walking with care in the darkened lobby. Darren opened a locked panel, turned on a main switch and began flipping circuit breakers. The inside of the building came to life, illuminated by brilliant lights. Overwhelming the cavernous interior was a gigantic, circular craft, suspended from massive trusses in the ceiling and pitched forward and banked in a manner that gave it the appearance of being in flight. The black, curved wall behind the display shimmered with pinpoints of lights, simulating the starry background of a night sky and giving the observer the sense of being in three-dimensional space.

"This is what your discovery in the Antarctic led us to," Darren said. "A time-ship from Pangaea, a super-continent that existed on earth 200 million years ago. You caught a glimpse of it when you stumbled into the Anomaly. On that continent, we found a whole civilization in trouble that we helped relocate to the future. As an expression of gratitude, they left this ship for us to study."

Skeeter, transfixed, stared at the immense black vehicle, its gleaming surface giving it an intimidating appearance. Mixed in with the clean, new smell of construction materials was a pungent, hot metallic odor.

"What is it I'm smelling?" he asked.

"When the craft reached its maximum speed, the very outer layer of the skin atomized in a sacrificial manner, and the surface became translucent. Once it cooled, some of the scorched particles solidified and re-bonded, but they continue to leach out into the atmosphere. Since we've had the circulating air blowers turned off for several days, the odor is noticeable. It'll go away when the blowers are back on. The metal skin is an alloy so sophisticated we don't know how it was made, but we're close to understanding it."

Skeeter could see portholes at the front. On the top surface, in front of the windows, unrecognizable characters were spread through an arc of 45 degrees.

"For the love of God," Skeeter said. "I'd heard about this, but never dreamed it was so awesome." He walked to the front of the ship and looked at the letters, trying to decipher them. Squinting did him no good.

"Roughly translated, the ship's name is the 'Spirit of the Ages.' It could carry 1,000 people, and it was the same kind as those in the fleet of time-ships that were refueled here at this very port on the way to the future. This ship brought Dwyer, the Pangaean emissary, to us. He helped bring a peaceful resolution to a potential conflict between our two civilizations. Dwyer—we named our son after him—lived near here until the 'The First Migration', as we called it, had been completed. Dwyer took the last vessel to the future and left this one as a gift to our people."

"What have you learned about it so far?"

"We've reverse-engineered most of its propulsion and time-warping systems. We still don't understand how they managed to transform matter into a zero-mass state to eliminate the problems created by inertia. Some of the components are so complex it will be years, maybe even decades, before we can understand them. We will continue working in this museum as necessary while it's on display. Visitors will be able to observe the actual process in real time."

"Will it ever fly again?"

"The Pangaeans made sure it couldn't. They destroyed the link necessary for the systems to activate. They didn't want to chance that someone, less benevolent than us, might use the ship to visit them in the future. We would not do that, but the ability to activate the systems would accelerate our learning process."

"A shame."

Darren thought a minute before continuing. He had to be able to trust Skeeter implicitly. He decided he could.

"We know there's an older ship here in the United States. We just don't know where the ship is."

"Incredible! How do you know that?"

"According to Pangaean history, a time-ship crash-landed in this region of the country around 400 A.D. It carried nearly a thousand people trying to reach the 21st century. Something went wrong, and they had to make an emergency landing in the desert. Most survived, but they were far short of the time period they were targeting."

Skeeter turned back toward Darren, amazed at what he was hearing.

"What happened to them?" he asked.

"They were forced to live off the land and in a few generations they reverted to a primitive people. The real history of their origins faded into legend. You know them as the Anasazi."

"Jesus, man, what happened to their ship?"

"We don't know. It's never been found."

Darren didn't mention Dwyer's comment about the lost ship. "Find it," Dwyer said before departing, "and you'll uncover the secret of our origins—and of your own."

Darren motioned Skeeter to the door and began shutting down lights. He pulled the main switch, and the building became dark once more.

CHAPTER FIVE

TRACEY

"Hello?"

"Darren, uh ..."

"Tracey? Is that you?"

"Oh, Darren. This wasn't a good idea."

Silence.

Darren paused, awaiting his wife's next words. He hadn't talked with her for months, and now she was calling him. Whatever the reason, he loved hearing her voice, but a part of him dreaded what she might say next. What if she had decided to make their separation permanent, or worse, pursue a ...

"Don't say anything, Tracey, at least not for a minute. I'll not argue with you or push you. I want for one brief moment to remember our phone conversations the way they once were."

"Oh, Darren, me too."

"Tracey, I miss you. I get up each day hoping it will be the day we try to get back together."

"Please stop, Darren. I have some news. That's why I called."

Once again, Darren worried that the news might not be good.

"Tell me."

"Well, I'm coming to Sedona to visit Dwy the last weekend of this month. I want to talk with you then. Could you come see me there?"

"Are you sure?"

"Of course I am."

"I'll be there. Do you want me to stay over at Dwy's place?"

"I think it's best for now that you not stay with us."

Again, a long silence.

Darren wanted to have some idea of her news. But he knew she didn't appreciate being pressed. He tried, anyway.

"Good news, I hope," he said.

"I think so, but we'll talk more when we're in Sedona. I have to go now," she said. "Good bye, Darren."

"Bye, Trace. I love you."

A click indicated the connection had been broken. Darren listened a moment, then hung up the phone. He looked at Vimmy lying in front of the fireplace, thumping his tail on the floor in response. Walking outside on the patio, Darren stared at the night sky to clear his head.

He knew he'd caused a mess—his separation from Tracey and his relationship with his only son—and swore to find a way to make things right. After all, he didn't have the excuse of being in a protective custody facility to blame for the loss of his own family. *It's my own damn fault*, he thought. He resolved that when Tracey visited later in the month he would take steps to reconcile their issues—or failing that, he would request they get divorced. He couldn't stand this never-never land of separation.

CHAPTER SIX

SHIPROCK

After work the next day, Darren caught Skeeter on the way out the gate and asked if he still had an interest in geology.

"Hell yes!" Skeeter said, "as long as I don't have to dig through a mile-deep ice pack to find rocks. I'm kind of burned out looking for them that way."

"Next weekend, we're closed for the Memorial Day holiday. I'm going to take my Jeep and camping gear and go north to the San Juan River to do some trout fishing. There're some amazing geological formations nearby. Want to go?"

"Well, yeah, but I don't have any gear."

"I've got enough for both of us."

"I wouldn't be a bother?"

"No, I'd enjoy the company and the chance to get to know you better. After all, we've both traveled through time warps—even though your trip was unintentional. And I guess I'd like to know more about your family."

Darren didn't expand on that point. But he knew that each of them was hurting in similar ways. Maybe they could learn something from each other.

"I'm game."

"Okay, then, we'll leave after work on Friday," Darren said.

* * *

The Jeep lurched and bounced on the desert road, mess kits and fly rods rattling in the back. Vimmy panted incessantly from excitement, and he paced from one side to the other in a tortuous path over the gear to poke his head out the open windows. A layer of dust now coated the interior, and both men were tired from the long day's drive. The deepening twilight made it difficult for Darren to find the road to his favorite fishing spot. Finally, just before dark, he spotted the turnoff and slowed the Jeep to a crawl, the transmission whining in protest as he descended down the grade to the river. At the river's edge, he braked to a stop, a dust cloud swirling around them.

Darren hopped out and walked the few paces to the river. Vimmy scrambled out and began tearing around the area in increasingly larger circles, sniffing the ground and rooting through the bushes. Darren shook his head in disbelief as he watched the dog run across the riverbed.

"Damn," he swore.

"What?" Skeeter asked.

"Nothing but a dry wash—sand, not even a muddy bottom."

Skeeter walked up beside Darren and laughed. "When's the last time you were here?" he asked.

"Just a few years," Darren answered. Then, after thinking, he added, "Well, maybe, uh … five. No, let's see. We brought Dwy here when he was 20. Shit, it's been over 10 years."

"What'd you expect?" Skeeter asked. "Twenty-five years of extended drought, the last seven being extreme. Hell, rivers and lakes everywhere on this side of the Continental Divide are drying up; the president has declared most of the Western Slope of the Rockies in a state of emergency, and you expected your favorite fishing hole to be just the way it was 10 years ago?"

"Something like that," Darren answered with the beginnings of a grin.

"Well then, what kind of bait are you planning to use?"

Darren let out a heartfelt laugh like he hadn't experienced for a long time. When he settled down, he turned his face into a serious expression.

"I don't know," he said. "What do you recommend for sand trout?"

Skeeter smiled in response. Since darkness had now settled in, Darren suggested they set up their tents, stay overnight, then drive west in the morning along the river until they found water—if they *could* find it.

Over the campfire, the two men talked at length about their experiences with time travel. Skeeter opened up more about the emotional stresses he had gone through. The more he talked, the more he shared, releasing the agony that had been bottled up for so long. Darren brought Skeeter up to date on his and Tracey's encounters with the Pangaeans.

* * *

After breakfast the next morning, with the gear and Vimmy once again packed into the back seat, Darren and Skeeter drove west but failed to find any spot where the former river contained water. Becoming more discouraged with each passing mile, Darren decided that if they reached the Four Corners area and still had no luck, it would be time to call it quits.

Rounding a bend, they came upon diamond-shaped, orange signs warning of the road being closed ahead and recommending a detour to the south. Darren ignored the signs, figuring the road had fallen into disrepair and thinking he could get through with his 4-wheel drive. He came up to a chain-link fence across the road with "WSP Construction" and "No Trespassing" signs posted on it. Beyond the fence he could see cranes and heavy equipment busy at work. Clusters of pipe sections large enough to drive a car through were scattered all over the area. The dust created by graders reduced the visibility to almost zero, even though tankers were busy spraying water on the ground behind them.

"What are they building, a new road?" Skeeter asked.

"No, I think it's part of the Ogallala project," Darren said.

"Ogallala?"

"Yeah, WSP, uh … Western Slope Pipeline was awarded the contract by the city of Los Angeles to build a line across the Continental Divide to tap the Ogallala Aquifer and pump water from it to the San Juan into the Colorado River basin. I didn't realize they were this far along."

"Okay, I'll bite. I've been on the other side of the mountains and never saw a drop. The desert there is as bad as here. How are they going to get water over there?"

"It's deep underground. The Ogallala Aquifer was created during the last ice age—more than 10,000 years ago—when water seeped into the earth. It's huge. It stretches from South Dakota to Texas. It's the water the farmers have used for their crops for the last century. But protests have led to riots over this project."

"What's the deal?"

"Two things. First of all, it's about water rights, the old issue that has triggered violence in the West since the homesteaders settled here and restricted the free range access of cattle to water. Second, the aquifer doesn't have any way to replenish itself. Once that water's gone, it's gone forever. The farms on the east side of the divide will dry up like they did during the dust bowl. It's a potential life or death issue for both sides. If Los Angeles doesn't find additional sources of fresh water, the city could collapse. I can't even imagine the diseases and social upheaval that would take place. And none of the states on the eastern side will sit by and see their water taken from them. People have gone to war over less."

A security guard approaching the fence from the inside caught the two men's attention. Vimmy bristled at the German Shepherd the man had with him.

"Easy, Vimmy," Darren said.

"Morning, gentlemen," the guard said.

"Morning," Darren replied.

The guard opened a pedestrian gate and walked to the side of the car. The two dogs glared at each other. Vimmy tensed and his whole body awaited a command from Darren. Vimmy could become very defensive whenever someone approached. He began to growl.

"Easy, boy, it's okay," Darren said, trying to get Vimmy to settle down.

The guard looked at the two men and scanned the inside of the car, but he didn't come any closer.

"Just checking that you boys weren't taking any pictures or anything like that. We have to be pretty careful. Last week, we caught two protesters inside the fence lugging a case of dynamite."

"No, we're just trying to find some water for trout fishing," Darren said. "I didn't even know you were here."

The guard laughed. "Trout fishing! Hell, this river doesn't even get damp until it joins the Colorado way up ahead. And it doesn't begin to pool until you get to what's left of Lake Powell; that's why they blew the dam up a year or so ago. The river had dropped below the intakes and they wanted to get it flowing again. But it's still too low even there for good fishing. Where've you two been?"

"Uh, we've been busy at other things," Darren answered.

"Well, those things must've been pretty important. I've got to go drive the fence line now, and I'd appreciate it if you two would move on. It makes my boss nervous when someone's this close. You see that camera over there? He's been watching and listening to everything we've said. Okay?"

"We'll head on. Doesn't sound like there's going to be any good fishing this trip, anyway."

Darren backed the Jeep a few yards, then turned around and drove away. After a mile or two, Vimmy became his old self again, excited by the passing scenery.

"Okay, Skeeter, since trout fishing is out, we're going to take a look at those rock formations I promised."

"Great! I'll bet they'll still be there," Skeeter said. "Rocks hang around a lot better than water."

* * *

Within an hour's drive, an intimidating monolith appeared on the horizon, shimmering like a mirage in the afternoon sun. The dark silhouette rose skyward from the desert terrain. As Skeeter concentrated on the formation, the ghostly image played tricks on his mind, but it resembled a nineteenth-century clipper ship in full sail. The black rock gave it a sinister look.

"Shiprock Peak," Darren said. "In the mid-1800s, the formation served as a landmark for travelers. But long before that, it had its origins in Native American lore. The Navajo call it 'Tsé Bit' A'í', he explained, stumbling a bit with the difficult pronunciation, "or, in English, 'Rock With Wings.' To them it's a sacred monolith, the legend being that a huge bird swept up the Diné—the Navajo people—and deposited them on top, saving them from their enemies. But, one day, when the men were down below tending the fields, a storm came over and lightning broke off the trail to the summit. The women, children and old men perished from starvation. The Navajo do not want anyone climbing the peak and disturbing the spirits of those who were lost."

Skeeter gazed at the rock through the eyes of an experienced geologist. He saw a line of intermittent outcroppings, much smaller than the peak, leading up to its base. He recognized its origin.

"A volcanic core," he said. "Once, it was an active volcano, but the lava inside cooled and solidified. Eventually the volcano eroded away, leaving that solid monolith. These smaller structures are called 'dikes.' They come from magma oozing through a crack in the earth's surface and cooling in place. Awesome formation! I'm glad I came."

Darren drove to a fence line and parked the Jeep at a gate.

"Come on," he said, grabbing a tote bag. "Whoa, Vimmy. Not you. You stay here in the car."

The two men walked a mile on a path through the desert to an eight-sided adobe dwelling, a hogan, surrounded by long-haired, cashmere goats, their curly horns looking like twisted slats of bleached wood. The clanking of a bell around the neck of one of the goats drew the attention of the hogan's resident, who came out to greet them. Darren had visited the area several times in the past and knew the Navajo man well. Darren rustled around in his tote bag and withdrew a tin of tobacco.

"Warren, my friend, I brought you tobacco," Darren said. "This is Skeeter. He studies rocks, and he's come with me to see Shiprock Peak."

The Navajo smiled and accepted the tobacco, taking a few pinches and packing the wad inside his lip with his thumb. Warren held the grazing permit for the land Shiprock Peak was on and Darren would need his permission to go further.

"We'd like to drive up to the base of the formation, but not climb it. We respect the sacred grounds above. We won't be long. If we find trash—bottles or paper—left by other visitors, we'll clean it up as a token of our appreciation."

"You are always welcome, Darren. Others don't even bother to seek permission, and we must chase them away. But you, you walked among the Anasazi. Even though they were our ancestral enemies, they were a great people. I am grateful that I know you."

"Thanks, Warren, you honor us."

Darren and Skeeter returned to the Jeep. The trail to the base of the peak was rough and, in places, deep with drifted sand. As it rose above the surrounding terrain, the vista became magnificent. At the trail's end, the men got out. Skeeter walked to the vertical face of the lava and placed his hands against its sun-warmed surface, sensing millions of years of history beneath his palms. Vimmy followed him and sniffed the rock, too, wagging his tail.

"Dr. Stewart," Skeeter said, "you have no idea what this does for the soul of a geologist."

Darren pulled a pair of binoculars from his tote bag and began scanning the desert floor. "Remember, there's a time-ship here somewhere. One made by ancient men, but it's never been found. Maybe someday it'll be discovered."

Darren believed the ship to be nearby. He shared the view of a number of reputable scientists that the ship carrying the colonists might lie within a triangular area defined by three major Anasazi sites—Mesa Verde, Chaco Canyon and Canyon de Chelly. Shiprock Peak was near the center of this area. Yet satellite imagery had failed to find any sign of the ship. Nor had hundreds of history buffs turned up a single clue.

"Do you think it's out in the open? Metal wouldn't last very long, even in this dry climate."

"According to legend, the survivors covered it with stones, so it wouldn't give away their location. It's buried somewhere. And the metal used in its construction would withstand corrosion and not necessarily show up on a satellite's ground-penetrating radar. I believe the ship is still intact. It's like many small plane crashes. After the initial search turns up nothing, a lone hunter will stumble on the site years later. Just imagine the treasure of information it would contain."

Darren handed the binoculars to Skeeter, who studied the land that stretched before him all the way to the horizon.

"I can see them digging the trench in the pipeline right-of-way," Skeeter said. "Look at the damn scar they're making!"

Handing the binoculars back to Darren, Skeeter turned back toward the peak and pulled a camera from his pocket. "Do you think Warren would mind me taking a few shots?"

"Not at all. Go ahead."

Skeeter snapped some photographs of the peak from its top to its base. His attention then zeroed in on a solitary pile of huge chunks of lava, scrambled like boulders in a giant's playground.

He walked to the outcropping, withdrawing a small tool bag as he neared. Darren heard the intermittent tapping and clinking of a hammer and chisel.

"What the hell are you doing, Skeeter?"

"Taking samples. This looks pretty interesting."

"Rocks?"

"Rocks to you, maybe, but history to me. Something's not quite natural, here."

The chinking and plinking continued while Skeeter went from rock to rock. He began to hum in time with the staccato tapping, reminiscent of Lionel Hampton on the vibes—never one of Darren's favorites. Finally, he completed his exploration and returned, carrying several sample pouches, neatly tied and labeled.

"I think it's you," Darren said.

"What?"

"That's not natural."

Darren laughed and glanced at his watch. He got a trash bag from the Jeep and began stuffing litter into it. Skeeter joined him, and in no time they had the area cleaned. Once finished, Darren opened two cans of soda and offered one to Skeeter. They sat in the shade of the rock and sipped the drink.

Skeeter broke the silence. "Your wife left you?"

Darren wasn't used to discussing his personal relationships with other people and didn't know for sure how to respond. He chose to be open. "About a year ago. My job's here, and her work is in D.C. We didn't seem to have enough time with each other. Neither of us wants anyone else, but the conflicting pressures created problems for us. At first, it was just easier when we were apart. Before long, we got comfortable with being apart. Then we decided it might be better if we stayed that way."

Skeeter remained silent for a minute, refusing to offer judgment on Darren's comments. "Your boy?" he asked.

"That's another story. Dwy and I are very different. He grew up resenting the regimen I imposed on his life. He rebelled. After each disagreement we had, he found a new body part to have pierced or tattooed in retaliation. He's done well in his business, but he has no love of science or the things I've accomplished. He's close to his mother. He and I try to get along, but it's always an effort."

"I'd have done anything to get my family back—*anything*," Skeeter said. "But my wife remarried before I got out. There's still some hope I can reconnect with my girls again, if I can get my life in order. At least that's my goal. But you're lucky; you haven't lost your wife, not yet, anyway. You can still see her and talk to her. I'm not one for giving advice, but I'll tell you straight. If I were you, I wouldn't be spending a holiday weekend out in the middle of nowhere bumming around with some over-the-hill geologist. I'd be going after her. And your son, uh … he's probably a whole lot more like you than you give him credit. That's why the two of you butt heads. He may be closer to his mother, but I'll bet he loves you, too. That's all I'll say."

Skeeter crushed his soda can in his hand and tossed it into the trash bag. Darren, stunned by Skeeter's words, remained silent for a few moments. After thinking about Skeeter's comments, he picked up the bag and said, "Not only are you a good geologist, you're a pretty fair psychologist. I appreciate your thoughts, but we'd better be heading back now. On the way, I want to hear some more about your daughters. Sounds like I may get to meet them someday."

Darren whistled for Vimmy and held the door open for him.

"Come on, boy, we're going home," he said.

The dog didn't know—or care—that they had a long drive ahead. He just loved the ride.

CHAPTER SEVEN

THE
COMMISSION

President Mitchell stood before the individuals assembled in the conference room. Acknowledging each person seated at the table with a glance, he smiled when he saw Tracey. She nodded her head and smiled in return. Nearly a dozen altogether, the group represented the best in their fields. From the Department of the Interior and the Corps of Engineers to industrial giants and academia—even military brass—the members had nearly unlimited resources at their command. Aides and deputies sat behind the principal members, whispering information back and forth.

Tracey had been selected for her press secretarial background since communications would be at the forefront of the challenge that lay before the task force. With a sense of apprehension, she turned to the two interns seated behind her, one a college major in political science and the other a journalist. She leaned toward them and whispered, "This is an opportunity of a lifetime. I'll need your total commitment. You will have no life outside this work until we achieve our goals. Make me proud ..."

President Mitchell's opening remarks interrupted her. She turned her attention back to him.

"There is no good news," he said. "No silver lining, no light at the end of the tunnel, and there's no cavalry coming to save us." He let those comments sink in, once again looking into the eyes of individual committee members.

"Let me share with you the ominous information I have about our situation. First, we are in our twenty-fifth year of drought in this country, and most of the area west of the Continental Divide—the Western Slope—has been at the extreme level the last seven years. We've declared six states disaster areas and more will follow."

Looking at the U.S. Forest Service member, he continued. "The incidence of wildfires has tripled since 2010 with last year's loss of life and property from the Santa Ana fires being a tragic record."

"Wells in the San Fernando Valley are salting up because we've recycled the water through the ground too many times. Prices for produce have skyrocketed, creating enormous inflationary pressure, and unemployment is at levels we've not seen for decades."

The president paused and sipped from a bottle of water. He gestured toward the appointee from the Centers for Disease Control.

"Hospitals in the United States are reporting a resurgence of cholera and dysentery, diseases we thought we had eradicated in the late 1800s."

He continued, the emotion building in his voice.

"All major cities in the West have implemented stringent water rationing plans. Green lawns are a thing of the past, as well as clean cars. Fire departments are fighting low water pressure at every fire, and just last week, one of the nuclear plants in Arizona was forced to shut down because of a lack of cooling water. The blackout extended across four states, and for a while we worried that it might take down the whole western grid."

He laid down his notes and walked to the side of the lectern, leaning his right arm upon it.

"But it gets worse. Climatologists see no change in the weather pattern that has led to all this.

The city of Los Angeles is against the ropes, losing 10,000 residents a day. People on the western side of the Continental Divide are seeking respite from the drought. Other cities will soon follow.

"But resistance to that movement is growing. Already there are vigilante groups at the Texas border observing—and intimidating—persons they see trying to cross back over the 100th Meridian. Texans are against outsiders coming into their state and taking water. 'Crossbacks' is the scornful term they use for them. There have been a number of skirmishes and even violent exchanges leading to fatalities. And Texas is not alone. We've heard similar concerns in Colorado and Wyoming."

The president walked to former President Earlman's side and placed a hand on his shoulder. "All this is why I announced the formation of this task force last week and named President Earlman as its leader. His choice of members has been second to none. Your charge is to develop a program to resolve this crisis—a crisis that could dwarf the Great Depression and the Civil War combined if it is unabated. You are the good news, the silver lining and the light at the end of the tunnel. I hope you can become the cavalry. Thanks for serving, and God be with you. I give you now your leader, President Earlman."

With those final words, President Mitchell left the room. President Earlman sat motionless for a moment. Nearing his 80th birthday, his white hair lent him the aura of a man of wisdom. His countenance reminded people of that of a favorite uncle, a trait supported by his personality; "Uncle" remained his Secret

Service designation. Yet those around him knew that beneath that exterior lay a demanding, accept-no-excuses manner of leadership. Woe to those who sought forgiveness for work not meeting his expectations.

He spoke in a measured tone. "Thanks for accepting my invitation to serve. It is my hope that you will look back upon your contribution to this task with pride. However, that is for you to decide—not me. My priorities are that we meet the charge given us by the president in the most timely manner possible, even though that work will take its toll on you. Here are my objectives for this group."

The video screen came to life with four bullet-pointed objectives outlined on a blue background.

"First, we must overcome enormous engineering challenges and provide additional sources of water. There will be serious social and political consequences because of these efforts. No choice will be without extreme downsides.

"Second, we must provide emergency relief to those who need it—medical, technical expertise, relocation assistance and so forth. One-third of our population is expected to become severely impacted by this crisis, perhaps more.

"Third, we must preserve civil order, a job that will become increasingly difficult.

"Finally, we must offer hope by communicating our progress. We will be open about our work and the issues we face as a nation."

President Earlman concluded, "That's our task. You have in front of you a briefing paper. Study it until you not only understand the problem we face, but you can personally identify the impact it will have on you and your family. We are all in this together. We will meet again next week and continue our work. At that time I will expect an outline of initial proposals from each of you. That is all for today."

President Earlman closed his notebook, stood and motioned for Tracey to join him.

She wasted no time. "Yes, Sir," she said.

"Tracey, it's nice to be working with you again, but I wish the circumstances were different."

"You can count on me, Sir."

"That's why I chose you. Now, what progress have you made on the assignment I gave you last week?"

President Earlman had asked Tracey to begin setting up an annex of the White House in Phoenix. He had offered her any resource she needed to make it happen. He planned to base the task force there, so the members would live in the area affected by the worsening drought. And he believed that President Mitchell should spend a significant amount of his time there also, so people on both sides of the Continental Divide could be reassured that the president understood their needs and would represent their interests.

"Mr. President, I have things moving already. We have located a federal building near the center of town that would work well. Architects have developed plans for renovating the interior and for installing the security and communications hardware. I'll be there next week to verify that the work is progressing well. We plan to dedicate the facility on the 4th of July."

"I knew you were a good choice. Thanks, I'll see you next week."

President Earlman walked out of the room, relying on a cane to ease the pressure on his arthritic hip.

CHAPTER EIGHT

SEDONA

After the short flight from Phoenix, Dwy's plane touched down at the Sedona airport with a slight chirp of the gear due to the crosswind.

"Nice," Tracey said as the plane rolled down the runway. "You inherited your dad's touch."

"It's about the only thing I inherited from him."

"No, I'm *not* going to let you do that to yourself or to your dad," Tracey said. "You've got his smile, his sense of humor, his wavy hair, his thirst for adventure and—whether you'll admit it or not—his brilliant mind. On the opposite side, you've also got his single-minded stubbornness."

"Okay, maybe you're right. But didn't I get anything from you?" Dwy teased.

"My looks, of course," Tracey said, smiling and grasping Dwy's forearm. She knew, but rarely let on, that even in her late fifties, she was still stunning.

Dwy taxied to the apron in front of his office, shut down the engine and helped his mom out of the plane. Aaron greeted them and secured the aircraft.

"Loloma, Mrs. Stewart," he said, offering a friendly greeting in his native language.

"Loloma, Aaron. Good to see you again," she replied. She chatted with Aaron in perfect Hopi, even with the difficult inflections, complimenting him on his abilities as an aircraft mechanic. Ever the master of communications, Tracey prided herself on her fluency in many languages.

Aaron beamed with a big grin. He liked both the Stewarts and always enjoyed Tracey's visits. He grabbed the luggage and walked to the car with the pair.

"Goodbye, Mrs. Stewart."

"Nú tus payni, Aaron," Tracey said, returning his farewell.

"Ta' á um ason piw a' ni," Aaron responded.

"All right, you two, *enough*," Dwy said. "We've got to go. Aaron, thanks for watching the shop the next several days."

On the short drive from the airport to Dwy's modest home, Tracey marveled at the breathtaking red rock vistas that surrounded Sedona. She loved the ambience of the town, with its mystical vortices and its rich culture of ancient civilizations. In previous visits, she and Darren had explored the cliff dwellings and the petroglyphs left by the Anasazi, always trying to learn more about the fateful destiny of a culture descended from the Pangaeans.

"I love it here, Dwy. Perhaps someday we'll, uh … maybe someday I'll move here," she said, embarrassed by her slip. Being with Dwy in an area where she and Darren had experienced many good times almost made her forget they were separated. "When does your dad get in?" she continued.

"Sometime later this afternoon. He's driving from Alamogordo. He wanted to bring Vimmy for you."

Tracey looked away, emotion welling up in her throat. She and Darren had come to accept their distant relationship, but the dog couldn't understand it. Vimmy continued to be, without question, Tracey's dog. Their romps before were fun-filled and joyous. One of the most difficult things for Tracey to do was to leave the dog with Darren because she had no place in D.C. to keep him. She hid a tear from Dwy. This was not going to be an easy reunion.

Dwy pulled into his drive and parked beneath the carport. He opened the door for his mom and showed her to her room.

"Like it?" he asked. "I've spent a lot of time fixing it up for you. I even replaced the old, lumpy day bed with a new queen. Nothing too good for my mom."

Tracey walked around the room, inhaling the rich smell of pine and juniper wafting through the open window. Her spirits buoyed by Dwy's thoughtfulness, she tossed her tote bag and business satchel in the corner, and stretched out on the new mattress, testing its comfort.

"Wake me when I have to go back to work," she said. "I'm in heaven."

Dwy laughed and suggested she take a nap before freshening up for dinner.

"I've got reservations at the Mountain View Restaurant this evening. We'll have a nice secluded table with an overlook so you and Dad and I can all enjoy the sunset playing on the red rocks. Then after dinner, we can catch up on each other's news. I can't wait to hear about your new venture, whatever it is."

"You're going to have to tell me about yours first, or you'll not hear a thing from me. I still haven't forgiven you for leaving me up in the air in our last phone conversation."

Dwy blew his mom a kiss and closed the door as he left the room.

* * *

An hour or so later, a commotion at the door woke Tracey. She heard a whining and a barking followed by the sound of a large dog scampering from room to room, frantically searching for someone. Her door opened, and she barely had time to brace herself before Vimmy bounded in and, in one flying leap with tongue hanging out, landed on the bed and began licking at her face. She grabbed him around the neck and shoulders, wrestled him onto his side and began petting him.

"Hi, boy. Have you missed me?" she asked, watching his tail thump the covers like a carpet beater. Vimmy had just begun to settle down when Darren poked his head through the doorway.

"Anyone going to say hello to me?"

Tracey jumped from the bed and rushed to Darren, grabbing *him* around the neck and shoulders. The two of them embraced. Tracey didn't let go because she knew she couldn't trust her voice until the wave of emotions running through her body subsided.

"Hi, Sweetheart," she finally managed to speak. "I shouldn't say it, but God, I've missed you."

"Me too, Trace, I ..."

Darren's response was interrupted by Dwy walking into the room and placing his arms around both of them. The poor dog then went wild, trying to bull his way into the center of the three, first by Darren's side, then by Tracey's. When he finally worked his way in, Tracey started laughing, laughter that caught on with the two men. She finally dropped her arms.

"Hey, I was promised a wonderful dinner tonight," she said. "I get the bathroom first."

* * *

Back near the Four Corners area, a chopper with a WSP logo settled to a landing near the pipeline construction field office amid a swirl of dust. Before the rotors had even begun to slow, Jackson Davis leapt out, one hand grasping the Australian straw hat on his head and the other clutching a briefcase. Wearing a tan, short-sleeve shirt with epaulets, jeans and construction boots, his outfit was accented by a turquoise and leather bolo. The man behind the sunglasses looked more like a movie director arriving on set than the manager for the six-billion-dollar project backed by the city of Los Angeles. After a few quick strides, he hopped into the waiting Hummer and slammed the door.

"Let's go," he barked to the driver, without asking his name. The nervous driver spun the tires in the rocky soil and with a jerk, headed for the office trailer. Skidding to a stop in front of the handful of waiting managers, he reached for his door, intending to assist his passenger. But Jackson swung his door open and jumped out without a parting comment.

Jackson muttered a few greetings to the men, then strode up the steps into the shack with the others hastening to follow. Once inside, he glanced around the room.

"Jesus, Evans, this place is a mess. It makes me wonder what it looks like when you aren't expecting someone."

"Sorry, Jack, I didn't—" Ray Evans, his field superintendent, said before being interrupted.

"—Jackson. It's *Jackson*, not Jack."

"Er ... uh, I'm sorry, Mr. Davis, we've been concentrating on getting the pipeline back on schedule."

"I expect you to do both. The next time I come, I want this place neat—and the project back on schedule."

"Yes, Sir."

"Now, show me where you are."

Evans motioned for Jackson to sit and offered him a packet of materials. Jackson leafed through each page as Evans briefed him on the contents. The deeper into the packet Evans got, the deeper the frown on Jackson's face. Before Evans could conclude, Jackson shook his head and interrupted him.

"You're not anywhere close to being on schedule. Your critical path diagram has 10 obstacles holding you up. Your survey team doesn't even have the right-of-way laid out yet. Damn it, man. You've got to get after it."

"Yes, Sir. We can catch up. The delay's only two weeks."

"Bullshit. Two weeks today becomes three weeks tomorrow. Then it'll be a month and before you know it we've missed the best part of the construction season. They'll have my ass if we aren't past the Sangre de Cristos by September."

"We'll be there, Sir."

"Not at the rate we're going now. If you can't get caught up, I'll find someone who will."

Evans, obviously stressed, promised he would have things in order for Jackson's visit the following month.

"Now what about security? You know we've had some protests at the San Juan terminus."

"We've set up aerial patrols along the entire route. We observe each point along the line every two hours. If the pilots see anything, they radio us directly, and we can have the law there in short order."

"You know we're not dealing with mere vandals. There're several militant organizations that would love to blow up an entire section. And at the Texas border, vigilante teams are already in place. They don't want us to cross their state line. Are your security guards armed? I don't want any of our crew harassed or shot at."

"They are, Sir."

"Can they shoot?"

"Yes, Sir. They're pros—not rent-a-cops. Most of them are ex-military."

"That's the first good thing I've heard you say today. Now get on with it. I'm headed back to L.A., and on the way, I'll have to figure what I'm going to tell them about this mess. And get me someone else to drive me back to the chopper. That fellow that brought me here couldn't find the right gear."

"He's new, Sir. I'll take you."

"Fine, let's go."

* * *

Dwy pulled into the parking lot and escorted his mom and dad to the foyer of the Vista Montagna Ristorante.

"Mom, you love Italian food; there's none better in Sedona than the Mountain View," Dwy said.

Once inside, they were surrounded by an ambience of the warm, subdued tones of a Tuscan residence. The terra cotta walls were illuminated by the soft glow of light spreading from bronzed sconces. The chatter from the guests added to the cozy atmosphere. Light notes from a piano softened the buzz in the room. The maitre d' welcomed Dwy, and after introductions led them to a small courtyard with an elegant, sculpted fountain at its center. At one time a soothing cascade of water flowed down the display's artistic curves, but now it was dry. Although there were several tables around the room's centerpiece, no other guests were seated there.

"I've taken the owner on a few flights," Dwy said. "He offered to let me have this room for a special occasion. This certainly qualifies."

"It's wonderful," Tracey said. "I can't wait to see the menu. I'm famished."

"Mom, if you want water, I'll see if they will serve it."

"That's okay, Dwy. I'm fine without it. Besides, the cocktails cost less."

After enjoying drinks and wonderful entrees, they watched a spectacular sunset. Darren could wait no longer. "Okay, it's time to catch up on the news. Who goes first?"

Dwy and Tracey each pointed at each other and laughed.

"Ladies first," Dwy said.

Tracey reached for Darren's hand, paused a moment, then said, "I'm moving to Phoenix in a few weeks to serve on a presidential task force on the water shortage. I'll be working with former President Earlman again. President Mitchell is setting up a Western Slope White House. The work will be very demanding, but exciting. The best part of it is that I'll be a lot closer to each of you."

Darren noticed her hand tensed as she spoke of being close again. He squeezed her palm and nodded. She returned the squeeze. Maybe the move would help them reconcile. He would pursue that possibility when they could speak in private.

Tracey reached for Dwy's hand, and holding on to both her men, she asked, "Okay, Dwy, I went first. Now it's your turn."

Darren thought Dwy tensed as he began speaking. He sensed the news wouldn't be as upbeat as Tracey's.

"Mom, uh … Dad, it's no secret my business has been struggling. I'm making ends meet, but I haven't been able to put away anything for tomorrow. Nor do I have any security with health insurance or other benefits."

"You're not selling your company, are you?" Darren interrupted.

"Darren!" Tracey said.

"No, Dad. I'm taking on an additional job. I won't be flying any more tours, unless it's for a special reason. I'll let my three pilots do them all and free me up for my new job."

"What is it?" Darren asked.

"He's going to tell us," Tracey replied, the first signs of a frown on her face. "Let him finish."

Dwy looked at his mom, then back to his dad. "I've accepted a pilot's position with Western Slope Pipeline. I'll be primarily flying pipeline security patrols, but sometimes I'll be called upon to fly execs around. The best part is that I'll have full health coverage and a great 401(k)."

"Dwy, you know I don't care for WSP—Jackson Davis in particular," Darren said. "He's nothing but a power-mongering, ego-centric hypocrite who will do anything for a buck. I don't trust him or his company. NASA turned down his bid for my project because of his shady dealings. Don't get involved with him, or he'll drag you down with him."

Tracey pulled her hand away. She tried to lighten the discussion. "Dwy won't be directly working for Jackson Davis," she said. "He'll be working for a company that's trying to save Los Angeles—"

"—by stealing water from an aquifer—the Ogallala—that belongs to the ages," Darren said. "Once it's gone, there's no replacing it. The crops will be lost as will those who grow them. It'll turn the plains into a dustbowl again. People will starve because of it."

"Dad, if people in L.A. don't get more water, they are going to die in droves. Most can't move out. The city approved this project to *save* people."

"Hey, you two. I'm in this game, too," Tracey said, with fire building in her voice. "One of the first things President Earlman said to the task force was that there would have to be difficult choices made with extreme downsides. This is one of them. The task force will be reviewing this project to see if it should be supported or opposed."

"Let's just hope the whole damn project is cancelled before your son gets his plane shot down."

"That won't happen, Dad."

"It very well *could* happen. You know the Texans have formed armed vigilante groups to protect their western border. There's even more and more talk of Texas exercising its option to become a republic once again. Constitutionally it wouldn't pass muster, but tell that to a bunch of Lone Star cowboys spoiling for a fight."

The waiter interrupted their animated discussion by asking if anyone wanted dessert. An awkward silence ensued until Darren said they did not. When the waiter offered the tab, Darren reached for it, but Dwy snapped it up. "This is *my* treat, Dad. It's the least I can do. I wanted you both to have a wonderful evening, but instead you and I let our differences put Mom in the middle again. Not the outcome I had hoped for tonight."

"I'm sorry, Dwy—" Darren began.

"Dad—we'll talk later. We all need to calm down. This is not the place for a family argument, especially since this is the first time we've been together in a long while. Besides, I don't want to spoil the surprise I've got set up for the two of you tomorrow evening. You're going on a real journey.

CHAPTER NINE

A SHAMANIC JOURNEY

Dwy picked up his mom and dad late the next afternoon. He drove along a bumpy dirt road toward one of Sedona's famed vortexes. "I thought you two might enjoy the experience of an ancient healing ritual, performed by a real Hopi shaman."

"New age stuff?" Darren asked.

"No, far from it. The new age stuff didn't begin until the woo-woo people arrived in Sedona in the mid-'70s."

"Woo-woo people?" Tracey asked.

"You know, the long-haired, linen-gowned, middle-aged types searching for a higher-level esoteric experience—we call them the 'woo-woos.' They can't say more than two words without including the term 'energy.'"

"So, we're going to work with a real shaman then?" Tracey asked.

"Yes, you'll find the experience authentic. And, if you keep your minds open, you may see things in a completely different perspective."

Darren looked at Tracey, touched her shoulder and winked. She saw his playful grin that had been absent for so long.

"I'm beginning to sense the energy building," Darren said.

Dwy laughed and the tension eased a little as they continued the drive. A line of red sandstone cliffs appeared on the horizon, and they drove toward it across miles of desert terrain, filled only with scruffy, dry vegetation. Dwy took a turn-off a few miles from the cliffs.

"I want you to see this first," he said, parking the car in the shadow of the cliff. He led them to a large, concave area at its base. They approached a rock and clay ruin of a dwelling.

"Palatki," Dwy said. "It's a Hopi word that stands for 'red house.' But the funny thing is that the Hopi didn't name the structure; a white man did. The Hopis have no direct connection to this place."

"Who lived here?" Tracey asked.

"The Sinagua, a branch of the Anasazi in Arizona. Sinagua means 'without water', and the ancient people who lived here had to survive on very little."

"They could teach us something," Tracey said.

"Remember, Trace, ancestors of the Anasazi were the Pangaeans, who were exceptional at conserving both water and energy," Darren said. "It's no surprise the Sinagua could adapt those skills to aid their survival."

"There's more," Dwy said. "Follow me."

He led them along a trail parallel to the base of the cliff. A half a mile away, a sight emerged that took Tracey's breath away. The concavity in the sandstone had grown into an opening the size of a small amphitheater. An ancient, rock-lined fire pit lay in the center, the arched wall behind it covered with black soot. On either side were scores of pictographs, subtle paintings on the rock portraying animals and geometric designs. The colors ranged from white through various shades of red to black.

"It's an ancient ceremonial site. These figures and symbols had important meanings to the Sinagua."

"What do they represent?" Tracey asked.

"Since the Sinagua had no written form of their language, the translations have all been lost. We can only make our own interpretation, at best a guess as to what they say."

Tracey found a pictograph that intrigued her. A large animal painted in whitish-gray with a rack of antlers stood at the base of a ladder outlined in a charcoal-black. The ladder's wavy lines ascended the irregular surface of the rear wall and disappeared into a massive crack in the stone above.

"This is beautiful. What do you think it depicts?"

"The animal is a large deer or perhaps even an elk. The ladder has a more spiritual connotation. Many times cracks or holes in overhanging ceilings represent the point of entry into another world, so the ladder might represent a means of ascending and emerging into a better place, perhaps a heaven."

"My take is that the ladder parallels the Anasazi emergence myth. They came from a civilization beneath the earth and climbed to the surface of the earth through an opening. The ladder could be a symbol for the way they got to the surface."

"Dad, you might be right. That's why the pictographs are so interesting to me. Anyone can make their own interpretation."

Dwy saw from the cliff's lengthening shadow that he had to get them moving again. He ushered them to the car and drove back to the main route. The road entered a valley carved into the cliff by erosion. Within a mile or two, the road steepened and climbed, the curves providing one outstanding red rock vista after another. The scent of juniper became overpowering. At last, they reached a level clearing.

"Ready for a hike?" Dwy asked.

"Of course," Tracey said.

Dwy pointed to a trailhead and told them to walk to the top of the knoll. The shaman was expecting them.

"Oh, turn off your phones," he said. "You don't want one ringing in the middle of the ritual. It would be a very bad sign. Here are a couple of backpacks with some water, food and blankets."

"Blankets?" Tracey asked.

"I'm going in to work this evening. I'll pick you up in the morning. Or call me if you need me before then."

"I thought Aaron was filling in for you at work," Tracey said.

"He was, but he needed the evening off."

* * *

"Hike?" Darren said. "This is a mountain climbing *expedition*."

Both were huffing in the thin air. Tracey scratched her arm on a cedar branch. Darren slipped on the red shale and banged his shin on a rock. Ignoring the pain, he picked his way along the path, but became confused about the proper direction. All the possible routes he saw required a steeper climb than he felt comfortable with.

"There's a cairn," Tracey said.

"A what?"

"A cairn, a stack of rocks that shows the way."

"That doesn't look any better than the rest," Darren said.

"Let's try it and see."

After a few yards, they saw a second cairn leading up the hill. Then another. The cairns gave them an increased sense of confidence that they were on the right track.

"Makes you feel better, like someone's been here before you, to guide you," Darren said.

"You're supposed to add a rock."

"Why?"

"Just do it. It's part of the mystique."

Darren searched for a suitable rock and tried placing it on the cairn. It fell off. Tracey giggled.

He finally found one of the correct size and shape, and it stayed. He turned to Tracey and pointed to it with pride.

"Powerful human scientist adds rock to pile," he said with a grin.

The last pitch of the trail required the use of both of their hands and feet. Darren caught Tracey's arm as her foot slipped. For a moment he looked into her eyes, a look she returned. He remembered how things used to be between them. He leaned forward and kissed her. She responded. They tried to embrace each other but their position was too precarious. Tracey started laughing.

"Darren, it won't do us any good to hug each other if it causes us to fall and break our asses. Let's see how this shaman thing goes, and then we'll take it from there."

Darren turned back to the rocky ascent and scrambled the last few yards to finally reach level ground. He stood, then bent forward, resting his hands on his knees while he caught his breath. He heard Tracey just behind him. He turned and hugged her.

"We made it."

"We almost didn't," Tracey said. "Wait until I see that son of yours."

"Mine?"

"Ours."

They looked around, taking in the view. Darren reached into his backpack for a bottle of water and handed it to Tracey. When he turned back around, he was startled by a man with long black hair in Native American dress, standing as if in a trance, holding a stick in each of his outstretched arms. The ceremonial paint on his face did not hide his identity.

"Aaron!" Tracey said. "Aaron, what a surprise."

Aaron remained in his trance, his face uplifted to the sky. He began a rhythmic chant, facing in turn toward each of the cardinal directions. When he completed the entire circle, he crossed the prayer sticks over his chest and looked at Tracey.

"Eagle-To-The-Clouds says Loloma, Mrs. Stewart."

"Loloma, Eagle-To-The-Clouds. Please accept my apology for any disrespect. It was unintended."

"Loloma, Dr. Stewart."

"Uh, Loloma, EagleCloud—er … I mean, Eagle-To-The-Clouds," Darren replied.

Aaron motioned them to follow him to the center of the clearing. Darren clutched Tracey's arm and walked behind Aaron, wondering what was to come. Always the scientific one, Darren had little use for mythology. He felt out of place subjecting himself to a ritual of another culture. He knew, however, that for Dwy's sake he must at least pretend to appreciate it.

Tracey, on the other hand, had no such reservations. "Isn't this exciting?" she asked. "A chance to experience something mystical. I love it."

They approached a geometric pattern of white stones, laid out on the red ground in the form of a maze, bounded by an outer circle with the four cardinal directions marked by a small boulder.

Aaron turned back to them and spoke in a hushed tone. "The circle represents the journey of life. In the East is the Sunrise and the Summer Solstice and to the West is the Sunset and the Winter Solstice—Life and Death. The northern half of the circle represents the world where we live now. The southern half represents the world we came from. Above the circle in the sky is the spirit world, and below the circle in the underground is our ancestral world. The center of the circle represents our individual center of the universe. From there each of us can see to the stars from which we came."

Darren started to ask a question, but Tracey restrained him with pressure on his forearm.

Aaron continued. "The maze represents the path we walk from birth. If we make the right choices, we die and re-emerge into a new world. Our present world is the fourth on which we have existed, and we have three more yet to come, or seven altogether. There are two worlds beyond our reach. The eighth world is where the spirits who maintain our universe reside. The ninth world is the sole domain of our Creator."

Aaron paused in his discussion, and the expression on his face changed back into a more relaxed one with a friendly smile on his face. "Dr. and Mrs. Stewart," he said, "before we go on, I must tell you some things. Your son, Dwy, said that your lives were out of harmony, and asked if I could help. I cannot take you through a Hopi ritual, because you are Anglo—you were not brought up in our ways, and you would not understand it. But I can call upon my powers as a Hopi shaman to open your eyes to some possibilities. I must caution, however, that what you might experience could shake the foundations of your beliefs. Trust me and do not be afraid. I will not let harm come to you. If you wish me to continue, let me know."

Darren looked at Tracey. She nodded. Darren turned back to Aaron. "We trust you," he said. "Go on."

Aaron asked that they step to the circle, Tracey to the North and Darren to the South. Aaron took the position in the West. "We reserve the East for the Respected Spirits, the messengers who may come to advise us."

Once in place, Aaron resumed the stoic demeanor of Eagle-To-The-Clouds. The deepening twilight turned the sky to a turquoise backdrop for the distant mountain ridges, now becoming silhouettes. The first of the evening stars sparkled in the skies above. Eagle-To-The-Clouds reached into a leather pouch that hung from his belt and drew out his hand, closed in a fist. He began a chant and opened his hand, palm side up. A flame flickered from his palm. With a flourish, he tossed the flame to the stack of greasewood twigs he had built at the center of the circle. With a whoosh, the wood ignited, and the fire whistled and popped as it grew in height to eye level, its light chasing the shadows from the faces around the circle.

As Darren watched in fascination, Eagle-To-The Clouds reached into the pouch with his left hand and threw a powder onto the fire. The flame became brilliant for an instant, then a bluish-gray smoke swept outward along the ground and rose to engulf the three of them. The thick smoke had a penetrating, sweet aroma. It caused Darren's breathing to be difficult—almost to the point of choking. Anxiety overwhelmed him at first, but this feeling was replaced by a calm detachment. He relaxed and his breathing became easier. He inhaled deeply with a slow rhythm. Looking across the circle at Tracey, he could see only her face, reflected in the light from the fire, seemingly suspended in the haze of the smoke. Darren felt a pressure in his eardrums that pulsated and resonated, sounding like what a swimmer hears deep underwater.

Before Darren could gain control over the sensations he was experiencing, Eagle-To-The-Clouds pulled a wooden flute from a quiver that hung from his shoulder. He raised the flute to the direction of the East, brought it to his mouth and began to play.

The first tones sounded like the low moaning of the wind rushing up a canyon wall, punctuated by yips of a coyote. The notes floated around the flame into Darren's head and swirled through his mind. The melody from the flute increased in complexity, overwhelming Darren with its beauty. He forgot about his inhibitions, his worries and his fears. His heartbeat was in sync with the tempo of the music. Darren lifted his face and didn't question the fact that he could watch the notes spiral around the circle and rise upward into the night sky.

Then he heard an echo, softly repeating the notes from the flute. The echo became more distinct and intertwined with the melody, increasing in volume and taking the lead. Darren brought his gaze back to the circle and was startled by the image of a figure playing a flute at the once-vacant eastern point in the circle. The image, transparent at first, solidified into the form of an elderly man whose long, white hair fell across his bronzed shoulders.

Eagle-To-The-Clouds placed his flute back in his quiver and rested his hands on his knees. He deflected his eyes away from the man opposite him, knowing it was unwise to look directly into the face of a Respected Spirit. He motioned for Darren and Tracey to look only at each other.

After a few moments, the elder ceased playing his flute.

"Why have you called upon me, Eagle-To-The-Clouds?" he asked.

"To help my friends."

"I cannot help them. They are Anglo. Our ways do not work with them."

"I ask only that you share with them what you see ahead on their road of life."

"I can tell *you* what I see. Then, if you wish, you may share my vision with them. Remember, they might not have the strength to learn from it."

"If they are willing, I will help them deal with it."

Eagle-To-The-Clouds looked to Darren and Tracey for consent. Darren saw Tracey nod her head in agreement. In a move completely out of character for him, Darren nodded his head also, wondering where his mind was to be taken.

"Go ahead, Respected Spirit. They are willing."

The elder raised his flute to his lips and played a lovely, but somber, melody. At one point, the notes became heavy and discordant. Then the music stopped. The smoke obscured the elder. When it cleared, he was gone. A serene silence remained behind.

After a few moments, Eagle-To-The-Clouds spoke. "The Respected Spirit shared with me that your paths begin to converge, yet remain separate."

"Is that all?" Tracey asked. "The music seemed to imply more."

Eagle-To-The-Clouds took a long time before answering. "He saw a mountain across your paths and could not see beyond it. He saw only the stars above it. That was all he shared with me."

"A mountain?" Tracey asked.

"It could mean an obstacle in your path."

The expression on Tracey's face darkened. "What kind of an obstacle?"

"One that will take strength to get beyond. But once you succeed, you will find harmony in your lives."

Darren rose and walked around the circle to Tracey. He hugged her. "Trace, we'll be okay. Remember, we traveled 200 million years back in time, so what's a little mountain?"

Aaron walked to them. He suggested the two of them remain there overnight and talk about their experience, trying to learn from it. "The Respected Spirits are messengers," he said. "Their message is to be one of help, not one of fear. Seek to find the help in what I've shared with you."

Darren started to reply, but Aaron walked away toward the path down the mesa and disappeared into the brush.

* * *

Jackson Davis hopped from the chopper and strode to the entrance of WSP's corporate headquarters. Acknowledging the receptionist's greeting with a brusque nod of his head, he hurried to his office in the construction division's suite. Once at his desk, Jackson's administrative assistant quickly reviewed his appointments and messages for him.

"Oh," she said, "Tracey Stewart called you. You remember—she was the one we met at the reception hosted by President Mitchell's task force. Wants you to call her."

Jackson perked up. He did remember Tracey—what man wouldn't?—as the woman rumored to be separated from her husband, probably some poor chump gone flabby with age and more interested in golf than his wife.

"What did she want?"

"Didn't say. Want me to call her back?"

"No, leave her number. I'll talk to her."

After his assistant left, Jackson flipped his cell open and dialed. After two rings, he hung up, not wanting to leave a message.

I'd rather talk to her in person. It might be worth it.

* * *

Darren added some wood to the fire. The last gleam of the setting sun faded from the sky. He picked up both backpacks and sat next to Tracey. He began to rummage through his to see what items Dwy had packed for them. On the very top, he found a headset connected to a digital recorder.

"Dwy left us music," he said, putting the earphones on. Tracey drew her feet up and grasped her knees in her arms, looking toward the sky. Darren hit the "play" button on the recorder.

"Dad," the message began, "I've tried to think of everything you and Mom might need. That's why the packs were so heavy. I hope you enjoyed your experience with Aaron. He's an amazingly complex individual, but he knows things that we in our world are not open to believing. You and he should talk sometime. His knowledge of the mythology of his ancestors would intrigue you.

"I'm sorry things ended the way they did last night. One of these days we'll find a way to get along. Mom says our problem is that we're too much alike. Well, Dad, I took that as a compliment. Bye, Dad. Have a good evening. I'll pick you up at seven in the morning."

Darren stared ahead without saying anything. *Dwy's a good man. How come we keep getting crossways with each other?*

"—the stars," he heard Tracey say.

"What?" Darren asked, returning to the present.

"Look at the stars. I've never seen them as brilliant as this, especially the Milky Way."

Darren raised his head. She was right.

"You can even see the Dark Rift," he said.

"The Dark *what?*"

"The Dark *Rift,*" Darren answered. "See that notch of blackness in the Milky Way's bulge at the center? It's an enormous cloud of gas."

Darren continued scanning the night sky, enjoying the vivid display. Even some of the dimmest constellations were visible.

Directly overhead was a smudge that looked like a sparkling thumbprint. The stars within ranged from bright to very dim.

"The Pleiades," he said.

"What?"

"See over there?" he said, pointing to the formation.

"I'm not sure which one you mean."

"You know the constellation 'Orion', don't you?"

"Yes."

"Well then, start at Orion's belt and follow its line to the right until you see—"

"Oh, I've got it now."

"That group is called the 'Pleiades.' It's not a constellation—some arbitrary, connect-the-dots outline—but a *cluster* of stars, almost the same age. They're very young, so recently born that they've not yet drifted apart."

Darren pulled a pair of binoculars from his pack and handed them to her.

"Look close," he said. "What do you see?"

Tracey gasped in surprise. "I see a miniature, sparkling dipper. It just jumps out when you look through the glasses."

"The 'Seven Sisters', the daughters of Atlas, according to the Greeks," Darren said. "Each sister had an affair with a different Olympian god."

Darren told her the cluster was well known throughout many cultures, from the Greeks to Native Americans. It was sometimes used as a vision test. The better a person's vision, the more stars could be seen. Many civilizations saw the Pleiades as a point of origin for knowledge and wisdom.

"The Greeks gave them the name. It means 'to sail.' The Pleiades marked the beginning and the end of the summer sailing season in ancient Greece.

"Asian civilizations believe all knowledge comes from the Pleiades, but most remarkably, the Hopi—Aaron's people—believe that they are the direct descendants of the Pleiadeans, that the

Kachinas come from the Pleiades and reside for the summer on the San Francisco peaks, north of Flagstaff."

"Did you see him?" Tracey asked.

"Who?" Darren asked, not following her abrupt segue.

"You know, uh … the guy in the circle. Was *he* a Kachina?"

"I'm not sure exactly what I saw. I think I was high on something."

Tracey laughed. "That'll be the day—old Darren Stewart high on something. About as likely as old Darren Stewart getting pregnant!"

"No, I'm serious."

"Well, then, did you see him, or not?"

"Okay—I saw him. I heard his flute, too. And for some reason, I didn't question whether he was real. Nor was I afraid. What did you experience?"

"The very same thing," Tracey answered, and then shivered in the night air.

Darren put his arms around her and gave her a longing kiss, a kiss she returned.

"Let's see what kind of gear we have in our packs," Darren said. "Hopefully, there are some blankets inside."

Darren and Tracey rummaged through the packs and found individual sleeping bags, pillows, bottles of water and snacks. Darren reached for the bottom of his bag and drew out a bottle of Tracey's favorite wine.

"Look," he said, reaching into his pocket for his Swiss Army knife. He opened the corkscrew blade. "I'll have it open in a second. We'll have to drink it straight out of the bottle, though."

Tracey smiled and raised two wine glasses that she had found carefully wrapped in her pack. She clinked them together and then held them out for Darren to fill. With a blanket draped around their shoulders, they sipped the wine and talked at length about the experience with Aaron. They came up with several theories for the mountain. Darren thought it could be Shiprock Peak or perhaps even the San Francisco peaks. Tracey saw the vision in a metaphorical sense, an obstacle representing an uphill climb to reach something they both sought.

"Life is full of mountains," she said. "Some are beautiful and breathtaking. Others are challenges. But I've had some time to think about it now, and I'm no longer afraid of the vision. Whatever the mountain represents, we'll manage."

Darren agreed. He poured the last of the bottle, and Tracey, a little giddy from the wine, giggled. He had not heard that happy sound for a long time. He reached for her, but she exclaimed, "Look! Oh, look! A shooting star!"

Darren looked where she pointed and saw the streak of light. Tracey said, "Quick—close your eyes and make a wish!" She squinted her eyes closed and smiled. After a moment she opened them and asked, "Did you make a wish?"

"Yes."

"What did you wish for?"

"She's right next to me."

Tracey giggled again. "Okay, but we're going to have to zip our sleeping bags together. There's not enough room for us in one."

It didn't take long before they were together, catching up on the pent-up desire they had for each other. Tracey's conversation faded to whispered suggestions, then to moans of pleasure. Later, she asked, "Did you get your wish?"

"Yes, I did, but—"

"—but what?"

"I made several more—just like the first one!"

CHAPTER TEN

A ROCKY ANALYSIS

The guest bedroom in Skeeter's apartment had been converted into a geology lab with rocks of all types stored in floor-to-ceiling bins along one windowless wall. A workbench cluttered with tools and instruments, including a microscope, precision scales and a digital scanner, stood against the opposite wall. A kiln on a hearth of bricks occupied one corner. The carpet and every other horizontal surface in the room were covered by a layer of gritty dust. Skeeter worked at a butcher-block table at the very center of the lab.

He focused a high-intensity desk light to illuminate the rock sample in his hand. He closed his left eye and squinted through the monocle over his right eye, gradually turning the specimen around for a close inspection. Satisfied, he placed the sample in the chuck of a carbide saw, adjusted the blade to the correct position and exchanged his monocle for a pair of safety goggles. He turned on the flow of coolant and flipped the switch on the saw. Once the blade began its cut, Skeeter left the room so he would not have to listen to the high-pitched scream of the saw. He closed the door and poured his third cup of coffee for the morning.

* * *

At sunrise, Darren awoke with Tracey snuggled next to him. He longed for a cup of coffee, but there had been none in his pack. Darren reflected on the fascinating night he and Tracey had experienced. *Maybe the mountain represented this mesa. Maybe we've climbed the mountain and can now get beyond it.* Tracey stirred and opened her eyes, a smile on her face.

"Morning," she said.

"Did you sleep well?" Darren asked.

Tracey turned her body to Darren, sliding her knee upward along the front of his legs. "No, some old man kept me awake most of the night."

"You keep doing that, and that old man won't let you get up, either."

"Promise?"

"Come on, Trace. Dwy's going to meet us at the trailhead at seven. We've got a long hike and worst of all—there's no coffee."

Tracey didn't handle mornings without coffee at all well. The absence of caffeine could turn an otherwise upbeat and happy woman into a grouchy, ill-tempered, dragon-lady.

"No coffee?"

"None. Our son's into green tea, instead. Remember?"

"Well then, dude, you know I become evil incarnate without my morning coffee. You'd better get me off this mountain quick."

"Let's do it."

The two scrambled around, picking up an assortment of bottles, glasses and articles of clothing and stuffing them along with the sleeping bags into the backpacks. It didn't all fit, and they had to carry the blanket and some of the other stuff on their arms. Darren poured a couple of bottles of water on the embers and kicked sandy soil on top of them. Satisfied the fire was out, he said, "Let's go."

Hiking down the trail proved to be more difficult than the climb up. The sand-covered rock made the footing difficult. Any misstep or slip could lead to a nasty fall. The two worked hand-in-hand to navigate the most difficult areas.

Darren glanced at Tracey and smiled. The woman never had a hair out of place, even when she worked in the yard. Now, she looked a little disheveled, her shirttail hanging half out of her shorts and red smudges all over her legs, arms and hands. Her hair hung down over her eyes and by brushing it back with her forearm, she smeared her face with dirt. She was not happy.

"Stop it," she said. "I know what you're thinking."

Darren knew she did. Try as he might to keep his thoughts to himself, he could never get away with it. He swore she was telepathic.

"You look beautiful."

The minute he said it, he knew he had messed up.

"No, I don't, and you know it. Keep me up on a mountain all night, and both of us act like a couple of teenagers oversexed on hormones; then wake me up with no coffee, make me do a death march down a mountain and expect me to look like a model? No way."

They didn't speak the rest of the way down. When they finally reached the trailhead, they sat exhausted on a bench to wait for Dwy.

After a few minutes, Tracey broke the ice. "I'm sorry."

Darren became serious. "What do we do now, Trace?"

"I don't know. I wish I did."

"But last night was how it could be for us again."

"Oh, Darren, we've never had trouble with sex. That's not the issue. A marriage is more than that. We're missing something. We've got to find it before we can even think about getting back together."

"We can't find it while we're apart."

Tracey thought a minute, staring at the ground.

"You have to become spontaneous," she said.

"What do you mean by that?"

"Everything in your life is by plan. Hell, you even go through a grocery store aisle by aisle. It's a big deal if you have to retrace your steps to pick up something you missed. Your son is a beautiful person, but you try to box him in. He resents it, and you can't see that you're doing it. And as for me, sometimes you're so predictable, sometimes you ... you *bore* me."

Her words stunned Darren. She had never—never—said anything like that to him in all their years. It hit him the wrong way. Something ignited inside him.

"*Bore* you? What am I supposed to be? Some kind of a court jester to keep you entertained? Well, someone has to be responsible. We can't both be free spirits chasing causes and cavorting with presidents all the time while leaving family behind."

"Do you think that's what I'm doing?"

"Do you think I'm boring?"

Before either could answer, Dwy's car pulled up. He jumped out to help them with their packs.

"How was it? Did you enjoy it?" he asked.

Tracey got in the front seat without answering, leaving the rear seat for Darren. Dwy got back in the car and wondered what he had done wrong.

* * *

The whine of the carbide blade stopped, letting Skeeter know the saw had finished its cut. He set his cup down and returned to his lab. Removing the rock from the saw's chuck, he polished the freshly cut face of the stone on a grinder. Once finished, he took some measurements of the sample under his microscope, and jotted them down in a notebook.

He checked the kiln to be certain it had stabilized at the proper temperature. Using insulated tongs and shielding his body from the heat, he opened the kiln's door and slid the rock sample into the flame, planning to drive off any moisture and organic impurities.

A rose-lavender aura of flame formed around the rock and quickly disappeared. Before Skeeter could close the door, a wisp of an aroma escaped, an odor that Skeeter recognized. As the awareness of the implications of his discovery dawned on him, Skeeter settled in his chair. *I'll be damned. Darren's not going to believe this.*

* * *

The next morning after breakfast, Dwy flew his mom back to Phoenix. During the flight, they managed to talk about everything except what had transpired the day before. Tracey's mouth remained in a firm, thin line the whole trip. Dwy wondered if he had helped the two of them or made things worse. He struggled with his uncomfortable role of trying to be a counselor to his parents.

At the airport, she thanked him and said farewell with a hug and a mother's kiss. Dwy taxied to the runway and began the trip home in a depressed state.

Darren had left for home at sunrise with Vimmy poking his head out the open window and excitedly sniffing the many tempting smells. Each time he repositioned himself for a better vantage point, his tail swished the side of Darren's face.

"Sit down, Vimmy," he said, in no mood for the dog's distraction. His mind kept going over the conversation with Tracey that had left them both irritated with each other. No matter how many times he tried, he could not change the outcome.

He jumped when his cell phone rang.

"Yeah," he answered.

"Darren?" Skeeter asked.

"Go ahead, Skeeter,"

"Darren, you've got to get back. I've discovered something monumental."

"What?"

"You're not going to believe it. When you get here, I'll let you experience it for yourself."

CHAPTER ELEVEN

WATER DIVINERS

Tracey worked at her desk, surrounded by boxes packed with papers and equipment from her old office. Amid the chaos created by the move to the federal building in Phoenix, she reviewed the plans for the inauguration of the Western White House scheduled for the following week. Events included a convening of all the major organizations responsible for water projects, ranging from the practical expansion of existing infrastructure to research and development focused on far-out, theoretical solutions. Each organization had been invited to present an overview of its project, with the hope of obtaining government funding.

She thumbed through the stacks of project abstracts on her desk. She had provided each group attending with a format designed to quickly cover the essence of the proposal and outline the relative benefit so that the Earlman Commission, as it had become known, could determine which to support. The competition for funds was fierce, with companies offering task force members perks—and, in some cases, outright bribes—from jet trips to major golf tournaments to vacation stays in corporate resorts, complete with discreet and beautiful escorts.

If the general public learned of some of the proposals before they could be properly introduced, a political backlash might result, costing many influential leaders their jobs. One of the projects in the stack contained a proposal to begin siphoning fresh water from Lake Superior, a move Tracey knew could lead to major conflict. Another proposal would draw water from the mouth of the Columbia River and bring it to San Francisco through a pipeline buried offshore. Still another would tow icebergs from the Artic Circle despite the failure of the first attempt. The iceberg moored in San Pedro Bay off of Seal Beach had yet to produce a drop of drinkable water. "We can solve the problems with additional funding," the report said. A major desalinization plant off California's coast seemed plausible until it came to the disposal of the salt generated.

Not all the projects had to do with water supply. Several major efforts targeted excess consumption. The proposals included setting strict limits on household use and finding alternative fluids to replace water in selected applications, like the washing of clothes and flushing of toilets.

Then, there were the recycling projects that would outlaw once-through uses of water in industrial cooling systems, geothermal applications, and other commercial uses. Tracey's least favorite involved the recycling of human liquid waste using environmentally high-tech, bio-treatment plants. What worked on a manned spacecraft with astronauts in a controlled and sterile environment could lead to a pandemic in the civilian population, should something go wrong.

She shuddered at the thought. The phone on her desk rang. Surprised that it functioned, she picked it up.

"Tracey Stewart," she answered.

"Mrs. Stewart, this is Jackson Davis, returning your call."

"Thank you, Mr. Davis," Tracey said.

"Please call me Jackson, I prefer it. What can I do for you?"

Tracey asked for the details of the presentation to be made by Western Slope Pipeline about the project to tap the Ogallala Aquifer. She wanted to know the names of the attendees and the order and topics of the speakers. "It's for our program," she explained. "You must conform to our protocols. Be sure you cover your request within the time allotted. Don't go over, or President Earlman will cut you off."

"Mrs. Stewart, I'd like to work with you to assure we comply with all the requirements. Could we meet—over dinner?"

Tracey knew of Jackson's reputation as a womanizer, but she had not anticipated such a blatant offer. She could not afford to accept his invitation. It represented an attempt to either gain a competitive advantage or to make a move on her, or more likely, both.

"I'm sorry, but I'm afraid not," she said. "Everything you need to know is in your information packet. We'll see you next Tuesday."

* * *

Darren's Jeep screeched to a stop in Skeeter's drive. Vimmy didn't wait for the car door to be opened. He bolted out the window and, with tongue hanging out and tail swishing back and forth, bounded toward an unsuspecting Skeeter, at the back porch pulling dead flowers from one of the dried-up beds. Skeeter heard Vimmy's excited barking and braced himself to try and keep from getting bowled over. It didn't work. The dog collided with him in full stride and both of them went tumbling to the ground, Skeeter laughing uncontrollably. He raised his arms in front of his face to ward off Vimmy's slurping attack.

"Vimmy, down!" Darren shouted. "Down—NOW!"

The dog finally obeyed but whined in anticipation as Skeeter picked himself up and dusted off his jeans. Still amused, Skeeter made a sudden move toward Vimmy, faking a playful attack. The dog couldn't stand it. He jumped toward Skeeter, and the chaos started all over again.

Darren, now pissed at Skeeter, yelled, "Damn you. How am I going to get Vimmy to mind if you tease him like that?"

"Aw, Darren, he's just an overgrown pup. Loosen up and let him play."

"Oh yeah, it's funny when he goes after a big hulk like you, but it wouldn't be if he knocked over someone's grandmother."

"No, I guess not. Anyway, come back to my lab. I can't wait for you to see what I found."

The two men left the dog on the rear stoop and walked into Skeeter's lab. It took some time for Darren's eyes to adjust to the dim room. The dust in the air irritated his nose, and Darren had to stifle a sneeze.

"Jeez, Skeeter," he asked, "how do you stand it in here?"

"You get used to it. Besides, the residue is pure earth—not some of the pollution you get in the cities."

"Radon's pure earth, but I don't want to breathe it either."

Skeeter motioned for Darren to join him at the table in the center of the room. He picked up one of the samples of the lava chips he had taken at the base of Shiprock Peak. He held it aloft, between his thumb and forefinger, allowing Darren to examine it.

"It's a smoking gun," Skeeter said. "The cluster of rocks I took this sample from broke off very recently, geologically speaking—about 1,500 years ago—but the peak itself is nearly 50 million years old."

Failing to get the point, Darren grabbed the sample and turned it over. "How can you tell how long ago it broke off?"

"Elementary, Dr. Stewart. Elementary," Skeeter said. "Patination."

"Patination? What's that?"

Skeeter explained that with time, a patina forms on a rock's surface from sunlight, weathering, and biological processes. "Takes about 4,000 years for a new surface to develop a full depth of a patina. The patina on this sample was less than a third of that."

"I still don't understand," Darren said.

Skeeter sighed and took the sample back from Darren. "This sample came from the fracture surface—where the rock broke," he said. "All the other surfaces had normal patinas. I think it places the fracture at between 1,500 and 1,800 years ago."

"What's so noteworthy about that?"

"Come here," Skeeter said, walking to his oven. He filed some particles from a different sample and placed the filings in a small ladle. He donned a face mask and heat-resistant gauntlets. "Stand back," he cautioned. He opened the door, put the sample in the oven and closed the door. After a few minutes, he opened a small sample valve in the oven's flue. He wafted the smoke toward his nose. Smiling, he told Darren to do the same.

Darren did and was nearly floored by a unique, but familiar, smell. "Damn, Skeeter, it smells exactly like the heated surface of Dwyer's time-ship in the museum. What is it?"

"One of the samples I took at Shiprock Peak came from a lava pinnacle that had a streak of color on its side. The sample in the oven is from that area."

Darren's mind whirled as he began to make the connection. But Skeeter beat him to the point.

"I think your lost time-ship hit the peak during its emergency descent and broke off the tips of the pinnacles. The streak of color came from the ship's surface."

Darren nodded. The time frame was in the right ball park. He sat on one of the stools and rubbed his brow, thinking through the possibilities.

"That's all I can tell you," Skeeter said.

"No, there's more," Darren replied, becoming excited about the finding. "Those rocks were on the southeast side of the peak. That means the ship was traveling in that general direction before it crash-landed. We can get an approximate bearing of its final route, but we don't know how long it managed to stay aloft before it went down."

"We could fly along the path. We might spot something."

"No, remember: there've been lots of history buffs who've looked. They've used ultralight aircraft, satellite photos, metal detectors, Geiger counters—everything to no avail. Somehow we've got to narrow the search."

Skeeter walked into his kitchen, pulled a soda and a beer from his refrigerator and tossed the beer to Darren. "Here you go, guy, let's drink on it."

* * *

Late Tuesday afternoon in the convention hall of the converted federal building, Tracey sat with a panel of members from the Earlman Commission listening to presentations from a host of project leaders attempting to secure federal funds for their water development efforts. She and the others had heard polished pitches from those who planned to tow icebergs, tap the Fraser River in Canada, build huge desalination plants off the coast and even dam the Yukon. Some of the most promising were the most controversial. The team members on the dais were detailing their plan to divert water from the Great Lakes to the Colorado River west of the Continental Divide.

Not a chance, Tracey thought. Even if they got past the hurdle of the Great Lakes Council of Governors with its compact—signed by each governor—expressly prohibiting the export of water from the lakes, there remained the technical challenge of crossing the Rockies at their highest point with a high-volume pipeline. And even if that could be accomplished, they still faced the most daunting quagmire of water rights to the Colorado River. Western history had been shaped by this contested river, a history that included high-level legal maneuvering, the emergence of water power-mongers like L.A.'s legendary water-services engineer, William Mulholland, and others, and their projects that led to the formation of activist groups such as the Sierra Club. Tracey shook her head when their presentation ended and scribbled "impossible" in the margins of the abstract in front of her.

She shrugged her shoulders and exhaled, puckering her mouth and puffing out her cheeks. Glancing at her watch, she worried that the commission's task itself would prove to be impossible. She tensed as the final group of the first day took the stage: Western Slope Pipeline, headed by none other than Jackson Davis, himself. She resigned herself to the ordeal of listening to the pitch from a man she had come to detest. She decided she must put her bias aside and remain objective.

"Working with the City of Los Angeles, Western Slope Pipeline can provide sufficient water with our project to sustain the current population," Davis began. "With federal funding support, we can cut our project completion time in half. Our project to tap the Ogallala Aquifer and route its waters across the Continental Divide to the upper reaches of the San Juan River, and from there to Los Angeles, is technologically feasible and can be done with a minimal environmental footprint at reasonable cost."

What kind of fudge phrase is that? Tracey wondered. She interrupted Davis with a question. "What do you mean by 'minimal environmental footprint'? From what I've read of your project, you will deplete an irreplaceable resource that's been in place for more than 10,000 years. That's not 'minimal' in my view."

Unfazed by the line of her question, Davis glibly explained that the well heads were in place throughout the plains states and were already pumping down the aquifer for agricultural irrigation. The bridge of using the aquifer had already been crossed.

"These well heads supply the center-pivot irrigation systems—wheeled sprinkler lines—for watering the arid plains. We don't have to drill new wells. Our project has a minimal environmental footprint because we connect these 3,000-gallon-per-minute wells with a manifold and collect the water from thousands of them for our pipeline. The manifold and the pipeline—which, by the way, crosses the Continental Divide at its *lowest* point—are underground. You'll never see them."

"But what about the displacement of all the people who can no longer farm?"

"They can continue to farm if they so choose. Their decision is an economic one that they make themselves. They may either sell us the rights to the water at a price that is more than most of them make in a lifetime by farming, or they can turn us down and keep their farm intact. Some might even choose to do both, sell us the water rights and continue to farm with natural rainfall. Our system is deep enough that it will not be disturbed by plows."

Davis watched Tracey for a moment to see if he had answered her question, then he continued his team's presentation, completing it in the exact amount of time allotted. Once the WSP team finished, the commission members adjourned to a private conference room for a caucus.

They discussed the projects covered that day, making assessments of their feasibility and the political viability of each one. Some were clearly destined to become funded; others could be ruled out. WSP fell in neither group. That project seemed technically sound, but it faced immense social resistance. The panel decided it must have further review before a final decision could be made.

* * *

Tracey hurried to her room to ready herself for the cocktail hour prior to dinner. She quickly showered, refreshed her makeup and brushed her hair. She detested the social pretense that came with the job. She hated nothing more than having some man with martini breath get in her face and talk business. Still worse were the encounters with those who got a little too friendly after a few drinks. Slipping into a conservative dress, she checked her appearance in the mirror and squared her shoulders. *I can handle this*, she reminded herself. Eight years as a deputy press secretary, hobnobbing with all kinds of politicos and international representatives, had battle-hardened her.

Arriving early, the first person Tracey encountered in the reception area was Jackson Davis. None of the other participants had yet shown up. *Happy hour nightmare personified*, she thought. Tracey didn't find him attractive. She despised his type—one who viewed women as some kind of a tally on a macho score sheet and didn't care if they were married or not.

Jackson saw her enter the room, raised his glass as a greeting and walked toward her with a huge smile on his face. "I hoped I could have an opportunity to speak with you alone," he said, motioning her to a seat at an empty table.

Time to face this jerk and put him in his place, Tracey thought. She sat, and Jackson took the chair next to her.

"So what did you think about our pitch?" he asked.

"Professional, crisp and to the point."

"Do you think we'll be granted federal funding?"

"You know better than that. No comment."

"Well, off the record, how did we compare with some of the others, then?"

"I won't discuss that either. Any talk about results would be off limits. Change the subject, Mr. Davis."

Jackson swirled the cocktail in his glass, staring at the ice cubes in the drink. "How can I help you better understand our project?"

"You covered the material today. Very well, I might add."

He leaned toward her, his shoulder nearly touching hers. "I could personally fly you to San Francisco and show you the work we're doing there. You'd enjoy it."

"Are we talking about your company's work or San Francisco?"

"Both."

Tracey felt the slight pressure of his knee. *That's it.* Repulsed by his obvious move, she slammed her drink down and stood.

"Stop it! Before you go any farther, I'm not some defenseless young girl attracted to your power. I'm married. I'm not interested in you, and your company isn't going to get any favorable treatment from me."

He taunted her. "What are you going to do? Run off to get help from Earlman?"

"No. You keep pressing, and you'll find I can take care of myself."

Jackson stood, glaring at her. "I've heard you can. Is that why you're no longer with your husband?"

Rage welled within Tracey, and she didn't just slap him—she punched him in the face, releasing her fury. He reacted in shock, the first authentic emotion Tracey had seen him exhibit all day. He pressed his fingertips against his aching jaw.

"Bitch," he muttered.

"You better believe I can be," she shouted.

Moments later, a member of the security staff appeared, apparently called by the bartender.

"Need any help here?" he asked.

"No, everything's been taken care of," Tracey said, grabbing her purse and striding out of the room leaving Jackson to explain the situation to the security guard.

* * *

The next morning, the members of the Earlman Commission reconvened their hearings. They triaged the projects that had been proposed, using a show of hands. Those with unanimous support—only a few—were placed in the "accepted" category while those at the opposite end were "denied." Tracey withheld a vote on the WSP project, a fact that did not escape President Earlman. That project fell in the "further review" category along with a long list of others. The commission planned to spend the next two days working through the middle category and reaching a position on each. Once all the projects had been categorized, those in the "accepted" group would be weighed and ranked according to a rigorous cost/benefit analysis.

Tracey exhaled, billowing her cheeks, depressed by how far the commission was from completing the initial phase of its work. Her butt, sore from hours of sitting, wore at her ability to concentrate. No amount of squirming made her any more comfortable. She slipped off her shoes and wiggled her toes in the plush carpet.

The skirt surrounding the table hid her departure from protocol, but she still felt a little pang of guilt from the subtle pleasure she enjoyed from her lack of decorum in the presence of the former president. She fumbled in her purse for a pain reliever to help fight the headache welling up from reading all the fine-print details in the project proposals. The meeting dragged on.

After four hours of project reviews, none of which had been accepted, the WSP project came before the panel. As the other members were shuffling through the project papers, Tracey cleared her throat and said, "Mr. Chairman, I must recuse myself from the discussion of this project due to a conflict of interest."

President Earlman looked up from studying the packet of WSP information and peered at her over the top of his reading glasses. His face morphed into a scowl. Tracey braced herself. She had seen that look before—but never had it been directed at her. When President Earlman shifted away from his "uncle" persona, the recipient was due for a harsh tongue lashing. Tracey had witnessed heads of state, congressional leaders, military commanders and numerous others sharply taken to task for expressing a position in opposition to the president's point of view. She swallowed, knowing her only course was to hear him out.

"Ms. Stewart," the president began, "what makes you think you have the luxury of recusing yourself? This is not a court, and you are not a judge. I'll decide whether or not it's appropriate for you to participate."

"Uh ... Mr. President," she began, baffled by her inability to find the words to respond. She became the center of attention. The other panel members stared at her, waiting for her response, thankful it was her, and not them, on the receiving end of the president's ire. "Mr. President ... uh, my son ... my son, Dwy, is employed by WSP and my ... uh, people might question my vote, particularly if it were the swing vote. I—"

"Stop right there, Ms. Stewart," the president interrupted. He removed his glasses and glared at her. "We have seven panel members, each chosen for the unique competence they bring to the table. Yet the ultimate decision is not made by the panel. That decision's mine, on my shoulders alone. And I will not make that decision without the input from every panel member. Do you understand me?"

Tracey slipped her shoes back on, not wanting to risk raising the president's anger. "But Mr. President, people—"

"*People* are counting on this commission to do its job. We'll be judged by the results of our work, not by how we abided by some grade-school notion of civics. I don't care that your son works for WSP. I care only about your perspective on this project. We've wasted enough time on this discussion. Are we clear?"

It would have been easy to acquiesce, but Tracey had her own set of convictions. She knew that if President Earlman could back her down on a point of contention, she lost stature in his eyes.

"I will give you my input," she said. "That should satisfy your need for information. But I will not *vote*." She looked back at him, never having felt so tense in his presence.

The two stared at each other for an extended, awkward moment.

"Okay, Tracey," the president said, a smile flashing back on his face. "Looks like we each get what we want. What is your *opinion*, then?"

Tracey's heart rate, at a rapid peak, began to slow. She breathed easier. As quickly as Earlman could step away from his "uncle" persona, he could return without holding a grudge.

"I think we should support it. You said in our orientation that there would be tough decisions, some with enormous downside risks. This project is already underway. The technology has been demonstrated. It can be finished in a comparatively short time. It could begin saving lives in less than a year."

"What about the Ogallala Aquifer?"

"It's a finite resource. It might last 50 years at the present rate of draw-down. Perhaps it will last only 10 if this project goes through to completion. That's a huge downside, but it will give us 10 years to find additional ways to deal with the problem."

The former president looked at the other panel members. "What do the rest of you think?"

Tracey leaned back in her chair, listening to the comments and hoping her assessment of the project had been correct. She struggled with her thoughts, trying to keep her judgment separated from her disrespect for Jackson Davis and his connection with her family. The amount of negative comments from the other panel members didn't surprise her. This was to be a tough call.

After an hour of debate, the president gaveled the discussion closed and called for a show of hands. Tracey withheld her vote. The remaining six members split; three were "ayes" and three voted "nay." President Earlman contemplated his options, then cast the tie-breaker, "Nay."

* * *

The next morning, Jackson Davis got the bad news by phone. Within seconds of hearing that the WSP project had been rejected for funding, he became furious. Red-faced and with purple veins showing in his temples, he cut the caller off. "Put me through to Tracey Stewart—NOW!" The caller could only offer a connection to her voice mail. Once prompted to record, Jackson said through gritted teeth, "You'll be sorry, bitch." In a fit of rage he hurled the phone's handset against the desktop. It ricocheted off the surface and clattered to the floor.

Jackson punched the intercom and snarled to his secretary, "I want Anderson in my office in three minutes."

Anderson, the chief of flight operations, burst through the door moments later, out of breath.

"What is it?" he asked.

Jackson walked toward him and stood in his face. "You know that new pilot, the Stewart kid we put on the line a couple of months ago?"

"Yeah, he's a good man. What about him?"

"I want him assigned to patrol the Texas segment of the right-of-way."

"But … but uh, we've pulled our flights from that segment. You know they've taken shots at our planes there. One came back with some pretty serious damage."

"I know it's dangerous. That's why we need a kid who's got a spirit of adventure in addition to being a damn good pilot. He can handle himself. And it's because of the possibility of trouble that we must have flights there. Doesn't do any good to fly only where everything's expected to be serene."

Jackson glared at Anderson until the man shifted his gaze to the floor and muttered, "Okay, I'll reassign him." Anderson turned away and left the room.

Jackson smiled and picked up the phone from the floor on his way back to his desk. He sat in his chair and swiveled it around so he could take in the view of the L.A. skyline from his window.

Nice! he thought.

* * *

That evening, Tracey got the disturbing message Jackson had left on her voicemail. She called the Secret Service agent assigned to President Earlman and relayed the message's content and threatening tone. The agent took note of all the details and promised to have Jackson Davis added to the security list. Tracey knew several of the task force members had been accosted by other funding applicants who had also been rejected. Some of the threats were much worse than the one she received. The FBI maintained oversight of these threats and would be alert for any actions that might endanger her.

The security agent advised Tracey to avoid further contact with Jackson Davis or with WSP, advice she had no trouble accepting.

CHAPTER TWELVE

CHACO CANYON

Darren dialed Tracey's number.

"Hello," she answered.

"Hi, Trace, it's your boring husband."

"Oh, Darren, don't even joke about that. I've felt terrible ever since I said it."

"I'm over it. Probably deserved it, anyway. How are things going with you?"

"Awful. You wouldn't believe the jam I got in with President Earlman. Worked in his administration for eight years and never came close to being rebuffed before. I thought I was off the panel."

"What happened?"

"I said I had a conflict of interest and couldn't vote on the WSP project."

"Sounds like a good point to me."

"I thought so, too, particularly since neither one of us cares for Jackson Davis," Tracey said. "Jackson … he's a—" She paused in mid-sentence. *Better not elaborate; Darren would come unglued.* "—he's enough to make anyone want a break."

"Forget that bastard. He's not worth worrying about. How'd you like to do something spontaneous with me, instead?"

"I'd love to. I have a couple of days off. What do you have in mind?"

"Meet me in Gallup tomorrow night. We'll have dinner and start early the next morning on a day trip."

"Where do we meet?"

"Let's meet at the El Conquistador Hotel at 7 p.m. Oh, and pack shorts and a sweater."

"Shorts and a sweater? Oxymoronic. Sounds like the first time we went out. And look what that led to. Got me in all kinds of trouble. Where are we going?"

"It's a surprise."

"You're on."

* * *

Darren greeted Tracey with a hug when she entered the hotel lobby. He thought she looked weary, even showing her age a bit, but still pretty. *God, I miss holding her*, he thought, as she returned the hug. He felt a tremor pass through her body, perhaps a signal that she felt the same toward him. The hug lingered until Darren began to feel aroused. Tracey pressed against him, then slipped from his embrace, catching her breath.

After exchanging some pleasantries, Darren showed her around the lobby. The rustic Western motif featured on its walls the paintings and photographs of the many celebrities who had visited the El Conquistador during its glamour years. Built alongside Route 66 in the late 1930s by a director who had made a movie in Gallup, the hotel quickly became a haven for celebrities shooting films on location in the area.

Tracey enjoyed reading the comments and the autographs from stars she had only heard her mom talk about—icons such as Kirk Douglas, Errol Flynn and Gene Tierney. Climbing to the mezzanine, she looked down at the hotel's great room and tried to imagine Reagan—long before he became president—lounging in a smoking jacket on one of the Navajo-blanketed sofas, drink in hand and reading the latest issue of the Hollywood entertainment trade paper *Variety*.

"They didn't have to worry about the availability of drinking water back then," she said, turning toward Darren.

"No, but they were in the middle of the Depression, about to enter the war."

"I worry sometimes that we're headed for both."

"That's why you need a break," Darren said, placing his arm around her shoulders. "Ready for dinner?"

They continued around the mezzanine until they reached the top of the grand staircase. Once downstairs, they noticed a group of guests gathering around a TV in the gift shop. Fearing bad news, they joined the crowd and listened in shock as the news anchor, backed up by a "Breaking News" graphic, reported from on the scene at the State Capitol Building in Austin, Texas. Tracey missed the first part of his report but was stunned by what she did hear.

"... passed the Texas House and is now being voted on in the Senate to close the Texas borders to residents from the states west of the Continental Divide. We should have the results of that vote momentarily." The reporter turned his face away from the camera and grabbed his earpiece, apparently listening to his producer. "We now have information that the Texas Senate has just passed its version of the border closure bill. A conference committee has been convened and a vote on the final bill is expected later tonight. The governor has already signaled his intention to sign the legislation. The White House is expected to issue a statement momentarily in opposition to the action."

Tracey watched with a sickening feeling in her stomach as the reporter went on to explain that a number of projects that crossed the Texas borders would have their approval rescinded by the legislation. The broadcast jumped to the station's affiliate in Los Angeles, and Tracey grabbed Darren's arm when she saw the image of the man she detested, Jackson Davis, being interviewed about the WSP Project. "Texas has no authority to take this action," Davis began, "and we are appealing to the Interstate Commerce Commission to step in and protect our interests. We are requesting federal protection of our personnel and equipment."

A look of terror crossed Tracey's face. Darren knew what concerned her. "I talked to Dwy the day before yesterday when I first heard some of the rumors surface about this. He's flying the central New Mexico route. WSP stopped flying over Texas last week. He's not in any danger."

"But that was two days ago," Tracey said, grabbing her cell phone and punching in Dwy's number.

"Hello, Mom!" he answered.

"Oh, thank God, Dwy. Are you listening to the news?"

Dwy reassured her that he had been staying on top of the developments. He reiterated what his dad had told her. "I'm flying in New Mexico. WSP stopped flying patrols over Texas when they started shooting at our planes."

He asked what she was doing in Gallup and she told him that Darren and she were going to spend a couple of days getting away from it all. He wished her a good time and said he would be okay, that he knew how to take care of himself.

After he hung up, Tracey held her phone to her ear for a moment, not wanting to let her son's voice go. She felt the comfort of Darren's arm and lowered her head so he would not see her cry.

Darren knew her too well. He lifted her face toward his and wiped away her tears. "He'll be fine. Remember, he's got the best of each of us in him."

Darren took her hand and led her to the dining room, filled with the happy chatter of other guests and decorated in the bright, primary colors of Mexico. The aroma of enchiladas, tacos and fajitas added to the festive atmosphere. Their waitress, black hair tied back in a bun complete with a red flower, brought them a pair of margaritas. She spoke with a heavy Spanish accent and gave the impression that she loved her work.

When she returned to take their order, Tracey spoke up. "These drinks are wonderful. I'll have another."

Darren watched with an amused expression. Tracey normally had a one-drink capacity, and these margaritas were huge. He had been careful to sip his, and his glass remained half-full. Tracey had quaffed hers like it was lemonade. Darren didn't order another drink. *She'll need me to finish hers.* But he didn't have a chance. Tracey downed her second margarita as quickly as she had her first.

Before the waitress brought their entrees, Tracey's face became flushed. She picked up her napkin and began fanning herself with it. "Don't you think it's hot in here?" she asked.

"No, but I don't have any trouble understanding why you might think it is."

"Uh ... Darren, I need to get to some cool air. Let's walk outside."

Darren left money on the table to cover the meal and the tip. He led Tracey to the patio and in a few minutes, she began to feel better. Her thoughts returned to Dwy.

"Are you sure he's going to be okay?" she asked.

"Trace, there are no sure things in life, but he's his own man. You have to have confidence in him."

They embraced. Darren leaned forward to kiss her, but she shivered in the crisp breeze and backed away. Darren led her inside. They climbed the staircase and walked to her room. Outside her door, he kissed her. This time she responded with passion. Memories flooded through his mind—memories that floated on the wave of her perfume, the smell of her hair and the touch of her body. She broke the spell by fumbling for her room key. After she unlocked her door, Darren turned toward his own room. She grabbed his arm and pulled him toward her. "Huh-uh. I know I'm the one who insisted on separate rooms, but you're not going to kiss me like that and then go off and leave me by myself."

* * *

At breakfast, Tracey looked cheery. After her first cup of coffee, a smile broke over her face, even though the sun had yet to rise. As Darren had suggested, she wore shorts and a sweater.

"No hangover?" Darren asked.

"Nope, I think we found the way to prevent them," she said, with a wink and a little bit of a grin. "Where are we going today?"

"Chaco Canyon."

"The Anasazi ruins?"

"Yep, and we better get going, too. We don't want to miss the show."

"Show? What show?"

Darren explained that archeologists had recently made a major breakthrough in their study of the ruins. The pueblos in the canyon were found to have been laid out precisely along sun lines. Not only the individual pueblos, but all the buildings in the canyon were aligned to each other in a pattern dictated by the annual cycle of the sun. The Anasazi demonstrated a far deeper knowledge of the stars and the universe than ever before thought possible. So much so, that a new science term, "archeo-astronomy," had been coined for the study of this phenomena.

"Pretty amazing, but you still haven't told me about the show," Tracey said.

"Today is the summer solstice. At solar noon today, the sun will be at its highest point for the year. And at that exact instant, you will see a rain of optical events at Chaco. Shafts of sunlight will pierce serpents etched in the canyon walls. Slivers of light will pass through the very center of spiral petroglyphs. The sun will peek through a narrow slit in a wall and will illuminate an interior room of a pueblo, only to quickly disappear for an entire year before it can be seen again. All these events and others yet to be discovered make for a show of unmatched brilliance."

"I can't wait to see it, but if it's at noon, what's the hurry?" Tracey asked.

"First of all, the road's terrible, especially the last 20 miles—that stretch alone will take an hour and a half. But you can see only one or two of the events, because they're spread so far apart. Everybody knows that, so we have to get there early to get a good spot."

"Okay, but you also promised to show me how an ancient civilization dealt with a water shortage. Tell me about that."

"You'll have to wait until we get there. And if we're going to make it there in time for the show, we'd better get our asses in gear. Let's go."

＊ ＊ ＊

At dawn on the longest day of the year, the gray twilight signaled the sun's intent to rise by sending a horizontal streak of searing reddish-orange across a large portion of the northeastern horizon. Tracey lowered her visor and shielded her eyes from the brilliance with her right hand. Vimmy, confined to the Jeep's cargo area, had managed to jam his head between the seats and lay with his nose in the crook of Tracey's left arm. Looking away from the sun, she smiled and stroked his forehead with her fingertips. Vimmy thumped his tail on the floor without bothering to open his eyes.

Wearing aviator sunglasses, Darren scanned the countryside ahead, watching for the turnoff to Chaco Canyon. They had seen no sign of human life for the past 50 miles, only reddish-brown soil speckled with desert grasses. The road, unbounded by fence rows, quickly diminished in perspective to its geometric vanishing point, miles ahead. With no visible reference available to measure distances or speed, Tracey felt like they were in some form of suspended animation, with only the wind and tire noise to reassure her they were indeed moving.

"How much farther?" she asked.

"The turnoff's a few miles ahead. After we reach it, we have about 20 miles left."

"That's not bad at all."

"Wait until you see the road!"

They topped a swale, and Darren saw a faded wooden sign by the side of the road with an arrow pointing to the left. Darren barely made out the word "Chaco" before they whizzed by. He glanced in the mirror—as if anyone else might be on the road—then jammed on his brakes to a force just short of a panic stop. Even at that, they shot by the road to the canyon and had to back up before turning onto it. A few hundred yards along the road, another sign arose with an admonition reminiscent of Dante's inscription at the gates of Hell: "Abandon hope all ye who enter." Though not quite as foreboding, the sign warned the unsuspecting visitor that the road was extremely rough and should not be used by vehicles with low clearance. Nor should it be traveled after a rain—at least *that* hadn't happened in the last decade. The posted speed limit of 15 mph soon proved to be someone's fantasy. When Darren reached 10 mph, the Jeep yawed back and forth on the washboard surface. The deafening roar of the vibration grew to more than an annoyance, it became maddening. A half-mile-long rooster tail of dust trailed behind the Jeep. It permeated every opening in the cabin, burning their eyes and coating their mouths with grit. Vimmy awoke with a sneeze and shook his head violently, snapping his ears. Panting, he circled the rear compartment, sniffing for clean air and searching for a quiet spot. Finding none, he flopped down, head between his paws in disgust and eyes looking first to Darren, then to Tracey, in the hope that it all would soon end.

Tracey began to laugh. Darren did, too, not knowing why she was laughing but caught up in the joy of seeing her laugh once again.

"What's so funny, Trace?"

"Darren, you are truly unique. Most women would love for men to ply them with romantic getaways—Acapulco, San Francisco ... you know, places like that—and treat them to a luxurious dinner with an ocean view. Me, my one chance to be with you away from the pressures I'm under, and you take me out into the desert and bounce the living daylights out of me. Even our dog doesn't understand it."

"Well, one thing it isn't."

"What's that?"

"Boring."

Tracey settled back into her seat and gave no reply. She thought of the times she had been in remote and unusual vistas with this man. Memories flickered through her mind of the dunes at White Sands, the cliff dwellings at Mesa Verde, that shamanic night on the mesa in Sedona and all the other special places, including the landscapes they saw during their travel through time back to Pangaea.

She leaned her head on Darren's shoulder. A smile returned to her face. "No, it's not boring—it's wonderful."

* * *

In the distance, shimmering like a desert mirage, they could see a paved road beginning at the park's boundary. When they crossed onto the improved surface, the vibration subsided, the vehicle tracked a smooth, straight line, and the dust cloud disappeared. Darren parked at the visitor center, rolled down all the Jeep's windows and got out. The once metallic-gray vehicle now had a coating of red dust. While Tracey grabbed her purse and checked her appearance, Darren took Vimmy's water bowl and filled it from a faucet next to the park's bulletin board.

"Here, boy, you drink some of this and stay with the car. We'll be back soon."

Vimmy slurped up some of the water, spilling more of it than he drank, and quickly climbed into the driver's seat to await their return. Darren and Tracey entered the visitor's center, its cool and pleasant interior a welcome relief from the noisy travel in the Jeep.

Native American flute music played in the background. Quite a few visitors were milling through the exhibits, a much larger crowd than normal because of the summer solstice.

"Come on," Darren said, grabbing Tracey's hand and leading her to the center's small suite of offices. He spoke to the receptionist. "We are supposed to meet Professor Bowen here."

"Who's he?" Tracey asked.

"She," Darren corrected. "She's from the University of New Mexico and is the leading expert in archeo-astronomy—the field of science that combines archeology and astronomy, in particular how astronomy is related to ancient structures. Jane served as an intern for the woman who proposed—and finally proved—the theory that Chaco's pueblos had been laid out along solar lines. Professor Bowen, uh … Jane, carried on after her mentor retired and has since discovered and catalogued more than a thousand astroglyphs here in the canyon."

"Astroglyphs?"

"Sorry, it's a term for petroglyphs that exhibit a precise solar, lunar or stellar moment. The simplest example is a carved spiral that has a sliver of sunlight bisecting its center at the summer solstice. The spiral was the Anasazi symbol for migration. In this case, it is used to depict the sun's migration through the sky. Other petroglyphs might have figures marking the exact point on the horizon the moon will rise at the maximum of its 17-year lunar cycle."

"How did you come to know her, Darren?"

"She theorized that some of the astroglyphs portrayed stellar events, but couldn't make sense of any of the alignments. Then she realized that some of these buildings were constructed nearly 2,000 years ago, a long enough time for the alignment of the stars to have changed. She learned of my work on stellar alignments for celestial navigation in a far distant time during time travel and contacted me. I provided her the software to determine any star's position at any given time in the past. With that tool, she made some amazing discoveries."

"Like …?"

Professor Bowen's arrival interrupted Darren's reply. Tracey had pictured an elderly lady with reading glasses on a gold chain around her neck, as prim as an English teacher.

Professor Bowen, whom Darren quickly introduced as Jane, wore hiking boots, khaki shorts and a sweatshirt with the University of New Mexico crest on the front. She was a young woman with a strong grip and tanned, muscular legs who obviously spent a great deal of time outdoors and looked to be an experienced rock climber. Jane greeted Tracey as if she had known her all her life and welcomed her to Chaco.

"Darren was telling me about your work," Tracey said. "He told me about his collaboration with you on stellar alignments that led to some major breakthroughs."

"I owe Darren a good deal. That's one reason I'm happy to be your escort today."

Jane went on to explain that one of the stops they were going to make was to view the "Gate of the Spirits," a carving and petroglyph whose mystery had been solved by applying stellar equations. She said archeo-astronomers originally thought the Anasazi petroglyphs merely provided important calendar information for crop planting and harvesting cycles. Then they broke the much more complex lunar cycle code, which showed the Anasazi had a much greater understanding of the moon's orbits than ever before believed. "At first, archeologists thought the Anasazi developed these glyphs through years of observation, watching the sunrises and sunsets and marking the extreme positions.

"Then we found the Gate of the Spirits petroglyph that turned out to be a Rosetta Stone of sorts for the Anasazi culture's knowledge about the sun and the universe. A huge stone slab, stood on end, it had a hole carved through its center. If you looked through the hole from a precise vantage point, you could witness the sun rise at its winter solstice.

Tracey frowned. "How does that differ from the other glyphs you've talked about?"

"The Gate of the Spirits glyph represents something far greater than we thought: our own galaxy. Our earth's polar axis precesses, or rotates its alignment, the way a spinning top wobbles. The cycle takes 26,000 years to complete. The North Pole during this cycle traces a circle in the sky. Currently, the North Pole points to Polaris, the North Star, but it hasn't always been that way, and it won't always continue to be. Now stay with me on this. Once every 26,000 years, at the winter solstice, the earth, the sun and the center of our galaxy are in perfect alignment, designated by a point on the Zodiac that medieval man called the 'Gate of God.'"

"A similar name. Is that a coincidence?"

"I don't think so. Carved on this stone slab around the hole at its center are a number of figures. As a background, there's a square-shaped spiral, an Anasazi symbol that can mean a migration in some form or even a point of emergence, or a birth canal."

"What would that have to do with the winter solstice sunrise?" Tracey asked.

"There was another clue that we missed for years. Also carved on the stone was an arc of lizards chasing each other, nose to tail. One of the lizards at the center had his jaws opened around the hole as if he had it in his grasp."

"What does that mean?"

"We struggled with it until all the hoopla a few years ago about 2012, the supposed time of the galactic alignment."

"Some of this is beginning to sound a little familiar," Tracey said. "Something about the Mayans?"

"You're thinking about the Maya Long Count. The Mayans believed the earth had been destroyed and reborn three times before, each cycle lasting a Long Count, a little over 5,000 years. The last rebirth was about 3,000 years B.C., approximately the time of Noah. Starting from that point, the most recent Long Count supposedly ended December 20, 2012."

"Now I remember," Tracey said. "All the hype about the world coming to an end. But 2012 came and went and nothing happened."

"Like many urban legends that start out with the basis of a few facts, projections are made that feed upon themselves and develop a life of their own, far out of proportion to reality. Remember the so-called 'Jupiter effect' years ago, about 1990?"

"No."

"That's my point. Every so often, the planets in our solar system line up on the same side of the sun. I think the most recent year was 1990. The alignment of the planets was projected to place enormous stress on the earth's surface, much greater than a lunar tide, and cause dormant faults to fracture, the most famous being the New Madrid fault. Crowds of people, drawn by extensive media hype, gathered at the anticipated epicenter awaiting the cataclysm. Nothing happened. That's why you don't remember anything about it. The same with Y2K. Another big nothing."

"But you were talking about this Gate of the Spirits and galactic alignment."

"If you remember, even the galactic alignment got caught up in the 2012 doomsday myth. Because of the sun's width, the alignment takes place over a period of 36 years, from 1980 to 2016. So people began to refer to it as 'era-2012.' Made a good story, but the precise alignment actually took place in 1998, not 2012. Most folks overlooked that small detail, but not the Anasazi."

"What do you mean?"

"Darren helped me run the calculations. He ran the cycle backward and found that precisely on the winter solstice in 1998, the sun aligned perfectly with the center of our galaxy. The center is known by several names: the nuclear bulge, the 'Dark Rift', and the birth canal."

Tracey remembered the evening atop the mesa in Sedona that Darren had pointed out that feature to her.

"The Dark Rift," she said. "Sounds intimidating."

"It looks intimidating, too. Because of its shape, some have even described it as the jaws of a crocodile," Jane said.

Now the point dawned on Tracey. "Or the jaws of a *lizard.* Then the string of lizards represents—"

"The Milky Way, our Galaxy, as seen from earth precisely at the point of alignment. The rising sun, when centered in our Galaxy, looks as if it has been captured in the jaws of the lizard."

"But the galactic alignment came and went without anything apocalyptic happening."

"Yes, but that doesn't let us off the hook," Jane said. "The earth undergoes a number of cyclical deviations that cause serious changes in the amount of sun we receive, and as a consequence, our weather pattern is shifted. In addition to axis precession, the tilt of the earth goes through a 41,000-year cycle. And the shape of the earth's orbit around the sun changes over time. This cycle takes nearly 100,000 years. When combined, these cycles have an enormous impact on our climate. It's been determined they correlate with the cycle of our ice ages."

"The last ice age began nearly 110,000 years ago," Darren added, "and now we're in a warming trend, an inter-glacial period, somewhere near the peak. The warm cycles don't last very long. Most of the time, the earth is much cooler than now. The question for us—and for our water supply—is just how much longer will the warming trend last? And what effect, if any, will man have on the trend?"

"Here's the incredible thing," Jane said. "The Gate of the Spirits glyph I'm going to show you today verifies the fact that the Anasazi understood these universal cycles and the impact they would have on their civilization. They knew the climate would get hotter and dryer and were aware it would be thousands of years before crops would again be plentiful at Chaco."

Tracey had an epiphany. "Maybe they didn't just disappear; maybe with all their wisdom, they *decided* to leave."

"Tracey, it's something for you to consider," Darren said. "Perhaps there comes a point in time when all the efforts to supply water to the cities on the Western Slope, all the projects, all the cost and the human effort, cannot forestall the inevitable. The Anasazi chose this Godforsaken landscape at Chaco because they had the skills to collect enough water—with their channels cut in the rocks and their wells in the dry wash and all their other conservation efficiencies—to survive. They knew their enemies couldn't. They were safe here. The Anasazi worked with nature, understood it and were a part of its natural cycles, yet even with their sophisticated capabilities, the Anasazi finally chose to move away. The people of Los Angeles may have to make the same tough decision. That's what I wanted you to see today."

Tracey rubbed her face with her hands, trying to absorb the meaning of all she had heard. She looked up. "My mind's on overload. I need a break to let this soak in."

"I'll give you a good break." Jane smiled at the two of them and told them to get their backpacks; she also suggested they put Vimmy in her office while they were exploring.

"Where are we going?" Tracey asked.

"To the top of Fajada Butte."

CHAPTER THIRTEEN

THE GREAT NORTH ROAD

Fajada Butte was situated off a broad, Y-shaped point in the shallow canyon that had been formed by the confluence of the Chaco, Gallo and Fajada dry washes. Protruding into the canyon like the prow of a ship, it had at one time been connected to the Chacra Mesa to the east. Eons of erosion separated it from the canyon's rim and left it a free-standing, dominating monolith that could be seen from most of the vantage points in Chaco. Shaped like a three-tiered wedding cake, with its layers stacked off-center to one side, it rose over 300 feet from the valley floor. The moderately difficult climb to its top had been made easier by the steps the Anasazi carved into the steepest pitches. Reminiscent of a pointed gnomon at the center of a sundial, Fajada—or "banded"—Butte represented the perfect setting for petroglyphs exhibiting solar events. At noon on the summer and winter solstices and on the spring and fall equinoxes, the butte came to life with a cascade of astonishing occurrences.

Yet few people were allowed to witness them because tracks from previous visitors eroded and altered the alignment of the most spectacular glyph, destroying a phenomenon in existence for more than a thousand years. To prevent further damage, the route had been closed to the public. Professor Bowen and scarce few others had the permits now required to climb the butte.

The morning sun, on its way to its annual peak, bathed the rocks in heat. Jane led the climb, with sure and swift steps. Tracey followed, taking care to follow Jane's footsteps exactly. She paused long enough to tie her hair back and don a sweat band. She looked back at Darren, who lagged by a dozen yards. His face had turned to a splotchy red.

"Come on, old man," Tracey teased. "The show's over at noon. There won't be anything left by the time you get there at the rate you're climbing."

"You better keep your butt going up the butte; otherwise it's going to get whipped once I catch up."

"I'm scared," Tracey laughed, and then became serious. "Seems like we're always climbing mountains."

At her mention of the word, Tracey tensed. "You don't think this is the mountain the spirit guy saw in his vision, do you?"

"No, I don't think so. He said that mountain lay *across* our paths. Hell, we're on top of this one."

And after one last series of steps, they reached the top, joining a handful of people already there. Jane cautioned Darren and Tracey to step only on the shale, not on the earth or sand. Above all, she told them to not touch any of the stone fragments leaning against the vertical rock walls.

"Oil from your hands will discolor the rock's surface, and worse, even the slightest force from your touch could shift the rock and change its alignment. Now, follow me carefully."

She led them to a section of the wall shadowed by a huge shale fragment. Glancing at her watch, she said, "Seven minutes. Be ready. It won't happen again for a year."

Darren stared and at first saw nothing. After a minute or so, his eyes adjusted to the dimness, and he saw a spiral etched on the wall. As he watched in awe, a dagger of light appeared above the glyph, pointing to its center. Tracey caught her breath and reached around Darren's waist. A photographer with a camera sporting a lens as large as a megaphone continuously snapped pictures as the event progressed. While Darren and Tracey watched in amazement, the shaft of light pierced the center of the spiral.

"Solar noon," Jane said, looking at the face of her watch.

Darren experienced something unexpected. He felt a direct contact from an ancient, lost civilization, a culture intelligent enough to be able to speak to him across a gap of a millennium.

"Learn from us," he heard them say. "We can teach you things you must know."

In a fleeting instant, the light faded in brilliance, then disappeared, the only evidence of its brief existence being temporary, lavender figments left on the retinas of Darren's eyes. Mesmerized, he remained still until a shout from Jane startled him.

"Come on, let's go." She grabbed Tracey's hand and pulled her, with Darren in tow, to a series of steps carved in the top tier of the butte. After picking their way across the rock-strewn summit to the eastern edge, Jane pointed to a massive stone turned edgewise.

"The Gate of the Spirits," Jane said. "If you were to come back this December at the winter solstice and stand at the marker back over there, you would see the rising sun through the hole at the center. In the dark prior to the sunrise, the Milky Way Galaxy would be perfectly aligned with the lizard petroglyphs; the Dark Rift at the galaxy's center would be in the lizard's jaws."

Darren recognized the significance of the Gate of the Spirits. All the other symbols had been made after the fact, based on actual observations. How many centuries had it taken for the Anasazi to discover the sun dagger's unique position on the Summer Solstice? Only then could they have chiseled the spiral design on the rock face so that its center would be bisected each year by the shaft of illumination. Difficult enough, but the event represented by the image now before Darren had not occurred for 26,000 years. The Anasazi never witnessed it.

"Incredible ... absolutely incredible," he said. "This means they understood the cosmos well enough that they could foretell an alignment they had never seen. And they could leave a record of that prediction carved in stone for future civilizations to see."

Darren knew it meant more. The Anasazi were pre-historic but not primitive. They were the descendents of the Pangaeans, who were well versed in the laws of the universe. Even in today's high-tech society, few people could describe the physical basis for the seasons, let alone the term 'solstice.' *We are unaware. We're clueless*, Darren thought. *And yet, some politicians would have us believe that all we have to do to stop the cycle of global warming is to fill up our lawnmower's gas tank in the evening, rather than in the heat of the day.*

Darren walked to the northern edge of the butte, gazing toward the horizon to refocus his thoughts. From his vantage point, he could look slightly down on the broad mesa beyond the canyon's rim. His roving eyes picked up an aberration, an arrow-straight thread-line etched in the desert terrain, a line that stretched to the north.

Jane and Tracey came to his side. Tracey offered him a bottle of water. He poured some on his bandana and mopped his face with the soothing, cool cloth.

"What do I see over there?" he asked, pointing to the horizon.

"The mythical Great North Road," Jane answered. She explained that many roads led to Chaco and some archeologists believe Chaco represented a trade center and warehouse for settlements hundreds of miles away, some as far south as Mexico. Corn cobs found in the refuse at Chaco had been grown miles away in the foothills of the Chuska Mountains. Timbers used for construction of the roofs at Chaco were not native; they were Ponderosa pines from 40 miles to the west. "Over 200,000 tree trunks were brought here," Jane said. "And there are no scuff marks on the logs. They were too big to be carted, and they weren't dragged; the huge beams were *carried* by the Anasazi!"

Other archeologists believe Chaco represented a spiritual center, the best evidence for that being the Great North Road. "It goes nowhere. It passes through no settlements. It ends in a badlands canyon more than 30 miles north. But it was well designed. The layer of topsoil was removed, and cuts were made through swales to keep it level. The road is far wider than necessary for horse and cart traffic. For 10 miles, there's even a two-lane stretch like one of our interstates. The whole road is over-engineered. That's why many archeologists, including me, believe the road's basis is spiritual. The north-south axis was sacred to the Anasazi. Their buildings are aligned with that axis. The Great North Road was constructed more than a thousand years ago to a bearing less than a degree from true north."

Darren raised a pair of binoculars to his eyes. Scanning the horizon for the road, an ethereal, dark monolith came into view. "Shiprock Peak," he shouted in surprise.

"It's over 70 miles away," Jane said. "On a sunny winter day, you can see it without binoculars."

Something clicked in Darren's mind—some connection that remained just below the surface of his consciousness. But try as he might, he couldn't put it together.

Jane checked the time. She had to get back to the visitor center for a mid-afternoon lecture. She suggested she would meet them at Pueblo Benito, the canyon's largest building, afterwards. "You'll have some time to explore the pueblo while I'm working. When I finish, we'll walk to the beginning of the Great North Road."

* * *

Skeeter dropped the blade of the dozer, letting it hit the ground with a metallic *thunk*. While he allowed the diesel engine to idle for a cool-down period, he took a big swig of water, wiped his chin with the back of his hand and looked over the last portion of his work. *Done*, he thought, pleased with himself. *So smooth I could practice my golf putts on it.* He scanned the terrain to the horizon west of the complex and saw no remaining evidence of Project Time, except for the museum, now within days of opening. Landscaping crews were at work spraying grass seeding atop the bare earth, leaving a translucent, misty green covering in its place.

Skeeter shut the engine off, raised himself from the seat and climbed down the dozer's side, hopping the last foot to the ground. He removed his leather gloves and beat his hands against his coveralls to remove the heavy layer of dust that had accumulated during the afternoon. His ears still ringing from the dozer's engine, Skeeter didn't hear his boss, Spence, coming up behind him.

"You look like a damned bionic dust-devil," Spence said, watching in amusement.

Skeeter whirled around. "I told you it'd get done in time."

"I never doubted it."

"How's the museum coming? You going to be ready to open next week?"

"We're ready now. Just doing some dry runs on the exhibits. You know Earlman's going to be here, don't you?"

"Yeah, I heard. What happened to President Mitchell? I thought he was coming."

"He's tied up in this whole Texas thing. May have to cancel," Spence answered. "Are you inviting any of your family to the gala?"

"Nah, they can't make it," Skeeter said. *Even if I could find them, they wouldn't come.*

"That's too bad. You're coming, aren't you?"

"Yep. I'm bringing a friend."

"Good. After watching you in those damned coveralls for the last two months, it'll be a shock to see you in a tuxedo."

"Not as much of a shock as it will be for me to wear one. Haven't done that since the senior prom."

* * *

Darren stood with Tracey in front of Pueblo Benito, a
D-shaped, Chacoan Great House that was imposing, even in
ruin. The structure contained more than 1,000 rooms, and at
one time parts of it stood five stories high. Completed centuries after construction had begun, the building's architecture
represented evolving styles, the most recent being the most
sophisticated. The huge walls were formed with a rock core and
covered with a carved stone veneer. The veneer contained rows
of thick stones aesthetically separated by layers of thin stones
similar to the style used in modern brick homes. The doors and
windows were perfect rectangles, with corners that were true.
The interior was a labyrinth of openings and levels, each with
a complex roof formed by crisscrossed layers of wooden beams.
Great circular rooms interrupted the checkerboard precision
of the small rooms.

A ranger met them on the walking path and explained that
a large portion of the building had been destroyed by an event
that occurred more than 70 years ago. A 30,000-ton rock, called
"Threatening Rock" because of its precarious, overhanging mass
looming behind the pueblo, split from the cliff in 1941 and destroyed the rear quarter of the pueblo, leaving rock fragments and
massive boulders strewn throughout the area.

"Imagine the Chacoans living unknowingly with this impend-
ing disaster for nearly a thousand years—sort of like present-day
people living on the San Andreas Fault. Yet they vanished nearly
600 years before it happened. In one respect the Chacoans were
lucky," the ranger said, "or perhaps they were very smart and knew
when to leave."

"What do you mean?" Darren asked.

The ranger led them inside. "See those windows there?"

Darren looked to where the ranger pointed and saw a series
of windows that had been bricked closed with the same precision
as the original stonework.

"Why did they do that?" Darren asked.

"We're not certain, but throughout Chaco, many of the buildings exhibit the same care. It's as if the Chacoans decided to leave Chaco Canyon and took the time to close up important rooms in the buildings. Their departure was no panic-driven exodus, but a plan that took years to execute."

"They planned to leave? Why?" Tracey asked.

"Most believe that the drought put enormous pressure on their social structure. They had sufficient water to survive as individuals, but not enough to function as a regional center for gatherings and spiritual ceremonies. However, there's no convincing proof of that theory. Some have even suggested that the mini-ice age in Europe during the Dark Ages cooled the climate here, too. So much so that it became too cold to grow enough crops for humans to survive. I don't suppose we'll ever know for sure."

Jane caught up with them on the path, obviously happy that her lecture was over and she could be outdoors again. She greeted the ranger and suggested she would be happy to take over the tour so he could return to his duties.

"Did he tell you about the pueblo's alignment?"

"Not yet," Darren answered.

Jane walked them to the front wall that stretched 300 yards from end to end. "It's perfectly aligned east to west. On the spring and autumnal equinoxes, you can sight along the wall and see the precise location on the horizon of the rising or setting sun. At solar noon, the wall's shadow disappears. The D-shape is bisected by a north-south wall, an alignment that emphasizes the sacred directions of life and death."

Darren couldn't get his mind off the Great North Road. "Tell me more about its direction," he said.

Jane explained that north represented the direction to the "Shipap," the point of emergence.

Darren remembered the emergence myth about the Anasazi— *they came from a great civilization underground, free of sickness and strife. They came to the surface of the earth through a passage called a "sipapu." Once they reached the surface, a coyote covered the opening with a boulder, and they couldn't return.* The parallels between the Great North Road and Darren's search for the missing time-ship were strong. But he still couldn't make a connection.

"Are you ready for another little climb?" Jane asked.

"Little? It better be," Tracey said. "Hiking up Fajada Butte turned out to be quite an effort."

"This won't be difficult, and the results will be worth it."

"Let's go," Darren said.

Jane led them to a ravine eroded into the cliff face. A trail led up the bottom for a short distance, then turned and ascended the ravine's wall by a series of steps carved into the stone. After a few switchbacks along the natural ledges in the stone, the trail made the final climb to the top of the canyon. The three were hardly winded.

Darren looked down on the pueblo, still fascinated by its complexity. A hot breeze flowed up from the canyon's floor and hit them like a jet blast.

"Come on," Jane said, turning away from the edge of the mesa and walking toward the north. A few moments later, she paused and pointed in the direction of the road. "There's the beginning."

Darren stepped to the path, only wide enough for two people at that point. He was confused, though. "It's not heading north."

"No, it goes northeast for a short while, then, at Pueblo Alto, it turns due north."

"Pueblo Alto?"

"It is a small structure atop the mesa that we think served as a signal post for the southern terminus of the road—either part of a sentry system or perhaps some ceremonial basis to announce the arrival of spiritual beings. You can see a light from the top of Pueblo Alto for more than a hundred miles at night."

The walk on the trail was enjoyable, and within minutes they reached the ruin Jane had described. True to her promise, the road turned due north.

Darren stood in the center of the path, raised his binoculars to his eyes and could not believe how straight a line the road followed. He tried to imagine the Anasazi or even ghostly spirits who may have traveled its length. He swept his binoculars to the left to spot Shiprock Peak. It came into his view, eerily shimmering in the summer heat. His scan slowly returned to the road.

Then it hit him … a realization so powerful it nearly knocked him over.

"Holy shit! Trace," he shouted, grabbing her arm. "We've got to get back. I know where it is!"

"What?"

"The time-ship."

* * *

Darren had been wired the whole trip back to the hotel, muttering about compass headings, true bearings, azimuths and all sorts of navigational terms. But he came down to earth as soon as they neared Gallup and regained radio reception.

"Wyoming announced its intent today to follow Texas and close its borders to persons west of the Continental Divide," the reporter said from on-scene at Cheyenne. "Meanwhile, the Texas governor called up the National Guard and began positioning soldiers at each highway crossing along the state's western boundary. Clearly, they intend to check IDs and turn away persons who are not residents."

"Not good," Darren said.

The reporter continued, "President Mitchell met with the U.S. Attorney General and a panel of high-profile attorneys prior to issuing this statement: 'Actions taken by the states of Texas and Wyoming are in violation of the Constitution, and I have notified both governors that the U.S. will not permit these illegal measures to continue. I called upon each of them to rescind their executive orders. Though I do not expect they will be necessary, I have placed our federal troops on alert.'"

"Hold on," the reporter said, "I have just been given the Texas governor's response to President Mitchell. I'll read it to you. 'President Mitchell, I must remind you of Article IV, Section 4, of the Constitution:

> *The United States shall guarantee to every State in this Union a Republican Form of Government, and shall protect each of them against Invasion; and on Application of the Legislature, or of the Executive (when the Legislature cannot be convened) against domestic Violence.*

It says the government can send its troops into a state only with the permission of that state's legislature or of its governor, neither of which you have. I will not rescind my order because in the absence of federal protection against invasion, our action is vital to our state's well-being.'"

Darren saw the worried look on Tracey's face. He reached for her hand. "Right now, it's all bluff and bluster," he said. "No one's going to do anything stupid."

"What if someone miscalculates?"

"They won't. Right now they are talking to each other through back channels to work out an agreement to save face on both sides. They got themselves into this mess. They'll figure a way out. In the meantime, life will go on. Most folks will pay more attention to the fireworks on the Fourth than anything going on between Texas and Washington."

Tracey wasn't so sure. "Will it affect your opening next week?"

"No. Everything's ready. President Earlman will be the key-noter. We even have a role for Aaron Eaglecloud. Lots of star power, too. You told me last week that you'd come. I hope you will. I loved spending today with you."

"I wouldn't miss it."

"Maybe someday soon, we can make more permanent arrangements."

"Maybe. Let's work toward that, okay?"

"Okay."

When they reached the hotel, Darren saw her to her car and said goodbye with a lingering kiss. He gave her a farewell wave as she drove away. Getting in his own car, he turned onto the interstate eastbound and headed for home. He punched Skeeter's number into his cell and talked to him about making some special arrangements for the following day.

"Tell Spence you're going to be with me all day," he said.

CHAPTER FOURTEEN

A DISCOVERY

With aeronautical charts folded under his arm, Darren knocked once and burst through Skeeter's door at sunrise the next day. He heard a belated and grouchy "come in" and rushed to the source of the sound in the kitchen area. Skeeter stood at the counter measuring spoonfuls of coffee for the pot. Ignoring him, Darren pushed aside the leftover dinner dishes on the table, knocking a salt shaker to the floor in the process. He spread out one of the charts and jabbed his finger repeatedly at a specific point on the map.

"There it is," he yelled. "Right there!"

"Jesus, Darren, keep your voice down. I haven't had my coffee yet. Do you know what time it is, for God's sake?"

"I told you I'd be here early. Did you get the NASA chopper lined up for us?"

"It's on the ramp. They're expecting us at 7:00. I told them I was you when I called yesterday. They wouldn't have rescheduled for just a dozer driver."

"Rescheduled?"

"Yeah, you're going to have some peacemaking to do. This morning the chopper was supposed to airlift some critical parts from Albuquerque. Spence will be pissed."

"That's okay. I'll handle it. He's ahead of schedule anyway. And, uh … thanks."

"About time you became civil. Now what's all this about finding the ship?"

Darren told Skeeter about the trip to Chaco and seeing the Great North Road with Shiprock Peak in the distance. He recounted Professor Bowen's point about the north being the "Shipap," or the point of emergence.

"Skeeter, it kept working at me. If as we know, the time-ship carrying the ancestors of the Anasazi crash-landed, then their escape from that craft would represent a beginning—or an *emergence*."

"Go on."

"If they journeyed to Chaco from that ship, the route they took would have later become the Great North Road, a spiritual commemoration of their journey."

Skeeter now began to understand Darren's excitement.

"But it could be anywhere along that route for hundreds of miles."

"That's where Shiprock Peak and your damn broken pinnacles come in. Look here."

Darren showed Skeeter two lines drawn in red on the map. The first line ran due north from the ruin at Pueblo Alto, tracing the Great North Road.

"But if we estimate from the direction the pinnacles fell that the ship descended on a southeasterly bearing, we can draw this second line."

Darren traced his index finger along a red line beginning at Shiprock Peak and running to the southeast. When that line crossed the Great North Road, he began jabbing his finger again.

"There! Where they intersect. That's the spot!"

It took a minute for Skeeter to comprehend Darren's theory. Then it dawned on him. He bent over the table and looked closely at the chart.

"It's in the middle of nowhere—no roads or landmarks," Skeeter said. "No wonder it's never been found. And it's farther away from Shiprock Peak than you thought. The time-ship must not have been too badly damaged when it hit the pinnacle for it to have flown that far before landing."

"That's why we need to find it. It's a treasure trove of information and spare parts, and it might even be flyable, depending on how well preserved it is. The Pangaeans took a critical link from the ship at the museum to be sure we'd never use it. They never counted on us finding a complete spare time-ship."

"You're not really planning on flying the ship if we find it, are you?"

"Skeeter, my whole life's been focused on time travel. I want to experience it once more, and that ship represents my only opportunity. You're damn right I want to fly it. But right now we've got a helicopter to catch. Let's go."

* * *

The receptionist waved Dwy Stewart into the office of WSP's chief of flight operations, David Anderson. The chief rose and greeted him, motioning for him to sit. Dwy eased himself into one of the leather chairs, trying not to gawk at the elegant décor that included a bronzed replica of the aircraft carrier U.S.S. *Abraham Lincoln* on the credenza behind his desk. *A different world than my office in a second-hand construction trailer in Sedona*, Dwy mused.

Seeing Dwy staring at the carrier, Anderson said, "I flew F-18 hornets in combat off the deck of that ship. Even though the damned Iraqis were throwing Triple A at us so thick it blackened the sky, it was the most thrilling time in my life. Wouldn't trade it for one hour of all the airline cattle cars I flew after the war."

Dwy squirmed, knowing that Anderson had not asked to see him in person to tell him of his flying exploits. He knew the meeting represented an exception from the normal assignment of pilots, communicated by a list posted on the master duty board in the field office.

Anderson's demeanor changed; a stern expression crossed his face.

"Stewart, the situation in Texas has worsened. We've withdrawn our personnel and can no longer maintain an on-site surveillance of the security of our equipment. We need to begin our over-flights again."

"What good would those do?" Dwy asked.

"Reconnaissance flights would let the damn Texans know we are watching our investment. They wouldn't want any video taken of sabotage that would embarrass them and cost them national support for their cause."

The chief became silent. He rested his elbows on his desk and interlocked his fingertips, supporting his chin on his clasped hands while he stared at Dwy. The silence extended to the point of tension. Dwy knew what was coming but remained quiet.

"We are scheduling you to resume Texas patrols, starting next week."

"I don't think I'm prepared to do that. It's too big a risk."

"The same could have been said about my fighter sorties off the deck of the *Abe Lincoln*. We did it for the good of the country."

"This is different. We're not talking national security, here. Thanks, but no."

Anderson opened a drawer in his desk and retrieved a document. He turned it so that Dwy could read it and slid it across the desktop toward him.

"I had this severance paper prepared, in case that might be your response. You may take it with you and think it over carefully. Let me know of your decision in the morning. Good day, Mr. Stewart."

The chief turned in his chair, picked up his phone and began talking with his back to Dwy.

* * *

The NASA chopper neared Chaco Canyon. Darren sat in the right seat, next to the pilot, and Skeeter sat in back. By far the happiest occupant was Vimmy, who loved to ride, no matter what kind of vehicle. His panting, turning and tail-wagging added to Skeeter's discomfort. All three men wore the classic green headsets to be able to converse over the incessant roar of the rotors. Trying to ignore the smell of jet fuel that permeated the cabin, Darren spread his chart out on his knees and tracked their position. The vibration of the cabin, coupled with the blast of air from the air conditioner, caused the chart to billow and flap. Darren had trouble holding it steady enough to read.

Damn choppers, Darren swore to himself, *flying in one of these mechanical nightmares is an unnatural act. No sane pilot would get caught in one.* Darren didn't care for the sensation of being suspended underneath flimsy rotor blades, spinning at an impossible rate and fastened to the helicopter by the single, critical "Jesus nut"—so named because if it ever failed, you were destined for a meeting with Jesus.

The low altitude they were flying didn't allow them to escape the thermals rising off the desert floor that caused the chopper to surf the atmosphere like a boat on choppy swells. Worse, at this low altitude, the air conditioner could not maintain the cabin at a comfortable level. Soaked with perspiration, the back of Darren's shirt stuck to his seat. Squinting into the haze, Darren finally saw Fajada Butte on the horizon.

Pointing, he turned to Skeeter, who looked uncomfortable, and said, "A few minutes more; hang in there."

"What's my other option?" Skeeter asked with his characteristic grin.

"Not one you'd want to consider."

The pilot climbed to 2,000 feet to comply with the air space restriction over the National Monument. Enjoying the aerial perspective as they crossed over Fajada Butte, Darren could see that two segments of the road, beginning at different points in the canyon, converged at Pueblo Alto, a confluence looking from the air like a giant wishbone.

Once beyond Pueblo Alto, the road began its journey due north. Darren traced the route from his map and called out key landmarks as they flew over them. "There's Pierre's Complex," he said, nodding toward some outlying ruins.

A few miles north, the road split into four parallel routes, mimicking a superhighway, but for a purpose unknown. Darren checked to see that the pilot had entered the longitude and latitude into the navigation system for the intersection on the chart.

"35.6 North Latitude and 107.9 West Longitude," he said.

"Got it," the pilot confirmed.

"There's Gallegos Crossing," Darren said, turning back toward Skeeter. "We're coming up on Kutz Canyon. That's where the road ends."

"But your intersection is north of the canyon. If that's so, the road doesn't originate at the ship. Doesn't that put a kink in your theory as to where the ship is?"

"Yeah, it's got me worried."

The chopper reached the badlands area known as Kutz Canyon a few moments later. The name "canyon" proved to be flattering—"confused arroyo" might have been more descriptive. Once they crossed over the northern rim of the gulch, the navigation system alerted them with a green light and an audible alarm that the chopper had reached the intersection.

"We're right above it," the pilot said.

Darren motioned for him to circle. "Look for anything unusual," he said into the intercom. "Metallic reflections, debris, gouge marks in the desert floor—anything."

One thing caught their immediate attention. Grading work on the right of way for the WSP pipeline followed the canyon's edge.

"They're messing up the terrain," Darren said. Graders, ditchers, and backhoes were working feverishly to string 60-foot sections of pipe together once the route had been cleared and excavated.

Beginning to feel pangs of disappointment at seeing no evidence of a crash, Darren asked the pilot to circle the area once more.

"We're running low on fuel," he said. "I can give you a little more time, but not much."

Darren looked along the pipeline route. The grading stopped short of a mound, then resumed on the other side. "Over there," Darren requested, nodding toward the mound. "Let's see what the obstacle is."

Above the mound, Skeeter shouted into his mike. "That's not a natural formation!"

Darren's senses perked up because of Skeeter's comment. "What do you mean?"

"Something's strange about it."

"Set us down here," Darren told the pilot, who glanced at his fuel gauges with some concern.

The pilot turned the helicopter into the wind and eased it to a landing, kicking up a cloud of dust as it neared the ground. He cut the engine to idle and motioned for the passengers to get out. Darren and Skeeter stepped off the landing skids, instinctively ducking their heads until they had cleared the rotor's arc. The pilot shut the engine down to conserve fuel.

Happy to be out of the cabin, Darren paid no attention to the heat. He trotted toward the base of the mound, Skeeter right behind him. Vimmy swept the area in circles around them, nose to the ground, tail high. Darren estimated the mound to be 500 feet in diameter and 200 feet tall. It had the shape of a flattened dome rather than the cone that might be expected.

The geologist in Skeeter came to the surface. "I told you it wasn't natural," he reasserted. "It's all small boulders, nothing like the eroded sandstone you normally see around here. These rocks are not native to this canyon. There's not much variation in their size, either. Most unusual, the aggregate and soil between the rocks looks like it has been packed in like a binder, or mortar of sorts."

"How do you think it was formed, then?" Darren asked, excitement building.

Skeeter shook his head. "I don't know. Even the glacial moraines you would find much farther north are more like gravel than this. And their shape is like that of a sand pile."

Darren scrambled to the top, but Vimmy beat him there, scampering up the rocky slope without difficulty. Skeeter followed but lagged behind. Once Darren reached the top, he spotted something that shocked him. Stone slabs had been placed vertically in a circle surrounding the center of a fire pit. Gaps in the stones existed to the north and to the south. The formation resembled a crude, shoulder-high turret on a castle.

"A signal tower?" Skeeter asked, breathing heavily, "or some kind of shrine?"

Darren walked to the northern edge of the stone circle and looked to the south through the gaps in its circumference. He could see the trace of the Great North Road as clearly as if he were looking through a scope on a rifle.

"This is it," Darren said, his voice shaking. "Damn it, this is it!"

"What?" Skeeter asked. "You're not going to go berserk on me again, are you?"

"The time-ship. It's *here!*"

"Where?"

"We're standing on it. It's right beneath our feet!"

Skeeter looked at the ground between his legs. He looked back to Darren. "What do you mean?"

"The myth of the Anasazi says 'A coyote covered the opening with stone,'" Darren recited. "But it was the *Anasazi*—not a coyote—who did it. They didn't want their enemies to find them.

They brought these rocks here, one by one, and covered more than the opening; they *buried* the whole damn ship!"

"Maybe," Skeeter said, looking back at the ground between his legs.

"I just don't understand one thing," Darren said. "If they disembarked and traveled south, why does the road stop on the other side of the canyon? It could have skirted the canyon and come right up to the ship's door."

Skeeter looked across the canyon toward the road's juncture with its rim. Then he looked to the left and to the right. "Once again, elementary," he said. "The road did come all the way to the ship—some 1,700 years ago. The canyon had not eroded past this point yet. Over the years, it progressed and cut through the road."

"Uh-oh," Darren said, breaking into Skeeter's explanation. "Trouble."

A white car with "Security" emblazoned on its side, pulled up to the base of the mound. An armed guard got out and, one hand resting on his holster, motioned them to come down. Darren and Skeeter climbed to the ground and walked toward the man. Vimmy bristled and came to Darren's side. He stood on full alert, staring at the guard.

"Easy, Vim."

"You're trespassing," the guard said. "Show me some I.D."

Darren presented his NASA I.D. to the man. Skeeter followed suit.

The man pressed the transmit button on the radio strapped to his shoulder. He spoke to someone, giving the names and occupations of Darren and Skeeter.

"What are you doing here?" the officer asked.

Darren explained that they were carrying out some NASA research on the alignment of the Great North Road. They had landed to take a closer look at the road's terminus. With one hand around Vimmy's collar to restrain him, Darren apologized for the transgression, saying they had not meant to trespass. Skeeter stood sheepishly in Darren's shadow, letting him do all the talking.

The radio came to life with a static-filled transmission. Darren could hear only a portion of what was broadcast, but he heard the comment, "They check out."

The officer said for them to return to their helicopter and leave without lingering.

Before complying, Darren pressed his luck and asked the guard, "What's with the mound?"

"You'll have to take that up with the superintendent. All I know is that they've arranged to bring in a special piece of equipment at the end of the month to drill and blast through it. They can't complete this section until that rig gets here. Now you guys better move on."

They boarded the chopper, and after a brief refueling stop in Farmington, flew back toward Alamogordo. The whole return flight Darren tried to figure out how to meet his obligations for the museum's opening in two days and, at the same time, prevent WSP from digging into the mound and possibly destroying the ancient time-ship. Skeeter kept his thoughts to himself. Vimmy, worn out from all his activity, sprawled out on the seat and slept with his head in Skeeter's lap.

* * *

By the time the helicopter reached Alamogordo, Darren had talked to dozens of people, cross-checking the final details about the museum's opening day the following Saturday. He concentrated on the arrangements for the V.I.P. reception, scheduled the evening before the opening. The list of guests ranged from NASA leaders, including the Administrator, to government officials in any department or cabinet having connections with the museum—the departments of State, Defense, Interior, Homeland Security, and the EPA, to name a few. Then there were the celebrity guests, musicians and of course, President Mitchell, though it looked doubtful that he could attend with the Texas and Wyoming crisis.

Weary from the phone calls, Darren made the one he felt most important.

"WSP Corporation. How may I help you?"

"This is Dr. Stewart with NASA. Please connect me with Mr. Davis."

"He's not in at the moment. Would you like his voicemail?"

Darren muttered that he would and at the prompt, said, "Davis, this is Stewart. I must speak with you immediately about the WSP pipeline right of way in Northern New Mexico at Kutz Canyon. We've got to work out a change in routing. Shouldn't be too big a deal. If you don't call me back right away, I'll come to your office. This can't wait. It's urgent."

He snapped the cell phone shut and sat back in his seat waiting for the chopper to land so he could get on with his business.

CHAPTER FIFTEEN

AN EVENING AT THE MUSEUM

The day of the museum opening, Darren arrived for work at 6:00 a.m. and spent the morning responding to last-minute phone calls and attending to the details associated with the itineraries of the celebrities and dignitaries. President Mitchell, as expected, had been forced to cancel because of the worsening border crisis. Incensed that Jackson Davis had not bothered to return his call, Darren finally got through to his secretary and warned her that he would be knocking at the door first thing Monday morning unless he heard back from Davis. By the time Darren left to meet Tracey and Dwy at the airport, his face showed the strain from the pace of the activity and the concern from worrying about WSP forging ahead and destroying the ancient machine.

Darren drove to the airport and waited at the gate to the ramp, listening to the chatter between the controller and the arriving planes. Dwy had not yet contacted the tower, and Darren paced the fence line, adding anxiety about the safety of his wife and son to his concerns. He knew the weather between Sedona and Alamogordo had deteriorated all day, with some heavy storms moving in. His focus had been on the weather's potential effect on the opening, not about the problems it might cause Dwy's flight. Guilt added to his burden.

"Alamogordo Tower, this is Citation, November 6232 Uniform, at the Holloman VOR inbound."

"Roger, 32 U. Cleared for visual approach to runway 03. Report on left base."

"32 U."

Darren exhaled in relief, chastising himself that he had doubted his son's competence. *A better pilot than I*, he had to admit. *Of course, he had a good teacher.*

He watched a dot on the horizon make a left turn and line up with the runway. The little jet touched down without even a chirp and taxied to the ramp in front of Darren. The lineman waved his wands, guiding the plane to a tie-down spot, and then signaled for the pilot to shut the engines down. The attendant approached the gate, barely getting it open before Tracey burst through it, running at full tilt toward Darren. She nearly knocked him over with a bear hug and then smothered him with a kiss that lingered until Dwy rolled his eyes and said, "Hey, you two, enough!"

Darren and Tracey drew apart. Darren's grin promised there'd be more later, when Dwy wasn't around.

"Nice plane," Darren said. "Your business must be doing pretty well."

"It's the WSP jet," Dwy said, "the one I fly the execs around in. One of the perks is that I have to maintain a minimum number of hours each month, so they let me use it to keep current when it's not otherwise scheduled."

Darren helped the two of them transfer their luggage to the car. "Come on, get in," he said. "We've barely got enough time to get home and change before we have to be at the reception."

When excited, Tracey tended to chatter. And during the ride to their house, she talked so much that neither Darren nor Dwy could complete a sentence without an interruption.

Reaching their driveway, Darren parked the car and waited for what he knew would come next. In a few seconds, Vimmy tore around the corner of the house and bounded toward Tracey. Paws on her shoulders, he slurped her face, his body wiggling with excitement. Tracey grabbed Vimmy's cheeks, shook his head in mock aggression, and blew directly at his nose. What had been joy turned into complete chaos, with Vimmy running from person to person, barking, sniffing luggage, and scattering papers, ticket stubs and other belongings across the yard.

"He's glad you're home," Darren said. After a long look into Tracey's eyes, he put his arm around her shoulder. "And so am I." He grabbed Dwy with his other arm and they tried—but failed— to stuff themselves three-abreast through the front door, laughing when they had to break apart and pass through, single-file.

* * *

Skeeter struggled to button the tuxedo studs in his shirt, dropping one in the process. It rolled underneath the bed. On his knees, Skeeter searched for it, cheek on the floor and butt in the air, thankful no one could see him. He retrieved the stud and got the wayward piece of jewelry fastened. He raised his chin and stretched his neck to get the tight collar buttoned. He stepped into his trousers, fastened them at the waist and battled with the elastic of the suspenders, trying to get them adjusted to the right length. He walked to the dresser to get the cummerbund, not liking the feeling of his trousers bouncing with each step he took. *Damn tuxedos. No wonder I haven't worn one since the prom.* He stood before the mirror, bowtie in his right hand and the instructions that came with the rented tux in his left. Seven frustrating attempts later, he had it tied, knowing the bow wouldn't make any fashion statement. He donned the jacket and walked out the door.

* * *

Darren finished getting ready before Tracey did. Waiting for her downstairs brought back good memories of all the times they had gone out. She always took longer than he, but the wait was worth it. Hearing the bedroom door open, he turned to catch sight of her. She paused briefly at the head of the stairs in a rose-colored gown that was the loveliest that Darren had ever seen her wear. She flowed down the stairs, her feet bedecked in high-heeled sandals. As she approached him, Darren could tell she was wearing the perfume—containing a hint of sage and juniper—that was Darren's favorite. The smile on her face made her absolutely radiant. Darren fell in love all over again. He reached to take her in his arms.

"Ah-ah-ah," she said, shaking her head. "That'll come later. No wrinkles in my dress or smudges on my face, remember? Not until we get there, anyway."

Darren gave her a pat on the rear instead.

✳ ✳ ✳

Jackson Davis and the head of the WSP Engineering Department pored over the prints laid out on the conference room table.

"There's some asshole from NASA that's been bugging me about our right-of-way along Kutz Canyon. For some strange reason known only to himself, he wants us to deviate around that knoll, uh … let's see … oh, right here," Jackson said, stabbing the drawing with the tip of his pen. "I don't care about his problems—screw him. He's some kind of physics nut with a real bitch of a wife. But that blasted bump in the road is going to cost us big time—hauling in specialty equipment, delays and God knows what else. What would it take to go around it?"

The engineer studied the map, paying attention to the topographical layout of the surrounding area. He drew an alternate route in red ink and then scribbled a series of numbers on the corner of the print, shaking his head at the result.

"You're not going to want to go around it," he said. "It would cost more and take even longer than blasting right through it." He went on to explain that the right-of-way in that section followed a ridge of high ground through most of the canyon. To deviate around the mound on either side would require that the line drop down onto the canyon's floor and resurface 10 miles later. Not only would a large portion of the existing pipeline have to be relocated, but the new route would require an extra pumping station to meet the added pressure requirements.

"Okay, that makes the decision easy. We're going straight through as planned."

Jackson's secretary poked her head into the conference room. Motioning to the phone, she said, "You need to take this call. It's urgent."

Jackson swore. "Urgent" was his secretary's code word for "bad."

He grabbed the receiver, punched line two and listened for a minute before slamming the handset back into the cradle so violently the engineer jumped.

"Some goddamned rogue Texans just blew up a section of our line west of Amarillo!" he yelled. "They set fire to three of our office trailers and poured sand into the fuel tanks on our dozers. If we ever catch them, I'll kill them myself." He called Anderson, his chief pilot. "You got those flights going yet?" he asked, then scowled at the answer. "I don't care if you've got them *scheduled*; I want them *flying*—and NOW!"

* * *

"Is Dwy ready?" Darren asked. "He's always running late. The limo will be here any minute."

As if on cue, Dwy bounded down the stairs. Sporting a two-day growth of beard and a silver earring, he wore a black, pin-striped suit jacket over jeans and a white, V-neck sweater. Darren sighed. *It's a black tie event, for Christ's sake. Even Skeeter said he would be wearing a tux.* He felt an elbow from Tracey.

"Let him be," she whispered. "He's your son, and he is so proud to be going with you."

Darren relented. The limo appeared, and Darren ushered his family to the car and opened the door for them. Once they were settled, the driver began the trip to the museum.

"Hey, Dad," Dwy said, "Aaron told me he was on the program tonight. What have you got him doing?"

"It's a surprise. Look, everyone, tonight's going to be fun. Let's roll with it and enjoy being together."

In a few minutes, the limo pulled to the portico at the museum's entry. A crowd had already gathered. To one side, a huge searchlight swept the evening sky, and the Alamogordo High School marching band played a series of Sousa marches, welcoming the arriving visitors. A lush, red carpet runner, bracketed with a line of stanchions connected by velvet ropes, led the way to the V.I.P. entrance. Darren's mood improved with each step he took. Happy that the preparations were providing good results, the weight lifted from his shoulders.

Huge, sliding doors at the front of the museum stood open, allowing the guests to stroll outside in the comfortable, evening air. On the patio, Darren saw a circle of stones had been laid out with boulders at the cardinal directions.

Inside, he could not believe the transformation that had taken place. The Pangaean time-ship had been cordoned off behind a floor-to-ceiling black curtain. Elegant tables around the perimeter were stacked with hors d'oeuvres. Members of a big band were seated on the far side, and the director raised his baton upon seeing the Stewarts enter. On the downbeat, the musicians began a lively tune that Tracey instantly recognized.

"Oh, Darren," she said, clutching his arm, "The Santa Fe Stomp. How did—"

"It's the same group we heard on our first date. Remember?"

"Of course I do. But it's been over 30 years."

"There're a few new players, but most of the original members are still around. Enough of that, though," Darren said, "let's dance before they finish the piece."

Without warning, he put his arm around Tracey and spun her into a swing dance position. Dwy stood dumfounded, having not seen his parents on a dance floor in years. The band leader increased the tempo and cued the lead trumpet player to take a solo. It didn't take long for both Darren and Tracey to be gasping for breath. Giving up, they stood, hands on each other's shoulders, with huge smiles on their faces. The band shifted to a slow tempo. Darren motioned for the crowd to join them and the floor became filled with dancers. He held Tracey close to him as good memories flooded back.

"I'll be damned," Darren said. "Isn't that Sandy over there with Skeeter?"

"Yes. You didn't know they were dating?" Tracey answered.

"Not a clue."

"Other people have lives too, you know. You think Skeeter has nothing better to do than crawl over rocks for you?"

"Yes ... er, uh, no. I mean ... but *Sandy?*"

"How long has she worked for you? You think this museum is her life? What else have you been oblivious to?"

"Well, I never realized Sandy could be so pretty."

"Oh, come on, Darren. You've never seen her outside the work environment. I guess in one sense, I should be happy you don't ogle other women, but your single-minded focus on your work amazes me. It makes me wonder what else you are missing in your life—that's what was behind my comment about you being boring, even though I wish I had used a better choice of words."

Darren led Tracey to the edge of the dance floor. "You sit here. I've got to kick this thing off. I promise you won't be bored tonight."

Darren strode to the podium and signaled for the band to stop playing. Once he had the crowd's attention, he spoke a brief welcome and recognized former President Earlman and other notables present.

"We are about to unveil the museum's centerpiece, the Pangaean time-ship—the *Spirit of the Ages*. Who better to introduce it to us than a descendent of the Anasazi?"

With a wave of his hand, the lights dimmed to a level matching the dusk outside. Flute music floated into the museum, enticing the guests to turn their attention to the patio. A figure emerged from the shadows and approached the stone circle. With a who-o-o-sh, a campfire at the center erupted in flame, and blue smoke billowed outward and rose into the evening sky. When it cleared, a Hopi shaman stood with prayer sticks held in outstretched arms, facing the audience.

"Aaron," Dwy whispered in surprise to his dad. "It's Eagle-To-The-Clouds!"

"Sh-h-h. Listen and enjoy."

Eagle-To-The-Clouds told the story of the Anasazi and of their emergence to the surface of the Earth from a great civilization underground. He spoke of the ant people at the center of the Earth and of their care for the Anasazi. He talked about the Earth being the fourth world inhabited by his ancestors and of other worlds to come. He described the skies and the stars and the galaxies beyond. Then he explained that above the skies were dimensional portals that led to other civilizations.

Darren became mesmerized as Eagle-To-The-Clouds talked of the fire-ship that brought his people from the great civilization underground, how it traveled through the skies as the stars changed overhead. Some of the myth, for the first time, began making sense to Darren. "As the stars changed overhead" might refer to a trip through time. Could the fire-ship have been the crashed Pangaean time-ship he and Skeeter believed they had located? Native Americans sometimes used the term "underground" to refer to lands below the equator, like South America—*or maybe even Antarctica, the homeland of the Pangaeans*, Darren thought.

Eagle-To-The-Clouds told how the fire-ship carrying his ancestors survived a battle with a rock borne by the wind, but the craft fell to the earth like a wounded bird.

A rock borne by the wind? Darren thought, then the idea occurred to him—*Shiprock!*—a rock with sails, a rock that could
be borne by the wind. Had the fire-ship collided with Shiprock?
Was the fire-ship in the legend the very one that he and Skeeter
thought lay beneath the rocks north of Chaco?

"With its last gasps of life," Eagle-To-The-Clouds continued,
"the fire-ship gently touched the ground and deposited its passengers. Once they were all safe, the fire-ship became still, never
to rise again. In reverence, the survivors buried the fire-ship, stone
by stone."

The legend came together for Darren. *The fire-ship was a time
travel ship!* he thought. *The passengers came from a great civilization
underground—Pangaea, in Antarctica. They traveled 200 million
years into their future but crash landed after colliding with Shiprock
Peak. They covered the ship with stones. The passengers became the
Anasazi.* Darren was certain the ship he and Skeeter thought they
had found was the one in the legend.

Darren reached for his drink, unaware that his hands were
trembling. Aaron, finished with his story, began playing his flute.
Darren recognized the melody, the same one that Aaron had used
atop the mesa to call the Respected Spirit into the circle. Darren
scanned the faces of the crowd, wondering what their reaction
would be if the spirit's image appeared before them. This time,
however, the music had no echo. When Darren's gaze returned
to Aaron, he nearly dropped his glass. In the dim light, flickering
from the flame of the campfire, the shadows played across Aaron's
face, eerily transforming it to that of an elderly man. An ancient
man. *An ancestor? A spirit?* Darren wondered. *An ancestor speaking through Aaron?* Darren sensed that no one else in the crowd
saw the image … except for Tracey. She sat still, oblivious to the
crowd, as if in a trance, absorbed in the drama being played out.
She sees, Darren knew. *She sees it, too.*

Eagle-To-The-Clouds stopped playing the music. In complete
silence, he faced the curtain behind the crowd. He stretched his

arms, a prayer stick in one hand, and his flute in the other. He stood with his head raised. Instead of his short black hair, long gray braids fell to his waist.

In a hushed voice, yet one that could be heard clearly by all who were present in the room, Eagle-To-The-Clouds said, "I am a spirit of the ages—here to give you the *Spirit of the Ages*. He tossed a fistful of powder into the campfire, and an orange flame erupted with blue smoke, obscuring his image. When the haze cleared, Aaron had disappeared. The curtain had been drawn and the audience saw the magnificence of the time-ship, suspended in flight with brilliant colors from the campfire reflecting from its glistening black hull. Gasps of awe came from the crowd. No one moved. No one clapped. All watched the scene before them in complete fascination and wonder.

Even Darren, who had seen the ship many times before, was shaken by the image—mythical bordering on dark intimidation. It took him a few moments to gather his composure. On his cue, the house lights came up to full intensity.

Darren, moved, spoke from his heart. "The *Spirit of the Ages* is a gift the Pangaeans left as a symbol of their gratitude. Here it will remain, for all to see and experience. Tonight for the very first time, it will be open for you to step inside and experience the wonder of its technology. Welcome to the opening of our museum."

A murmur rippled through the audience, then grew to a cheer. Applause broke out. The band played a majestic fanfare and the room filled with excited conversations. People rushed to greet Darren, but Tracey reached him first.

"Did you see him?" she asked, knowing that he had. "Do you think anyone else saw him?" She knew they had not. "Do you think he was the same spirit we saw on the mesa? What does it mean?"

Darren placed his index finger on her lips and whispered, "I wish I knew."

* * *

Darren escorted the first group of attendees through the time-ship: President Earlman, the NASA Administrator, Skeeter and Sandy, Dwy and Aaron—who had changed back into his normal dress—the Governor of New Mexico, representatives of the Hopi and Navajo nations, and a few other dignitaries, but not Tracey.

"I flew in that ship once, with Dwyer," she told Darren. "I'll not relive the memories of the devastation we saw in our future. Nor do I want to come even close to experiencing the nauseating effects of the transition to a state of zero mass that's required to travel in time. I've done that."

Darren tried to persuade her, to no avail, that she would neither see any climate change devastation nor encounter any major physical effects.

"Nope," Tracey said, "you just go on. I'll stay here and enjoy the music."

After the group rode the elevator to the entry door of the ship, 90 feet above ground, they stepped inside. Pausing a moment to allow for their eyes to adjust to the dimness of the interior, Darren let them absorb the details of the cavernous cabin, larger than most theaters. "There's room for 700 people here plus another 300 on the level above us, next to the ship's bridge. That's where we're headed now. Follow me up this escalator."

When they reached the second level, they could see out the front of the ship through a series of wide portals, looking much bigger from the inside than they had from the ground level outside. Darren asked them to find seats close to the front and introduced Spence, who had been waiting in the sidelines. "Spence is our Construction Superintendent and before that, the Operations Manager for Project TIME. I don't think there's anyone on earth who knows more about time travel than Spence."

"Except for Darren," Spence quipped. "I know the mechanics of time travel, but even after all these years, I have to leave the theory to him." Spence stepped to the commander's chair, sat in it and swung around to face the bank of instruments and controls that stretched across the entire front. "Bring the ship to life," he commanded.

Techs rushed to the seats of the crew members. Computer screens, gauges and panels glimmered in a kaleidoscopic array of multi-colored lights. Whirring sounds, beeps and chirps accompanied each new instrument brought on-line. The cabin lighting level was reduced to the dim red glow suitable for the best night vision. Automatic check sequences surveyed all settings and controls. A hum pervaded the cabin and a vibration could be felt by the passengers. Some clasped the armrests of their seats with growing tension. Aaron, in the seat next to Dwy, leaned over and spoke to him.

"I'm getting out of here. I think this damn thing's getting ready to fly."

Dwy smiled at his friend. "Hang on, Aaron, you're fine."

"Don't worry," Spence said to the audience as if in response to Aaron's concern, "this is only a simulation. Enjoy the experience of time travel."

The view outside the portals changed from that of the museum's interior to one of a night sky, brilliant with stars.

"Begin transition to zero mass," Spence commanded. Zero mass was the state necessary to allow the ship to accelerate rapidly and make instantaneous changes of direction at high speed without the consequences of inertia. NASA engineers through retro-engineering had yet to solve the technology used, but they were getting close. For the purpose of the simulation, a complex, oscillating motion was transmitted through the ship's suspension cables to fool the inner ears of the passengers, causing them to experience physical effects similar to that of the state of zero mass. "If you begin to feel queasy, stare at the stars outside. You will adjust to the sensation in a few moments, I promise."

"Stations, call your final checks," Spence barked. "HULL?"

"Hull closed and pressurized!"

"INERTIA?"

"Zero mass achieved!"

"POWER?"

"Power is go!"

"VORTEX?"

"Vortex ready."

"GUIDANCE?"

"Go!"

"CONTROL?"

"Go!"

Spence eased the power forward and the passengers felt the acceleration. The stars fell and rotated as the ship ascended in a climbing turn. Aaron grabbed Dwy's arm to the point of numbing pain.

"Dwy, if this damn thing leaves the ground, you're going to be one dead Anglo."

"It won't, trust me."

"Begin vortex generation," Spence commanded.

The passengers heard a low pitched hum that smoothly accelerated to a whine, then into a scream before abruptly vanishing to silence.

"The ship achieves time travel by riding through a time vortex, like a surfer on a wave. The longer we remain in the vortex, the farther through time we travel. The whine you heard was a synthetic fluid, with an atomic weight near zero, rotating through a circular tube surrounding the perimeter of the ship. The rotation quickly reached a frequency above our human ear's capability of hearing. That's why it seemed to become silent. The fluid accelerates to nearly half the speed of light and distorts the time continuum, forming the vortex, much like a whirlpool that would be generated by stirring a pot of water rapidly with a spoon."

The stars began to change position.

"In a zero mass state, we can reach speeds unheard of with conventional rockets. We're already over Illinois. In a moment, when the vortex is formed, we will begin our time travel. You'll know when we do by the fact that a white mist will obscure the view out the portals."

"Where are we going?" President Earlman asked.

"Pangaea."

"Will we land?"

"Yes, but remember this is a simulation. We're still inside the museum. Here, I'll show you."

Spencer flipped a switch. The view out the portals changed back to the brightly lit interior of the museum. He left the view of the interior on long enough to satisfy the passengers, then flipped the switch back to the simulation.

After a few minutes, he banked the ship and allowed it to begin its descent back to the surface of the earth. When the mist cleared, a strange landscape appeared before them.

"It's Pangaea," Spence said, "as it was two hundred million years ago, when all the continents were one. The home of our ancestors."

The ship flew over the continent for a few moments and then landed. Spence suggested the passengers exit by a door opposite the side on which they had entered.

"Be careful," he cautioned. "There're some pretty mean reptiles out there."

Darren led the group through the exit into the arid, and quite cool, terrain of Antarctica as it had once been. Animatronic dinosaurs roamed the edges of the display, and replicas of Pangaean dwellings allowed the visitors to experience a sample of the ancient culture. After passing through the exhibit, Darren led the group to an elevator that took them deep underground to the first segment of the Project TIME facility, known as Sector 1, the only sector left intact. Darren stepped to the project's main feature, a section of the highly polished tube that was once 100 miles in circumference. "This sector of the ring contains the home position for the VME, The Vehicle for Mass Extraction," Darren explained. "We called it the 'Vimmy.' I won't go into a great amount of detail, but just to refresh your memory, here's how it worked. We ran Einstein's equation, E=MC2, in reverse, drawing massive amounts of dark energy—the energy that binds the universe together—from the vacuum in front of the Vimmy. The resulting negative force drew the vehicle forward, accelerating it to more than half the speed of light. The shock wave caused by the high rotational speed—60,000 circuits of the ring per minute—created the time vortex through which we traveled. Now, let me show you the VME." Darren pressed a button on the control panel, and an arc of the ring opened silently. Inside rested an intricate device that resembled a projectile covered with complex electronic circuits and metallic tubes.

Darren closed the door and said, "Well folks, there you have it. The time-ship you just toured uses the same basic science, but the Pangaeans were the pioneers in this field. Eons before we began our research, they developed the technology, miniaturized the components, and made our Project TIME look like a relic from the Dark Ages. That's why it's now a museum. Enjoy the rest of your visit. You may return to the museum's lobby whenever you like."

All too soon, they finished their tour and were led back to the sterile interior of the museum. President Earlman grabbed Darren's hand and pumped it. "Excellent, Darren. Excellent."

Aaron's face regained its color once he returned to the museum. Dwy stood in the hall and waited for his dad to finish with the former president.

* * *

A taxi pulled to the front of the museum, and a pretty girl in her late twenties got out, paid the cabbie and rushed up the steps. Clad in blue jeans and flip-flops, she stepped to the entrance and brushed past the ticket booth.

"Ma'am. Excuse me, Ma'am, but I need to see your ticket."

"Oh, I don't have one yet. How much do you need?"

"I'm sorry, Ma'am, but we're not open to the public. This is a private event. You can come back next weekend. We'll be open to the public then."

"Oh, I can't do that. I've got to see my dad. He's here, isn't he?"

"Who?"

"Mr. Johnson."

The attendant scanned the list of dignitaries, searching for the name. "I don't see that name on the list."

"I know he's here. Please let me go in and see. It's an emergency. I've come all the way from Chicago."

"Hold on." The attendant dialed Sandy's cell phone. He explained the situation to her.

"Who is she looking for?"

"Johnson. She says a Mr. Johnson, but there's no one on the list by that—"

"Oh, God, it's his daughter. I'll be right there. Don't let her leave."

Sandy raced to the museum's entrance, stepping as fast as her heels would allow. She reached the ticket booth, out of breath, and stood transfixed by the sight of the young woman.

"Hi," she said, "I'm Sandy. And you must be … uh, you're … oh, heavens, you're the youngest, so you've got to be—"

"—Jenna."

"Oh, Jenna, he'll be so excited to see you." Sandy gave her an enthusiastic hug.

"You know me?"

"I'll explain. Just wait here with me while I call Darren."

* * *

Dwy caught his dad in the hallway and asked for a minute with him in private. Darren looked at his son, wondering what Dwy had on his mind.

"Dad, you have to promise you won't tell Mom."

"I'm not sure I can do that without knowing what you're going to say."

"Dad, this is between us. She can't know. It would be too hard for her."

Darren motioned to a bench. They both sat. They remained silent for a moment.

"Okay, Dad, the decision's yours, but I'd rather we kept it between us."

"Go on, Dwy."

"Dad, you've always said that I was my own man. No one else could make my decisions for me. I've always looked up to you and watched you when you had to make tough choices. Now, it's my turn. Uh, Dad … WSP has insisted that I resume flying the Texas patrols again."

"Damn it, Dwy, you can't do that. It's too dangerous. Texas is on the verge of a border war. They've already had vigilante groups shoot at people. You'd be a sitting duck in your plane flying that low."

Dwy stood and paced down the hall, his back to his dad. He stopped, took a breath and turned back, determination on his face. "My job's at stake. My business is at stake. I've got to do it. Besides, I'll be careful. They've raised the patrol altitude in Texas to 1,000 feet."

"Even that's too low. They'd still be able to hit your plane."

"Dad, I'm not asking for your permission. I only wanted to let you know. I wanted you to be aware that I've made a tough decision. I'm sorry you don't support it, but it's been made. I start next week."

Darren rose from the bench and put his hands on Dwy's shoulders, staring into his eyes without saying a word. The two of them connected. "You're my son. I'd do anything to keep you safe. Anything short of not letting you be your own man. I would not take that away from you. Your decision is not the one I would make, but you do what you feel you must. And God be with you."

Before Dwy could answer, the ring of Darren's cell phone broke the moment. Seeing it was Sandy, Darren flipped the phone open.

"Dr. Stewart, you need to come to the front right now. You're not going to believe who showed up."

"Who?"

"Skeeter's youngest daughter, Jenna."

* * *

"Jenna's here?" Skeeter asked. "Here? She's *here* in the museum?"

"In the conference room with Sandy," Darren said. "I thought I'd give you a moment to collect your thoughts."

"God, Darren, I haven't seen her since she was 12. She must be … she must be … oh, Jesus, she's got to be 27 or 28. I won't even know her."

Darren put his arm on his friend's shoulder. "You'll know her. And better still, she'll know you. Somehow, she found you and came here."

Approaching the door to the conference room, Skeeter stopped. He put his hand to his forehead and took a deep breath. "Darren, I'm not sure I can do this. What if she … uh, what if she came back to … uh, ask me to stay out of her life or something?"

Darren smiled and opened the door. Jenna sat at the table next to Sandy. The moment she saw her dad, she rushed toward him and whispered, "Daddy!" She put her arms around him and the two embraced, both crying tears of joy. Sandy rose, patted them both on the back, grabbed Darren's elbow and led him back outside. "Let's give them some time alone," she said.

When the door closed, Skeeter sat on one of the sofas and motioned for Jenna to sit next to him. Jenna explained that she had been trying to locate him ever since she graduated from college and began living on her own. "But every trail turned into a dead end," she said. "Then, last week, I saw a picture of Dr. Stewart in a story about this museum opening and nearly fell off my chair when I recognized you standing next to him. The paper had your name wrong in the caption, but just the same, I knew it was you."

"No, they had it right. Myers is my name now—Jim Myers."

"But—"

"Jenna, I stumbled onto something terrible in the Antarctic. I saw good people lose their lives, and I nearly lost my own. I knew the cause of their deaths was something we discovered in some kind of a time warp. It represented a serious threat, but the government didn't want to take a chance on my leaking any of the details, so they put me in a witness protection program. They locked me up. Your mom didn't even know why I was there. I couldn't tell her, either, because they would've locked her up, too. After a few years, she left me and took you two girls with her."

"She told us you were in jail. She never said why."

"How is she?"

"Oh, Daddy. You don't know, do you?"

"Know what?"

"She remarried. Some guy with a lot of money. He spends most of it on her. Carrie and I never see her anymore."

"How is your sister?"

"She's married, too. Never asks about you. Mom kind of poisoned her mind. She lives in New York."

Skeeter searched for the words … the question he had to have answered. He took a breath.

"Jenna, why'd you try so hard to find me?"

"I don't like what Mom's turned into. I don't have much in common with my sister. I had good memories about you. I never understood you being away. I need my father back."

Skeeter hugged her, again fighting back tears.

"How long can you stay?"

"A week or so. Oh, and Daddy? I, uh …"

"Yes?"

"I could stay longer if I could find a job. NASA doesn't have any openings for a climatologist, do they?"

"I don't know. Can you drive a dozer?"

They both laughed. Then Skeeter became serious again.

"You met Sandy? The woman I brought to the museum opening?"

"Yes. She's nice."

"She and I are going to be married."

CHAPTER SIXTEEN

THE MOUNTAIN

Luggage packed in the plane, Tracey and Dwy lingered on the ramp, not yet wishing to say their goodbyes. Darren stood between them, one arm around Tracey's waist and the other on Dwy's shoulder. They chatted about Jenna and Skeeter and how happy they were that Skeeter was regaining a life. Dwy began the preflight inspection of the aircraft, meticulously checking all the external surfaces and linkages.

Tracey leaned against Darren. "Hey you," she said. "If you'll have me, I'm ready to move back with you and try to work things out. It won't be easy, though. I don't think we can do it on our own. We'd need some help."

"*Have you?* I've wanted nothing more," Darren said. Then the meaning of her statement soaked in. "Do you mean counseling?"

"Yes."

Darren remained quiet as he weighed the implications. "Okay, Trace. I agree. Let me know when your schedule will let you come back. I need to get the place ready. In the meantime, we can be looking for someone we feel is qualified."

Tracey answered that she had to return to the Earlman Commission to help complete the final report. She had spoken to the former president about the lessons she'd learned from the Chaco Culture—that perhaps the best answer to the water shortage was to reduce the population through attrition rather than employ Herculean methods to prop up a culture that in the end would still be unsustainable.

"You told me when we were at Chaco Canyon that the citizens of L.A. may have to make the same tough decision to move away as did the Anasazi," she said. "Earlman may not like the concept that L.A. is our Chaco, but his commission should consider the implications."

Tracey said she could return to Alamogordo within a week or 10 days and commute to Phoenix until she finished her work. Darren told Tracey that with the museum now open, his work had come to an end. Skeeter had been appointed the museum's curator, so they could be free to live wherever they chose. Tracey stood on her toes and kissed him. Darren reached for her, but the squeal of tires from a pickup turning into the parking area distracted him.

"Skeeter's truck," Darren said.

The doors popped open. Skeeter, Sandy and Jenna got out and hurried toward Darren and Tracey.

"Good morning," Darren said. "I hoped you could make it."

"We have some news," Skeeter said, taking Sandy's hand. "Sandy and I are engaged."

Tracey rushed to Sandy and hugged her, both of them beaming at each other. Darren slapped Skeeter on the back and congratulated him. Dwy, hearing the commotion, came back toward them. Once he learned what the fuss was about, he joined in the celebration—until he saw Jenna standing by her dad's side. He caught her eye and walked toward her. "We haven't been introduced," he said.

"Jenna," she said. "I'm Skeeter's daughter."

They looked at each other for a moment longer, oblivious to the chatter around them.

"Jenna, I'm Dwy Stewart—Tracey and Darren's son." A smile broke across Dwy's face. A tinge of crimson appeared on Jenna's cheeks. Dwy glanced at his watch. "Hey, Mom. We've got to get going."

After one last round of goodbyes and congratulations, Dwy and Tracey walked to the plane. He followed her up the entry stairs and paused at the top. He turned and smiled again at Jenna. With a subtle wave to her, he ducked inside, closing the door behind him.

* * *

On the drive home, Darren made mental notes about some of the things he needed to do to make their house comfortable for Tracey again. When he opened the front door, he realized how much needed to be done. Computers, printers, paper and clutter had taken over the family room. Even worse were the dust bunnies that had collected along the baseboards.

Vimmy ambled up to Darren and nuzzled his hand. *Oh, yeah,* he thought, chuckling, *Vimmy, old boy, you're going to have to get used to sleeping in your doggie bed again. No more sprawling out on the mattress.*

Darren's mind soon turned again to the threat the WSP pipeline represented to the ancient time-ship. *I'll call first thing Monday and try to gain some time. All we need is a week or so to do some test excavations. That should prove it, one way or the other.*

He poured himself a drink. The museum opening represented a milestone in his life, a milestone he had difficulty facing. *I've worked myself out of a job with NASA. What's next? Retirement?* He couldn't visualize himself without a job, but the prospect was staring him in the face. *Consulting?* He knew what he thought of consultants. *Can't be one of them. Teach physics? And live in a college environment again? I don't think so.*

With a few quick swallows, he finished his drink. *What if Tracey and I were both out of work?* The two of them had lived their lives trying to balance conflicting priorities between demanding, high-profile jobs. *What if the work priorities vanished?* Darren laughed at himself. *I can't paint. I never played golf—even when there was enough water to have lush greens. I don't think Tracey could ever become a quilter.* Darren gulped down the last of his drink. *If Skeeter and I don't find that ship, what am I going to do with the rest of my life?*

* * *

The next morning, Darren gave Vimmy his monthly heartworm pill, always a tussle, because the dog would fake swallowing the tablet only to spit it out moments later. He would then sulk in a corner with his ears laid back. Darren poked a hole in a chunk of cheese and stuffed the tablet inside. He first threw Vimmy a piece of cheese that had not been spiked, to gain the dog's confidence, and then he threw him the doctored one. Vimmy gulped it down without blinking and eagerly awaited the next treat. Darren reached for another piece on the counter but got interrupted by his cell phone ringing.

"Hello," he answered.

"Dr. Stewart?" a woman's voice asked.

"Speaking."

"I'm the executive assistant to Jackson Davis," she said. "He's returning your call. I'll get him on."

A moment passed. Then Jackson's clipped voice came on the line. "Stewart?"

"Yes."

"Davis here. You wanted to talk to me about the pipeline right-of-way through Kutz Canyon? I don't see how that's any concern of yours."

"I'm making it my concern. I'm a director for NASA, and we believe there's a major archeological relic under that knoll you're about to blast through." Darren knew he had stretched the truth a little, but it wouldn't hurt to have Davis believe NASA was behind the request.

"What do you expect us to do?"

"Deviate around it. Preserve the site for an archeological dig."

"Screw that. I've checked it. The cost is prohibitive. Worse than the money, though, circumventing it would upset our whole timetable. We're late now and don't need anymore delays."

"Could you hold off for six weeks? Or at least a month? That would give us time to get the equipment in and do some exploratory drilling."

"Hell, no. As I said, we're already late. Our equipment will be on-site at the end of the month. I remind you that we own the right-of-way. Our security personnel are on high alert. Don't trespass again or you might be shot."

"And don't *you* threaten me. I'm tired of your attitude. It wouldn't take much for me to come after you." Darren allowed himself a quick thought about how he might work through NASA to get a legal injunction to stop WSP. *NASA moves at the speed of a tank*, he thought. *Going through normal channels won't get it done in time.* Then it hit him.

"That knoll's on Navajo lands. You don't *own* the right-of-way there. All you have is *permission* from the tribal chief, permission that can be withdrawn. I've got a friend who sits on the tribal council. Believe me, you don't want the negative press resulting from Native Americans protecting their heritage. I'll give you more bad publicity than all your PR types can handle."

The rude buzz of the dial tone let Darren know that Davis had hung up on him. *Good. I hit a nerve.* He punched in Skeeter's number. When he answered, Darren said, "Skeeter, next week after I get my schedule cleared, I'm going to drive back to Shiprock and talk to Warren—he can't be reached by phone. Do you want to go with me?"

"Sure. Do you mind if I bring Jenna?"

* * *

On his fifth patrol since resuming flights over Texas, Dwy made a fueling stop in Santa Fe. Once the tanks were topped off, Dwy took off and flew east with the southernmost tip of the Sangre de Cristo mountain range off his left wingtip. In the pilot's seat of the company's patrol aircraft—a well-worn, high-wing Cessna—Dwy intercepted the WSP right-of-way and tracked it eastward, scanning for any signs of vandalism. *Nothing unusual so far. But we're not over Texas yet.*

He checked his charts and made a progress report to Flight Service. Right on schedule, he complimented himself on his choice of an early morning departure from Farmington to take advantage of the clear weather. With any luck, he could finish his flight before the afternoon storms built up from the summertime heat. He planned to fly his patrol to Texas and then make a stopover in Alamogordo to surprise his dad. Well, that wasn't the primary reason for the stop.

He and Jenna had managed to see each other a few times since they first met. The previous night he called Jenna to set up a dinner date in Alamogordo, and she accepted. They talked for hours by phone, like they had known each other for years. The prospect of spending another evening with her excited him.

East of the Sangre de Cristos, he turned slightly north to track the pipeline toward its terminus in the far northwest corner of the Texas panhandle. That was the point where the feeder lines from the center-pivot wellheads were connected to a major pumping station, the facility that had been damaged by vigilantes.

He crossed over the border and could see the town of Dalhart on the horizon before him. Before reaching Dalhart, though, the right-of-way turned due north and traveled through the high plains in some of the most remote terrain of the region.

Dwy dropped down to 1,000 feet and kept the pipeline in sight out his left window. *No unusual tracks, no activity, no vehicles.* He came upon the section of the line that had been damaged but since repaired. The charred remains of the office trailers were the only evidence of the destruction. He circled the pumping station yard several times looking for anything suspicious. *Nothing.*

Breathing a sigh of relief, he leveled his wings and began a climb.

Crack! A sound like a pebble smashing into a car windshield jolted Dwy. He swiveled his head, looking for the source of the sound. Clang! Crack! Two more. This time several of the gauges on the instrument panel stopped functioning.

I'm taking ground fire! Dwy applied full throttle and pulled the yoke back to his gut, climbing for dear life. He took evasive action, swerving violently left and right. Heart thumping, he shouted into the microphone, "Mayday! Mayday! Mayday!" No response, not even static. *Radio's dead,* he thought. In a couple of minutes, satisfied he was out of range of the ground fire, he leveled off and turned toward Santa Fe. Taking a few deep breaths to try and calm himself down, he took inventory of his situation.

No radio, no gauges powered by electricity, including those for the fuel tanks. He checked the circuit breakers and found one had popped and would not reset. *Flight controls okay.* Dwy made a check of the visible portions of the plane's wings and engine cowling. *No sign of damage. Engine's fine.*

Still trembling, Dwy considered his options. He could set down on the high plains once safely back in New Mexico, but that would only be his first choice if the plane's ability to stay aloft were compromised. *I'd die of thirst or heat stroke before I walked out.* Next, he could land at a small airport. *They'd have no repair services and it would take days to fly in mechanics and the necessary parts.*

He decided to continue to Santa Fe, keeping in mind all the small airports nearby in case his situation deteriorated. *We can make repairs on the spot at Santa Fe and get back in business quickly. The bullet must have hit an electrical circuit. I don't see anything worse.*

What Dwy couldn't see was a thin wisp of fuel siphoning out of his right wing-tank and streaming behind the plane. The tank had been punctured by a fragment of the bullet that hit the plane's main breaker panel.

* * *

Nearing Shiprock after more than six hours on the road, Darren continued chatting with Jenna, who sat with one leg curled up underneath her in the Jeep's passenger seat. Skeeter reclined in back with Vimmy's head and forepaws in his lap. The stereo sound of snoring indicated that both man and dog were dozing. Darren had come to like the young woman next to him and found her to be well-versed in her field of climatology. Staring at the arid terrain out the window, she asked Darren if he believed in climate change.

Not an easy question to answer, Darren thought. Should he speak his mind and risk an answer that might be counter to her education or offend her political view? Or should he duck the question, instead? Darren had sensed the chemistry between Jenna and Dwy. He had no desire to come across as an old contrarian and offend her. *But now's not the time to try and be something I'm not*, he thought. *She asked the question, and she wants my best answer.*

"Our climate *is* changing," he said. "It's continuing a change that began more than 10,000 years ago in the depths of our last Ice Age. We're in a rare, warm climatic period—an interglacial era. Our whole species, everything we are and have, has developed since the waning days of the last glaciers. Some say the temperatures have reached their maximum already, some say we have a ways to go. Many believe we have caused the warming, others that we have merely accelerated it. In either case, by the geological scale of time, we're destined to plunge back to freezing conditions. It's a cycle that's happened hundreds of times in the past, and it will happen again. There. I hope you don't mind my directness."

Jenna laughed. "You sound just like my dad. You would have pissed off most of my professors and many of my colleagues, but not me. I do think the jury is still out on the question of man's influence, but here's the hook. Even if we are totally responsible—and that's a *big* if—we are not unified enough as a civilization, nor are we willing to make the sacrifices that would be necessary to turn things around, even if we could."

The road topped a small rise in the desert terrain, a weathered sign marking its crest.

"The Continental Divide," Jenna said. "It divides the rivers, but a more significant, lesser-known boundary is the 100th Meridian."

"What about it?"

"On a map, it's a vertical line through the U.S. that forms the eastern border of the Texas panhandle. Rather than the rivers, the 100th Meridian divides the *rainfall.* East of it, the land is fertile, receiving more than 40 inches of rain each year. On a total world basis, that area of our country is a literal Garden of Eden, lush green and capable of producing a bountiful harvest, enough to feed much of the rest of the world. West of that line, however, most of the area receives 20 inches or less. Only desert plants and scrub can survive without irrigation. And since the drought began, the rainfall amount has diminished to 5 inches or less. Can't get much worse."

"It did in Pangaea," Darren said. "One huge continent stretching 10,000 miles from coast to coast in some places. Rainfall became non-existent a few hundred miles inland. The interior portions were the most desolate wasteland imaginable. The areas of our country today that are the greenest were at one time in Pangaea's barren core. They came back, but it took millions of years."

"Your point?" Jenna asked.

"On this planet and in this universe, we're along for the ride. Mankind better make the best of it, because at some point, we're in for one hell of a shock.

"You don't think we can escape that fate?"

"Mass extinctions come and go. The last one got the dinosaurs. The next one may get us. We may stave off our destiny by surviving a relatively minor occurrence, like a short-term climate change, but there are natural forces in play that we have no control over."

"Such as?"

"Oh, consider a super-eruption from the collapsed mega volcano at Yellowstone. We're already past due for that one. Or, perhaps another comet strike. Look what happened to Jupiter back in 1994. If any one of those comet fragments had hit us instead of Jupiter, we'd be toast. We know that New York will someday collide with Europe due to continental drift. Beyond that, eons from now, the sun will use up its fuel and go out. Then there's the black hole at the center of our galaxy, consuming stars with an insatiable appetite. But the ultimate is that the Andromeda Galaxy is headed our way and will collide with our Milky Way in a few billion years."

"Oh, come on, Dr. Stewart, you're making me feel like a gnat. How do you keep from being depressed?"

"Easy. As confident as I am that some or all of those things will happen, I'm even more confident that they will not occur during our lifetime, leaving us free to appreciate what we value in life, and not to be so arrogant as to think we can control those events. We should work *with* the natural laws, not in *opposition* to them."

"Bring that down to an understandable level for me."

Darren thought a minute. "Take Los Angeles. We're pouring billions of dollars of resources into shoring up a populace that never should have been there in the first place."

"Why not try to save them?"

"Because in the long run, we'd be doing them no favors. In fact, we'd make their ultimate fate far worse, by supplying water at ever-higher costs and prolonging the hard decisions that ought to be made now. One day, the whole system will collapse and an unimaginable loss of life will occur."

They reached the trailhead to Shiprock Peak. Darren stopped the Jeep, and they jumped out and began walking. In 20 minutes or so, Warren's hogan could be seen at the base of the rock formation, the small dwelling dwarfed by the intimidating backdrop. Darren called out Warren's name and fumbled in his pocket for the tin of tobacco he had brought. He pulled it out. Jenna spotted the can and said, "I didn't know you used tobacco."

"I don't. But it's a custom to offer tobacco to a Navajo upon greeting him. Otherwise, he would feel your greeting was insincere."

Warren came outside and waved. When he neared, Darren offered him some Skoal.

"Thanks," Warren said, taking a pinch. "Won't you join me?"

Darren took a pinch for himself and offered some to Skeeter and Jenna. Skeeter followed suit, but Jenna withdrew. Darren raised an eyebrow. "Take some," he whispered.

Jenna pinched a wad between her thumb and finger, and following Darren's example placed it between her cheek and gum. She became immediately repulsed by the tobacco's acrid-sweet taste. In a moment, her mouth filled with saliva, and she turned her head away, looking for a place to spit. Trying to hide her embarrassment from the others, she spat, but tobacco juice flowed down her chin. Turning her back on everyone, she grabbed a tissue from her pocket and wiped her mouth, secretly disposing of the rest of the tobacco. Taking a few deep breaths to clear her sinuses, she gained the courage to turn back around and face the men. Red-faced, but with her tongue poking her cheek, she hoped to fool everyone that she still had the tobacco in her mouth.

The men were all onto her charade but didn't let on. They respected her for trying to honor a custom.

"Warren, my friend," Darren said. "We need your help. Skeeter and I think we may have found the final resting place of the great winged bird in your legend, but it is soon to be disturbed and perhaps even destroyed by people who have no respect for your heritage."

Darren went on to explain the situation with the pipeline. He asked Warren to bring the issue before the tribal council and for them to rescind the permission for the right-of-way. "It's the only means we have to stop them."

Warren said, "Darren, you have my word. I will not rest until these Anglos are stopped. Our meeting is tonight. I'll be there. I'll make the case to the tribal elders. I can't promise how they might respond, but I'll do my best. And Darren—"

"Yes?"

"Next time, don't make the young woman take a chaw of tobacco, just to please me. The custom doesn't require that she make herself sick. I'll understand."

The three of them walked back to the car, Skeeter playfully elbowed his daughter, and she snickered in return. After driving a few miles, Darren's phone rang.

"Darren," Tracey said in a voice that indicated something was terribly wrong. "The FAA just called. Dwy's plane is missing. Oh, God, Darren, get here as quick as you can. I don't think I can deal with this by myself. I need you."

Darren reeled from the news. He tried to reassure her that usually a flight being listed as overdue means the pilot had merely forgotten to call the FAA and close his flight plan with them upon the flight's conclusion. Other possibilities, like being diverted because of weather, could also explain the situation. But inside, Darren knew Dwy was in serious trouble, if not worse. His stomach knotted.

Skeeter overheard half the conversation and when Darren hung up, he asked, "What is it, Darren?"

"Dwy's plane is overdue."

"Oh, no!" Jenna said. "What are you going to do?"

"I'm going to Phoenix. I've got to get to Tracey."

"Dr. Stewart, could I go with you?" Jenna asked.

"Jenna, no," Skeeter broke in.

"Dad, I want to hear any news on Dwy as soon as anyone has it. Besides, I could keep Dr. Stewart company on the drive—maybe even do some relief for a few miles."

Darren realized that Jenna really was concerned about Dwy. He would welcome the young woman's company. "Skeeter, I'd be happy to have her come with me. Just remember, Tracey's pretty upset, and, uh … things could get much worse."

Skeeter took a long look at his daughter. She returned his gaze, and he saw a mixed expression of care and concern in her eyes, the eyes that were no longer the young girl he once knew, but the beautiful eyes of a mature woman.

"Okay, Jenna. You go. Just keep in touch with me. If Darren will drop me off in Farmington, I'll catch a flight back to Alamogordo and monitor things from there. I've got a friend in Flight Service. He'll keep me posted."

"Thanks, Skeeter."

After Darren left Skeeter at the airport, he drove as fast as he dared toward Phoenix, worried about what kind of news the next call from Tracey might bring. Jenna bravely kept up a conversation. She talked about everything from the roadside scenery to her childhood, trying to keep Darren's mind occupied. Darren appreciated her efforts, but they didn't keep the terrible thoughts from his mind.

* * *

Darren parked in front of Tracey's apartment.

"Jenna, give me a moment alone with Tracey," he said. "I'll come and get you."

Jenna nodded. Darren paused at the entryway, collecting his thoughts. He knocked. In a moment he heard the chain lock slide open and the deadbolt latch turn. When the door opened, Tracey fell into his arms, shaking. He walked her back into the apartment.

"Have you heard anything more since we last talked?" he asked.

"I just got off the phone. The FAA said they've changed Dwy's status from 'overdue' to 'missing.' They've initiated a search."

She began sobbing. Darren tried to comfort her as he stroked her hair.

"Sh-h-h," he said. "We'll find him."

Her body stiffened, and she withdrew from his embrace, a look of terror on her face.

"But will we find him *alive?* This very moment he could be lying in some tangled piece of wreckage, praying for rescue. My God, Darren, is this our mountain? I can't believe I worried about something that might happen to us, when all along it was to be Dwy."

Darren pulled her back into his arms. "We'll find Dwy. He'll be okay. You've got to believe that."

She turned her head and laid her cheek against his chest, tears streaming down her face. "They told me that they last heard from him over Texas. *Texas!* Why did he ever fly over Texas? Oh, damn it, why?" She became silent a moment, reflecting on something. Then, in anguish, she began talking rapidly in a high pitched, sing-song voice. "Because of Jackson Davis. He made Dwy fly that route because I humiliated him. He did it as a payback."

Darren grasped her shoulders and forced her to look at him. "You humiliated Jackson? What do you mean?"

"Oh, Darren. I should have told you. At one of our meetings, he hit on me."

"That son-of-a-bitch." Darren felt an anger grow inside him to a level he'd never experienced before in his life.

"I stopped him cold," Tracey said. "I popped his jaw."

"You *should* have told me. I'd have taken care of it."

"I knew what you'd do. I didn't want you to get into some kind of a fight or something and get hurt. I handled it."

Now it was Tracey who tried to calm Darren down. She turned Darren's attention back to Dwy. "It's my fault. Why didn't he tell us he was flying over Texas? We would have stopped him."

"Right now we don't even know if being over Texas has anything to do with him being missing. Planes get lost on routine flights. Likely some mechanical problem forced him down. Dwy's probably sitting under a wing in the shade somewhere in the high desert flats, sipping a drink of water, waiting for someone to spot him. He's more worried about us than we are about him."

"I don't believe that," she said. "He got in trouble somehow over Texas."

"Look, Dwy's a grown man. He's both smart and tough. He thought he'd be all right making those flights. He'll come out of it okay."

Tracey's demeanor chilled, her face paled. "What do you mean by that? Did he tell you? Did you know?"

Darren stared at her. His slip had been unintentional but proved to be devastating. He had never lied to her. He couldn't begin now.

"Yes, I knew. He told me at the museum. Asked me not to tell you because he knew you would be worried. I didn't promise him anything, but—"

Tracey screamed at him. "You *knew*? And you didn't tell me? Damn you!" She raised her forearms, clenched her fists and began to pound his shoulders, striking him ferociously.

Darren wrapped his arms around her, drawing her to him so she couldn't continue to hit him. She sobbed. Her body became limp, and she slid to her knees. Darren eased himself down with her, gently rocking her, both of them on their knees.

"NO!" she yelled. "I don't want you back! I can't trust you. You go find Dwy, and when you find him, you send him to me, but don't you come with him. Get out!"

The intensity of her outburst left no room for doubt. She meant it. Darren stood and placed one hand on her shoulder. "I'll find him. I promise. He'll be okay."

Tracey made no reply, staring at the floor.

Darren left.

CHAPTER SEVENTEEN

SEARCH

The Alamogordo Civil Air Patrol Squadron Commander, Major Richard "Rick" Gordon, spoke to the senior members assembled in the C.A.P.'s hangar. "The FAA last heard from the missing aircraft at 9:23 a.m. in a position report to Flight Service. The aircraft, flying a route along Victor Airway V-190, reported crossing the Texas border and nothing has been heard since. Once across the border, the aircraft descended to an altitude too low for Amarillo Center to maintain radar contact. The aircraft's flight plan called for it to fly to Alamorgordo-White Sands Regional Airport via a direct route to Tucumcari and Roswell. The pilot planned to reach Alamogordo at 11:41 a.m."

Checking his watch, the major continued. "The aircraft is now nearly six hours overdue and has been declared missing. No signal from the emergency locater transmitter has been received, but all commercial aircraft flying over the area have been advised to monitor the emergency frequency. The aircraft is a single-engine Cessna Cardinal, white with blue trim. One soul on board, the pilot, a 31-year-old male, Dwy Stewart." The major laid down his notes. "That's all the info I have. We have been asked to search the flight segment from here to Roswell. This is what we train for. Let's do it well."

* * *

Darren walked halfway to the Jeep before he remembered Jenna. *Damn! How long have I kept her out here?* He reached the car, and Jenna knew from the look on his face that things had gone badly.

"Jenna, I, uh … I have something I must do, and … and I need you to stay with Tracey for a while."

"Dr. Stewart, I'll stay with her."

"She's in bad shape right now. We … we had a, well there's no other way to say it—we had a fight. I'm going to find Dwy. I don't want to impose, but Tracey shouldn't be alone right now."

"Dr. Stewart, I know how difficult a situation this is. I know the pressure you both are under. I can be with Tracey. If that will help you focus on finding Dwy, I'll stay with her. Dwy's going to be okay, I know he is. You see, he has to be. Dwy and I need to be able to see if we have a future, so he's got to come back. You go on ahead. I'll stay here. Don't worry about me. Don't worry about Tracey."

"You don't know what you may be walking into."

"Dr. Stewart. I can handle it. Your wife's a wonderful woman. She's just upset and afraid. My mom never needed me. Tracey does. That's important to me. You go. Things will turn out okay."

Jenna's words helped settle Darren down. He eased into the Jeep and made a call on his phone as he left the parking lot.

"Hello?"

"Aaron?"

"Yes."

"This is Darren. Get Dwy's plane prepped and have it on the line. I'll be there in a couple of hours. Then we're going to find Dwy. You're going to help me."

"Dr. Stewart, I don't fly."

"You're going to this evening."

"I can't."

"Aaron, you do what you have to do to get through your fear. Dwy needs me, and I need you. It's as simple as that. You be ready when I get there. Right now I don't have the luxury of catering to any damn phobias."

Darren snapped the phone shut and gunned the Jeep toward Sedona. After an hour of driving into the growing darkness, Darren found himself nodding off at the wheel. Good sense prevailed. *Over seven hundred miles of driving today and a fight with Tracey. My stress level must be through the roof. I won't do Dwy any good trying to fly in this condition.*

He called Aaron back and rescheduled the flight for early the next morning. Pulling off at the next exit, Darren found a cheap motel and crashed for the night.

* * *

On the road since before dawn, Darren tried to call Tracey before he reached Sedona but got no answer. *Not good at all. She doesn't want to talk to me.* He didn't leave a message. *Don't have any idea what I'd say.* Sipping the last dregs of coffee from a Styrofoam cup, Darren grimaced at the awful taste. He then called Sandy and found that the search for Dwy's plane had yet to find anything. When he pulled up in front of the Flight Tours office in Sedona, he saw that Aaron had at least fulfilled his demand that Dwy's plane be ready. It sat on the flight line, gleaming in the morning sun. Darren opened the office door and barged inside. Seeing his son's empty office, with family pictures and mementos on the desk, caused a twinge of dread. *He can't be gone. He can't. I've got so much to make up for. It can't end like this.* But he knew that with every ticking second, the odds in favor of Dwy's survival were diminishing. A noise startled him. Aaron came through the door, his face ashen and somber.

Obviously leery of Darren's mood, Aaron offered a subdued, "Good morning."

"'Morning, Aaron. Thanks for getting the plane ready."

"Why do you want me to go with you?" Aaron asked.

"Aaron, I'm sorry for the way I talked to you yesterday. But you're the only one who can help. The FAA can't find the plane. The search crews have all come up empty-handed. No airliner has heard an emergency transmitter. If you and I don't find Dwy, he'll die."

"Why do you think you can find him?"

"I can't. But you can."

"I don't understand how."

Darren sighed. He knew he was in way over his head. "Let's back up a bit. If we're going to work together, I've got to know who I am talking to."

"Aaron," Aaron said, dumfounded.

"Aaron can't help me. How do I talk to Eagle-To-The-Clouds?"

"I have to call on him."

"Then do it."

Both men stared at each other. Aaron closed his eyes, inhaled deeply several times. His posture strengthened. The expression on his face firmed. His fists clenched. He exhaled slowly, uttering a guttural sound. He raised his forearms and crossed his wrists in front of his throat and spoke, "This is Eagle-To-The-Clouds. Why have you called on me?"

"I need your help to find your friend, Dwy, who is in grave danger. I ask you to go with me and guide me to him."

"I must have time to consult with the Respected Spirits. It is the way. Leave me alone. They will not come with you here."

Darren nodded. He grabbed a few aeronautical charts from Dwy's desk and stepped outside. Darren sketched out a route of flight to Santa Fe. He kept glancing at the office door but saw no sign of Aaron. *Damn*, he swore. *We've got to get moving.* Darren pre-flighted the plane. When he finished, he thought, *Five more minutes. That's all the time he gets. If he's not out by then, I'm going in to get him.*

With relief, Darren saw the door open and someone emerge. *Oh, God, it's no longer Aaron. He's become Eagle-To-The-Clouds.* In full paint and Native American costume, the shaman walked with a determined stride to the aircraft and climbed in. He placed a pack filled with objects on the floor between his feet. He sat in a rigid brace, eyes gazing ahead, saying nothing. He raised his right hand and with a stiff wave, motioned in a forward direction.

Darren took the cue, started the engine and taxied to the runway, trying to ignore the smell of whiskey on Aaron's breath.

* * *

Jenna poured Tracey another cup of coffee; the rich aroma teased her need for caffeine. The two women had stayed up most of the night, trying to reassure each other about Dwy. At times the conversation would drift toward Jenna's background and her search for her father, but Dwy's safety dominated their thoughts. By summoning an inner strength, Tracey had regained her composure. But her resolve to be brave remained fragile. She had faced many difficult situations in her life, but nothing as terrible as the potential loss of her son.

During the night, there had been several bouts with the terror of imagined, but horrible, outcomes. Each time, the women would reach to each other to climb out of the depths of despair.

But not once—not even in passing—did Darren's name come up. As far as Tracey was concerned, Darren no longer mattered.

Tracey sipped her coffee. The phone remained silent. She feared it might ring with news she could not accept, but the longer it didn't ring, the more the thought grew in her that time was running out for Dwy.

* * *

Darren landed the plane at Santa Fe to refuel. After asking the fuel truck driver to top off the tanks, Darren suggested to Eagle-To-The-Clouds that he step outside and stretch his legs for a minute, but the only response he got was a stoic shake of the shaman's head. Darren walked inside to the flight desk and checked the records from Dwy's stop the morning before. *All routine. Correct time. Proper grade of fuel. Dwy's signature on the receipt. Nothing out of line.*

Darren returned to the plane. He planned to fly to the Texas border, retracing Dwy's route and hoping Eagle-To-The-Clouds could sense something that would lead to the downed plane. But when he re-entered the cockpit, the stench of whiskey was even stronger. The shaman remained in a rigid position, staring straight ahead.

"Did you consult your spirits again?" Darren asked, before he started the engine. "What kind were they, anyway?"

"Eagle-To-The-Clouds needs powerful medicine to fly. Doing this for Dwy, not for Dr. Stewart."

"Well, keep reminding yourself of that. And another thing …," Darren looked at Aaron, not sure how to proceed, "uh, we've had our butts jammed together in this cockpit for more than three hours, with God knows how many more to go before we find Dwy. I can't keep calling you 'Eagle-To-The-Clouds.' It's way too formal and takes too long. No disrespect, but you call me 'Darren' from now on, because I'm going to call you 'Eagle.'"

Darren noticed a flicker of a smile cross the shaman's lips, but it quickly disappeared. Maybe the two could work together across the huge cultural gap that existed between them. Darren felt a little better.

They climbed to altitude and followed the same route that Dwy had filed in his flight plan.

"Okay, Eagle, it's time for you to help me. Give me a lead to where Dwy is."

The shaman pulled two greasewood sticks, adorned with eagle feathers and secured with rawhide, from his pack. He tied each to the ceiling of the plane's cabin, one dangling in front of Darren's face, distracting him from monitoring the instrument panel.

"What are those?" Darren asked.

"Páhos—prayer sticks. I use them to communicate with the Spirits," the shaman answered, fumbling again in his pack and withdrawing a pipe. He filled it with incense and lit it. With his eyes closed, he inhaled and blew into the pipe. A pungent smoke filled the cabin, obscuring Darren's view. His eyes burned and began to water. Blinking didn't help, and he wiped the corners of his eyelids with the back of his hand. Darren's throat turned raw, and he sneezed and coughed, all the while trying to keep the plane flying straight and level. The overwhelming stench of whiskey combined with the acrid smoke made him nauseous.

Waving his hand through the smoke, Darren swore, "Damn it, Eagle, stop it. I can't see! You're making me sick."

"It has to be done. The prayer sticks must be purified before I can sense the Spirits."

Once again, Darren felt the odd sensation of being high, the same as on top of the mesa. This time, though, he couldn't afford to lose his faculties. *Won't do Dwy any good to crash this plane, too.* He wrestled frantically to open the vent in the left window to draw out the smoke. Once open though, the noise generated by the 150-mile-per-hour slipstream only added to the confusion. Darren could see nothing outside and focused on the gauges to keep the plane under control. He grabbed the pipe and tried to take it away from Eagle, but the man's strength was more than Darren could overcome. The plane wallowed and rocked. *This was not a good idea*, Darren thought.

Eagle extinguished the pipe and untied the prayer sticks, holding them with outstretched arms, eyes remaining closed. He began a loud, rasping chant, oblivious to Darren's concern.

"Now what?" Darren asked.

"I am speaking to the Spirits. Turn left."

"But Dwy didn't make a left turn at this point. He went on east to Texas."

"Turn left, now!"

Darren fumed, but complied with the shaman's directive. He added power to climb above the southernmost portion of the Sangre de Cristo range. Although the smoke began to clear, the plane got buffeted by turbulence caused by the winds crossing the mountain ridges. Darren swung the yoke from lock to lock to maintain control. In a more normal time, discretion would have suggested he turn around, but not today.

Eagle remained resolute, but his face took on a definite, greenish cast. He continued his chant.

"Don't you go getting sick on me. We're both in this until we find Dwy, so hang on."

The chanting grew louder, as if to drown out Darren's voice.

Darren followed the shaman's directions, first turning left, then a little right. He swerved to avoid the ridgelines. It bothered Darren that the Eagle's eyes were closed, but he kept chanting and periodically barked a change in direction.

After a few minutes, Eagle gasped, "Here! He's here." Then Eagle-To-The-Clouds passed out and slumped against Darren, head drooping, breathing heavily. Darren, struggling to maintain control of the aircraft, shoved Eagle, trying to get the dead weight off his body and arm. The third time he tried, the shaman's body fell against the right side of the plane, his head jammed between the head rest and the cabin wall.

Intoxicated, Darren seethed. When he turned back to the front, his peripheral vision caught the image of an aircraft converging rapidly on a collision course. Fear-induced adrenaline hit Darren like the shock of a pitcher of ice water being dumped onto his lap. Instinct screamed at him to pull the stick back to his gut and jam the throttle forward. He stomped on the right rudder to counter the engine's torque. The stall warning horn began bleeping. When the other craft passed under his plane from right to left, Darren yelled in astonishment, "It's an eagle. He came close to taking us both out." He swung his head to the right to follow the eagle's path. The bird soared in a graceful arc, pinfeathers gingerly sampling the wind, tail constantly twitching to make minute changes in direction. Hearing a groan from the shaman, a flash of recognition broke over Darren. *Wait a damn minute. That's not just any eagle—that's Eagle's spirit!*

Darren racked the plane into a right turn so steep the wings went beyond vertical. He aligned his path of flight with the eagle and cut the throttle, placing the plane in a gentle dive to follow in trail. After a few moments and having nearly caught up with the eagle, he saw it soar upward, flapping its wings and disappearing in a layer of mist overhead. The point was not lost on Darren. *An eagle to the clouds!*

Darren marked the position of the eagle's disappearance and put the plane in a steep left bank, scanning the forest below for any sign of a downed plane. Eagle-To-The-Clouds roused from his state of unconsciousness and became Aaron again. Bewildered by his surroundings, he grabbed for hand holds, terrified by the plane's bank.

"We're okay. Focus on the ground below. Watch for anything—and I mean *anything* unusual."

On the third circuit, a flash of sunlight blinded Darren for an instant. It happened a second time. And then once more. Darren searched for the source and saw a gash in the woods. At the very tip of the streak he saw what he thought might be wreckage. The flash hit him again.

Certain he had found something, Darren flew lower and expanded his turn to get a better visual angle on the point. A moment later he saw it. Not only the tail section of a plane, but an arm sticking out the cabin's window holding a piece of reflective metal. His heart leapt, jolted by a bolt of excitement.

"Eagle, that's him! It's Dwy. He's alive! Great God, he's alive!"

Darren tuned the radio to the emergency frequency and keyed the microphone. He shouted, "Center, this is Seven-Two Juliet, I've located the downed plane. There's a survivor. Get a rescue chopper here immediately." Darren radioed the coordinates of the wreckage, waggled his wings to Dwy and set up an orbit above the sight to await the rescue unit.

Aaron, shaking with tension and relief, grabbed a barf bag and filled it to the brim.

* * *

Within a matter of minutes, Darren spotted a rescue helicopter heading for the crash site. He called the chopper on the emergency frequency and established contact, giving the pilot vectors to the downed plane. Once overhead, the rescue team lost no time in lowering two members and a basket to the wreckage. Before the team reached the ground, a news helicopter from Albuquerque arrived on the scene and circled 1,000 feet above the rescue chopper.

Darren anxiously awaited news about Dwy's condition. Then it came.

"Seven-Two Juliet, the pilot says you're his dad, and he wants you to know he's okay. He's busted up some, but his vitals are good," he heard the pilot transmit. "Looks like a broken leg and maybe a couple of ribs. He's complaining about back pain, too, but he's got motion and feeling in all his extremities. We've got him on a back board in the basket. As soon as we raise him up and get him on board, we're taking him back to St. Vincent's in Santa Fe. And ... oh, yeah, he wanted us to tell you thanks. He'll talk to you at the hospital."

The strain and bottled-up tension whooshed out of Darren, and he gave Aaron an impromptu high-five. "Eagle, you did it. Thank God, you did it. You saved my son. I'm sorry I've been so gruff with you."

"My Respected Spirits and your God saved your son. You should thank them, not me."

Darren said a quick prayer to both and once the basket reached the safety of the chopper's interior, he turned on a bearing that would take them back to Santa Fe.

* * *

"Hello?" Tracey answered, filled with panic at seeing the caller I.D. *The FAA. I don't know if I can bear to hear the news. Oh, God, let him be alive.* Jenna placed a reassuring arm on Tracey's shoulder.

"Mrs. Stewart?"

"Yes," Tracey answered, overcome with dread.

"This is Ed Matthews in the flight safety office of the FAA. Mrs. Stewart, we found your son's plane this morning. He's banged up pretty bad, but nothing life-threatening. He's at St. Vincent's Hospital in Santa Fe—"

Overhearing the news, Jenna squealed in excitement, patting Tracey on the back.

"He's alive, Tracey. He's *alive!*"

It took a moment to sink in. Tracey raised her head and cupped her hands over her mouth.

"Alive? My son's alive!" She jammed the phone against her ear. "How bad is he hurt? Tell me!"

"Uh, Mrs. Stewart, he's going to be okay. The hospital let us know he has a couple of broken ribs, a broken femur and dehydration. He's in surgery now, but it shouldn't be too much longer."

"Oh, thank you. You don't know how relieved I am. Thank you, Mr… . uh, Mr… ."

"Matthews. Do you have someone with you?"

"Yes, I do. A wonderful young woman."

"Then I'll say goodbye."

"Goodbye, and thank you again, Mr. Matthews."

Tracey put the phone down and smiled at Jenna. "Come on, girl, we've got to get to Santa Fe."

* * *

When Dwy awoke, he sensed someone sitting next to his bed, but he drifted off again before he could recognize the person. His eyes fluttered back open. Confused by his surroundings, it took him a few minutes to become aware. He squinted.

"Dad? Is that you?"

Darren took his son's hand, concerned by the weakness of his grip. "It's me."

"Dad, you found me. I knew you would. If you hadn't, I …"

"I had help," Darren said, motioning toward the foot of Dwy's bed.

"Aaron!" Dwy said. "Dad, you called out the special forces."

"I wouldn't have found you otherwise."

Dwy tried to raise his head, but quit when pain in his chest overwhelmed him. He lay still for a few moments. "They shot me down, Dad."

Dwy's statement confirmed Darren's worst suspicions. "Easy, son."

"I knew the plane had been hit, but I thought I had escaped major damage. Must've been a fuel leak, though. Just before I topped the ridge, the engine quit." Dwy gasped for breath, his ribs hurting something terrible."

"Where did it happen?"

"Across the Texas border, above WSP's pumping station north of Dalhart. Texas vigilantes, most likely."

Darren clenched his teeth, his temples reflecting the tension. *Maybe Texans, but could even be WSP's goons.* Anger roiled inside him. Both men were quiet for a time.

Darren stood. Dwy's grip strengthened.

"Dad, I have to tell you something."

"Go on."

"We've had our times. But … well, you've always been my dad, and today … today, you were my hero. No one else could have done it."

Darren, touched by the emotion, could only smile. "You would have done the same for me; besides I had the help of an eagle."

"An eagle, Dad? Do you mean Eagle-To-The-Clouds?"

"Yes, Eagle, as I call him—but an eagle, too. I'll fill you in when you're better."

Darren withdrew his hand. "Your mom sent word she'd be here soon. She's not talking to me right now. I'd stay, but I've got something to do. Goodbye, Dwy."

"Dad, I'm sorry. It's my fault she's mad at you. What have you got to do?"

"I'm going to L.A. to settle a score," Darren replied, nodding for Aaron to take his place by Dwy's bed as he strode from the room.

CHAPTER EIGHTEEN

THE CITY
OF ANGELS

Darren entered the Los Angeles basin on I-10 via Cabazon Pass. Uncontrolled wildfires raged through the San Bernadino Mountains to his right. The beleaguered forest service had long since given up any hope of containing the blazes, although every few minutes Darren saw truckloads of weary firefighters headed toward the most threatening of the fires. Trapped by L.A.'s notorious temperature inversion, dense clouds of smoke filled the air and decreased visibility on the highway to almost zero. Darren switched the Jeep's A/C to recycle to keep out the fumes, but the smell of charred fir and pine filled the interior, causing his eyes to water and his nose to burn. Vimmy whimpered and paced the cargo area, sniffing for an area free of the acrid air.

"Easy, boy, it'll get better soon," Darren said, more trying to convince himself than the dog.

He had stopped by Tracey's empty apartment on his way through Phoenix and picked Vimmy up from a neighbor. On the ride to L.A., sensing Darren's vile mood, Vimmy kept to himself in the rear, not wanting to chance a harsh rebuke.

Darren seethed with anger. One man—a man he already detested—in a brief period of time had made a move on Tracey and then, with malicious intent, put his son in a position that could have cost him his life. *That sleazy bastard's going to regret he ever crossed paths with me.* Darren had no idea what he would do when he caught up with Davis, but at the very least he wanted to bust him in the face and turn that movie-star fake smile into a bloody, toothless pulp.

It had been years since Darren had traveled to L.A., and the deterioration he saw as he drove brought home to him the enormity of the ravages caused by the long-term drought. Traffic no longer choked the freeway, but many lanes were instead clogged with debris, junk from abandoned automobiles, discarded belongings and trash of all kinds, remnants of the ongoing exodus from the city. Gangs of young men brazenly picked through the refuse, unconcerned about any civil authority. Whenever rubble forced Darren to slow to a crawl, these groups would eye him as he passed, sizing him up for a possible attack. At one point, when Darren had to put the Jeep in four-wheel drive to crawl over some trash, they kicked and slapped the side of his vehicle, daring him to confront them. Vimmy bristled and growled, snapping in frustration at an arm on the outside of the window. Reaching a clear area of roadway, Darren gunned the Jeep to put some distance between him and the youths. *I'm not even to the bad part of town, yet. City of Angels? No more.* The real Angels had vacated the city along with a vast portion of the population years ago. No way could a baseball franchise survive in the God-forsaken, crumbling mass of civilization and infrastructure that now existed. *City of Angst, maybe.*

Darren took the Santa Monica Freeway west until he could turn south on the Harbor Freeway. The WSP offices were in an industrial park adjacent to the Port of Los Angeles. The closer he got, the worse were the surroundings. On a bridge across a dry and dust-filled aqueduct, filthy men with shopping carts and wagons filled with bottles of water from unknown sources were hawking their wares. *'Cholera canteens'*, Darren mused. *Can't imagine anyone thirsty enough to even think about drinking the stuff in those bottles. And judging from the appearance of the characters selling the water, they'd rather pop you and take all your money than make a sale.*

Darren left the freeway and picked his way along an inner-city road. Through the haze he could see the ghostly shadow of an abandoned iceberg tethered offshore. *Another grand program gone awry.* The government's plan to help quench the city's thirst for fresh water fell apart when the bill came due. There weren't enough people left in the city to pay for it, and the citizens on the eastern side of the Continental Divide didn't support it. *Why build a city in the desert? Why prolong the inevitable? You got just what you deserved.*

Darren pulled up in front of the WSP headquarters, a magnificent building surrounded by squalor. He left the engine running and sat back in his seat, contemplating his next move. Reason began to intrude on the anger he had hosted for more than two days. *If I attack him, he'll play the role of the victim to his advantage. If I threaten him, he can use all his resources to get back at me. He's done enough damage already.*

An idea came into Darren's mind. The more he mulled the thought over, the more he became convinced it represented his best course of action. He could bring about the downfall of Davis in a public and humiliating way. Darren exhaled several times, taking a few moments to calm down. He turned to Vimmy and patted him on the head, causing the dog's tail to wag for the first time during the whole trip. "Vimmy, do you want to go back to Chaco with me? I'm over being mad."

Vimmy whined in response and leapt into the passenger seat, peering eagerly out the front. Darren pulled away from the curb and began the trek back to New Mexico.

CHAPTER NINETEEN

THE RELUCTANT ACTIVIST

Two days later at the WSP pipeline construction site near Kutz Canyon, the superintendent of the demolition team arrived on the scene to make the final checks prior to authorizing the detonation scheduled for 30 minutes after sunrise. The area around the knoll had been cordoned off since the day before. The explosive charges had been put in place and connected to the main control terminal inside the construction shack more than a quarter of a mile away. He removed his walkie-talkie and cell phone, shut them off and tossed them on the desktop. He stood in front of the detonator panel, a device with an electro-mechanical interlock that prevented inadvertent activation of the switch. In order to throw the switch, not one, but two unique keys were required to be inserted and turned. He fingered his own key, securely fastened to a chain dangling from his belt and turned to the foreman.

"Show me your key," he said. The foreman did as requested, his key on a lanyard around his wrist. "Good. Sound the horn."

The foreman punched a button and a klaxon horn blared in short intervals, shattering the pre-dawn stillness. Over the P.A. the crew boss said, "All personnel, clear the area. This is a test." Allowing a few minutes, the crew boss reached for the switch and attempted to pull it. Satisfied that it would not budge without the two keys in place, he turned to the crew and said, "No one comes near this damn thing, understand? I'm going to walk to the site."

Not even daring to take a flashlight with him, he walked to the perimeter fence. The sky had begun to lighten, exposing eerie silhouettes of construction equipment and storage materials. He opened the gate and walked toward the darkness of the knoll. A moment later he stopped in mid-stride; a look of amazement crossed his grizzled face as he stared at the image in front of him.

What the hell? After shouting commands to a shadowy figure standing there and hearing responses that unnerved him, the boss turned and walked back to the shack as fast as his 60-year-old legs would take him. He burst through the door. "Shut it down," he yelled, grabbing his phone and jabbing in the WSP main office number. "Scrub the detonation. We've got a major-league situation. Nobody move."

* * *

Jackson Davis, anticipating the news that the detonation had taken place, took the call directly.

"Davis here."

"Mr. Davis, we need you to get out to the site right away. We've got a real problem."

"Have you detonated the explosives?"

"No, Sir, that's just it. We can't."

"Damn you, don't you tell me you can't. That's what you're paid to do. I want that hill blown to smithereens."

"There's someone standing at the base of the mound, Sir. Some guy and a dog."

"Clear the son-of-a-bitch out. How many men does it take to do that?"

"Can't take the chance, Sir. He's got a phone. Says he's got a TV reporter briefed on the story. Something about this being Navajo land, sacred ground, stuff like that. He said if we even got close to him, he'd call. That call could blow everything up."

"Not much chance of that. You know that."

"I don't care if it's one in a million. I'm not going to be inside the perimeter if he calls."

"You're telling me you won't follow my orders?"

"Uh … no, Sir. I won't take the chance."

"Send one of your men to do it."

"I won't do that, either."

"You're fired, then. I'm terminating your company's contract. Lock everything down and get out. Let the guard know I'll be there in a couple of hours."

The superintendent slammed the phone down. He took a minute to calm down, and then said to his crew, "You boys pack up your tools and lock up. We're off this job. Give me the other key. That sorry ass will have to come begging to me for both of them before he can blow that hill with another outfit. Let's get out of here."

* * *

Tracey and Jenna reached the hospital and found their way to Dwy's room. Dwy heard them enter and gave them a big smile. Tracey reached over and hugged him, but he winced at her embrace. Realizing the pain she had caused him, she apologized. Jenna offered her hand to Dwy, and he squeezed it and winked at her, a wink that triggered a welling of emotion inside her.

"Jenna, I don't think you've met Aaron," Dwy said. "He helped Dad find me. He's been doing hospital duty the past couple of days."

Aaron nodded and said, "Hello."

"Where is your dad?" Tracey asked. "I expected him to be here."

"I wish I knew. He was here when they brought me out of surgery, but he left shortly afterward. Said he had to go to L.A.; seemed pretty agitated, not like his usual self."

Tracey's heart missed a beat. She knew there could be only one reason for Darren to go to L.A., and she worried he might do something drastic. Would this ever end? First she, then Dwy and now perhaps even Darren—all because of Jackson Davis.

Dwy and Jenna chatted. Seeing an opportunity to get some lunch, Aaron excused himself and left. Tracey sat on a stiff-backed chair, beginning to regret the way she had acted toward Darren.

* * *

The WSP chopper settled to a landing in the construction yard. Jackson Davis wasted no time in debarking. He burst through the shack's door and growled at the guard. "Stay away from the explosives panel. I'm going to have a talk with that asshole."

He stormed out of the shack, not worrying about powering down his phone, and hurried toward the lone figure at the base of the mound. Getting closer, he recognized Darren, and he boiled with anger. He stepped in front of Darren and glared. Vimmy growled and got between them.

"I'm not afraid of you, your dog or the explosives. You get off my property or you go up with the damned hill when it blows."

"Go ahead. The news team is on the way to cover the story. I called them as soon as I heard your chopper. You lose either way. You drag me away, and they'll be all over you. You won't be able to stand the heat. You're trespassing. You're in violation of the sacred rights of the Navajo. You may destroy an ancient machine that's been lost for a millennium. For what? To steal water from some poor souls on the other side of the divide? The publicity will force you to shut down."

"One word from me and you're not going to be around to see that happen."

"Do it," Darren said, hearing the news chopper approach. "Do it, and you'll not only be a front page story for a year, you'll spend the rest of your sorry life in prison, trying to save yourself from other perverts like you who would see you as a delicacy."

Jackson raised a fist to hit Darren, but Vimmy snarled and grabbed his leg, throwing him off balance. Jackson had a rock concealed in his left hand and made a move to strike the dog's head. With all the pent-up anger and frustration behind him, Darren smashed Jackson's face as hard as he could. Jackson, stunned by the blow, fell to the ground. He lay there for a moment before wiping his bloody mouth and spitting out a broken tooth.

Darren stood over the man, shaking his fist at him. "That's for assaulting my wife, for nearly killing my son, for threatening me, and damn you, for trying to hurt my dog." Darren motioned to the chopper circling overhead. "They're out of Albuquerque. Smile, you're on TV."

Davis picked himself up. "This is just the first round. When I come back I'll have a team of my best lawyers and a sheriff with a warrant for your eviction. We'll see who ends up in prison for assault, battery and trespassing. And I'll have your dog put down, too. You're going to regret this day forever. Enjoy the desert sun while you wait. I hope it gives you a heat stroke."

Davis turned his back on Darren and stomped toward the shack, muttering every curse word he knew.

* * *

Aaron rushed back into Dwy's room and grabbed the TV remote from the night stand. "I caught the news coming down the hall. There's a bulletin about some incident at Chaco Canyon."

He clicked the set on and frantically switched channels until he came to a live aerial shot from a news helicopter. The camera focused on a small mound. The image, blurred by turbulence, swirled as the chopper circled. When the lens zoomed in, a solitary figure could be seen standing with a dog alongside.

"Who's that?" Aaron asked.

Tracey looked up and instantly recognized the figure. "Oh, my God, it's Darren. Look! What's going on?"

They watched, overcome with anxiety, as a reporter did a voice-over with the story.

".... We're on the scene. We have an unidentified man protesting the Western Slope Pipeline Company's plan to blast through a hill that is obstructing their right-of-way. We have no information as to why, but the situation is critical. The hill is laced with high-explosive charges, and the man is in imminent danger. We will monitor this story and break back in to your regular programming with updates as we get them."

Tracey closed her eyes, saying a silent prayer. Aaron stared in complete bewilderment. Jenna took Tracey's hand in one of her hands and Dwy's in the other.

Dwy broke into a huge grin and said, "Look at my dad. He's an activist! Who would've ever thought it? Way to go, Dad." He turned to the others. "We've got to help him."

* * *

The afternoon dragged on and Darren could see no sign of life at the construction shack, except for the security vehicle parked outside. Sweat soaked his shirt. *Must be over a hundred degrees and no shade.* He scrounged through the backpack he pulled from his Jeep before he crossed on foot through Kutz Canyon in the predawn darkness. He found several bottles of water, a blanket, some camping gear, rope and tent pegs. He fashioned a small lean-to for Vimmy from the blanket, using the tent pegs and the pack's metal stays. Once he got the panting dog to lie in the shade, he filled a tin plate with water and petted him as he lapped it up. *Sorry, Vim, didn't plan on getting you into this. Hang in there with me; it'll be dark in a few hours.*

Next Darren stuffed his handkerchief under the brim of his cap to keep the burning sun off his neck. He sipped some water and splashed a bit on his forehead and wrists to help provide some relief from the heat. He heard the rumble of a heavy piece of equipment and peered down the road to try and locate the source of the noise. Not seeing anything, he attributed the sound to his imagination.

He looked at his watch, discouraged to see how little time had elapsed since the last time he checked. The reality of his situation settled in. *I'm in real trouble. The heat could kill us both. Even if it doesn't, I'll be lucky to stay out of prison. I can't fight WSP's legal staff. Tracey's gone and …*

That noise again. This time louder, and from his right. It sounded like the growl of a big diesel engine. Turning, he saw a plume of black smoke rising beyond a swale in the desert. Then a huge caterpillar bulldozer topped the ridge, headed right for him. Vimmy rose and barked.

Perplexed, Darren couldn't believe WSP would use brute force to shove him off the site. The blade of the cat was raised, blocking his view of the driver. The dozer clanked toward him and at the last minute, squealed to a stop not four feet in front of him. With a huge clunk, the blade slammed to the ground, causing a shudder.

A familiar voice boomed out, "Hey Darren, you want some company?" A big man crawled down the side and turned toward Darren.

"Skeeter! Damn you, I thought it was the end. But am I happy to see you."

"It's been a while since I've driven one of these things. Need to keep my hand in, you know."

"Where'd you get it?"

"WSP's equipment yard. I don't think they worry too much about security out here in the desert. That geezer's asleep in the shack. Want a sandwich? I've got a cooler."

Skeeter reached Darren and gave him a high-five slap, a strong-armed one that nearly wrenched Darren's shoulder. Vimmy weaved in and out of the two, happy to see Skeeter. The men sat on the shady side of the dozer and snacked on the food from the cooler. Skeeter wiped peanut butter off his mouth and said, "Tell me, Darren, what's your plan?"

Darren shook his head. "I don't have one. I didn't think it through."

"You mean you just did this on impulse? You, the physicist, the organized, deliberate, conservative, and—what was it you told me your wife said?—oh, yeah, *boring* person? You mean you don't have a plan, or some mathematical formula, or a guaranteed outcome?"

"You could say that."

Skeeter laughed as hard as Darren had ever heard him laugh. When his laughter subsided, Skeeter wiped his eyes and elbowed Darren so hard in the ribs, it hurt.

"Welcome to the club, my friend. So tell me, what's going on."

Darren filled him in on the situation with Jackson Davis and WSP ... that he would bring the sheriff with a warrant for his arrest and eviction.

"It looks pretty hopeless," Darren said.

"Before they come, I'll put the dozer at that entrance gate. They'll have to get past me to get to you. Believe me, with the TV cameras rolling, they'll not shoot."

"I can't ask you to do that."

"You can't ask me not to."

* * *

Tracey suggested she and Jenna step out to get a bite to eat in the hospital cafeteria. On the way, Tracey told Jenna she'd catch up with her and ducked into the women's room. She dialed President Earlman's number.

"Hello, Tracey, what can I do for you?" he answered.

"You shouldn't have asked. Because I need a big favor."

"What?"

"You remember those times when I did things that saved your butt? All the times you asked me how you could pay me back, and I said I'd figure out something someday?"

"Sure, Tracey, go on."

"Well, that day's come. I need your help."

"Anything, Tracey, name it."

Tracey briefed the former president on what she needed. She waited with some trepidation as he mulled her request over. He laughed and said, "No problem, Tracey, but you know this wipes the slate clean, don't you? We're even after this."

She thanked the president and hurried to catch up with Jenna. Reaching her, Tracey explained that she had been called back to Phoenix for an emergency meeting. She'd catch a cab to the airport once she said goodbye to Dwy. Leaving Jenna to her lunch, Tracey returned to Dwy's room.

"I've got to go back to Phoenix, Dwy. Duty calls."

"But, Mom, you just got here."

"I know, but you've got good company around you. Jenna and Aaron will see that you stay out of trouble."

She leaned over Dwy and kissed him.

"Mom, call me when you get there."

Tracey agreed, extracting a promise that Dwy would call *her* if he heard any new information about Darren. Dwy watched her leave and listened as her heels clicked down the hall. A moment later, Dwy sat up and swung his feet over the edge of the bed. He groaned in pain. Aaron rushed to him. "Are you crazy? You can't get up. What are you trying to do?"

Dwy reached for his pants in the closet adjacent to the bed and pulled them on, having some difficulty getting one of the legs over his walking cast. Every tug on his pants caused excruciating pain in his ribs. Gasping for breath and feeling lightheaded, he stuffed his hospital robe in the waist. "I'm going to help Dad."

"No, no, no. Oh, no you're not. You can't even walk."

"Yes, I can. I've been making it to the bathroom with my crutches. Get me that wheelchair."

Aaron pushed the wheelchair to the side of the bed, protesting Dwy's request. Dwy grabbed a stationery pad from the night stand and scribbled a note to Jenna. Dwy eased his good leg to the floor and, using Aaron as a brace, stood and pivoted to sit in the wheelchair, exhaling in relief as he settled back. He motioned for the crutches and Aaron handed them to him. He clutched them against his side, taking care not to let the tips drag on the floor.

"Let's go."

"Your mom's going to kill me."

"No, she's taken bigger risks for Dad. She would do the same thing if she were in my shoes."

Aaron wheeled Dwy down the corridor to the elevator, taking it to the first floor. Aaron left Dwy at the entrance while he retrieved his car. A few moments later, Aaron had Dwy in the car and was folding the wheelchair to place it in the trunk when Jenna ran out the door, screaming for them to wait.

Dwy stared at her. "Jenna, my dad needs help. There's some risk involved. I thought it'd be better if you stayed, but you can go with us if you want. I'd like to have you. You decide, but do it quickly."

Jenna looked back to the hospital entrance, then to the car. She hopped in and closed the door.

"Let's do it. You're not going to leave me alone to worry about you again. I'm going to be with you."

* * *

Skeeter and Darren lay with their heads and shoulders leaned up against the dozer, gaining some relief from the cooler air that followed the sunset. Neither man felt sleepy. Vimmy curled up between them for warmth. Darren tried to think of a way to secure a good outcome from his predicament, but he came up empty no matter what course he considered. And now he had put his friend in jeopardy, too.

"Paradise," Skeeter said, startling Darren.

"Paradise? What do you mean, *Paradise?*"

"Well, as you physicist types like to say, it's all relative."

"You're not making sense."

"Compared to what I've been through, this is paradise. You should've spent three years in Antarctica. Seventy below, no sun for three months, one-hundred-mile-an-hour gales. Hell, this is a snap. Even worse than my stint in Antarctica was my time in protective custody. Locked up, no visitors, terrible food and not knowing—about family, future, what was going on or anything."

"I'm experiencing some of that now."

"Yeah, but you'll get through it, trust me. There's only one thing that worries me."

"All the explosives?"

"Nope, that risk would be kind of like lightning. If it ever hits you, you'll never know it. The same with the explosives. What really worries me about this is I may miss out on my lottery winnings.

"You *won* the lottery?"

"No, but I left my ticket in Santa Fe. If I win, I'll never know it."

Darren realized he'd been had. He fell asleep with a smile on his face.

* * *

At sunrise the next morning, a battered old car trailing a rooster tail of dust sped past the guard and careened through the open gate. It slid sideways, skidding to a stop in front of the dozer.

"Who the hell are those fools?" Darren yelled, wiping dust from his eyes.

He watched in amazement as Jenna got out from the driver's side. "Hi, Mr. Stewart," she shouted. Then, spotting Skeeter, "Hey, Dad, how did you get here?"

Both men scrambled to their feet. Skeeter hugged Jenna, and Darren rushed to see who the passenger was. He couldn't believe it when he saw Dwy struggling with his crutches in an attempt to get out. "Damn it son, you shouldn't be here."

"Neither should you, Dad, but I'm proud to be able to stand with you. It'll be great to be protesting again. Haven't done it since college."

"Where's your mom?"

A shadow fell across Dwy's face. He told Darren about her being called back to Phoenix.

"She's still pretty mad at you, I guess. I'm sorry, Dad." Then he brightened back up. "We brought Aaron, too. Dropped him off in Shiprock. He said he had an idea about how he could help, but wouldn't explain anything."

A wave of guilt came over Darren. The ante had been raised another notch. *Now my son and Skeeter's daughter are at risk, too.* He watched anxiously up the road for any sign of Jackson Davis. He had second thoughts. *Maybe now's the time to call the whole thing off. Get out now before Davis gets here.* That fleeting thought vanished as quickly as it arose. *Nope, I'm in this to the end. No turning back now.*

Darren saw the guard, now awake, peering at them through a pair of binoculars. Jackson Davis and the sheriff couldn't be far away. Overhead he saw the news chopper, back in the sky after apparently setting down somewhere for the night. Darren told the other three that he promised to stay to the end, but he would risk no violence. If the sheriff made arrests, all of them should comply without resistance.

An hour later Darren saw a strange sight on the horizon to the north. A big yellow vehicle bumped along a desert road in a cloud of dust and headed their way, swerving to avoid deep ruts and axle-busting rocks in its path. As it came nearer, Darren could see it was an old school bus. The others saw it, too. Dwy and Jenna cheered.

"That's Aaron," Dwy said. "He must be coming with the whole town of Shiprock."

Their joy proved to be short-lived.

"Look," Skeeter said, pointing to the main road. "Here comes a whole convoy of trouble."

Two black SUVs, following a sheriff's car with its lights flashing, were speeding for the gate. When they reached the entrance, they stopped. Doors on all three vehicles opened and the occupants got out. Darren could see the sheriff in his uniform and beside him, of course, was Jackson Davis. The rest of the group wore suits. *Lawyers*, Darren surmised.

The school bus topped the last swale and pulled up next to the dozer. The smell of hot brakes and oily exhaust fumes wafted over the entire scene. The passenger door opened and the first person out was Aaron in his shaman regalia, followed closely by Warren. Warren waved other Navajo townspeople off the bus. Led by Aaron, they formed an arc around the base of the mound and stood facing the entrance gate. Aaron scrambled to the top of the hill and turned toward the WSP contingent. He stretched out his arms, prayer sticks in hand, and began chanting.

Davis and the sheriff walked through the gate and approached Darren. Dwy stayed close to his dad's side; Skeeter and Jenna fell in place immediately behind them. The six of them stood without making a sound, sizing each other up. The news chopper circled closer, the rotor making a deafening noise and a downwash that blasted everyone with sand. Agitated, the sheriff waved for them to back off.

When things had quieted somewhat, Jackson Davis stood nose to nose with Darren. Darren stifled a grin at the sight of the butterfly bandage on Jackson's swollen upper lip and a temporary crown on his front tooth. Seeing the corners of Darren's mouth turn up made Jackson even angrier.

He scowled and waved a document in Darren's face. He spoke in a measured and clipped tone. "I have a warrant for your arrest and eviction. The sheriff is here to make that happen. You may avoid arrest if you agree to leave voluntarily this minute—you and your, uh, ... uh, whole entourage. That's as good an offer as you're going to get."

"Go piss up a rope," Darren said.

Davis could barely restrain himself. He barked an order to the sheriff, but something caught his attention from the top of the knoll and interrupted him in mid-sentence. Darren stared at the distraction, too. He saw Aaron had turned to face the other side of the hill, waving his arms at something. The shaman began an excited dance, hopping from one foot to another, his chant elevating to a scream.

As the two men watched Aaron's strange antics, an olive helicopter with a white top rose from behind the knoll. It climbed above the hill and flew overhead until it reached the road beyond the construction shed. Then it turned into the breeze and landed.

"It's President Earlman!" Dwy shouted.

Sure enough, a white-haired man stepped down from the passenger door. He stopped and raised his hand to assist another passenger, a woman.

"Tracey," Darren said, "it's Tracey."

Jenna began jumping and cheering. She grabbed Dwy, forgetting about his injuries. He groaned but held Jenna tight and shouted, "Mom!"

The former president lost no time in joining the gathering. Tracey ran to Darren but resisted his hug. Standing next to him, she whispered, "When this is over, we'll work out how to get back on track, but you have to promise me you'll be boring every now and then. I don't think I could stand this too often." She squeezed his hand.

The president, in his famed manner of a favorite uncle, said, "Everyone stand back and calm down." He looked at Tracey, still whispering to Darren. "Mrs. Stewart, would you care to rejoin us?" He motioned for Aaron to silence his chanting. He waved the news chopper away. This time, out of respect for the former president, they complied.

"Now, tell me what's going on here," the president said.

"We're here to arrest this man for criminal trespass," Jackson Davis answered.

"You'll do nothing of the kind. We'll have a little talk first," Earlman said. "I'm sure these minor differences can be worked out to everyone's satisfaction."

"It's gone past that point," Jackson said.

President Earlman's "uncle" persona vanished in a flash. He did not appreciate being challenged. He bristled. "Mr. Davis, when I told you things can be worked out. I meant it. I've butted heads with the Russians, Chinese, Israelis, Palestinians, with Arabs and even terrorist groups, so I have a little experience with negotiations. You come with me along with Dr. Stewart. We're going inside that construction shack and talk things through."

He told Tracey to bring Warren to represent the Navajo and Aaron to speak on behalf of the Hopis, too. "Everyone else should just stay loose," he said. "It's best that you all get yourselves and your vehicles off this rock pile and a safe distance away. The sheriff will help you stay out of trouble." With that statement, he ushered the key players inside and closed the door.

* * *

The president took a seat at the side of a rectangular table and motioned for Tracey to sit next to him on his right. Darren sat at the end of the table around the corner from Tracey. Jackson Davis, once he saw where Darren had chosen to sit, walked with a swagger to the other end of the table, pulled the chair out, turned it around and straddled it. President Earlman stared at Davis with a raised eyebrow. Warren and Aaron sat on the side opposite the president. Tracey had seen sessions like this unfold many times in her work with the president. She knew what was to come.

The president looked around the table focusing on each individual in silence. The smile left his face. He spoke. "Here's the process. Everyone here will be treated with respect. There will be no talking over one another. If you have a disagreement, you must bring it to the table. Failure to do so will mean you choose to accept the solution without making your case. In that event, you will not be permitted to bring the issue up at a later date. You had your chance to do it here. Understood?"

Davis rolled his eyes and exhaled.

"And another thing—decorum. This shack has now become the Oval Office. You will act here as you would have in my former office. That means, Mr. Davis, you should turn your chair around and sit like a gentleman. We will address each other by name or gentleman or gentle lady."

Silence prevailed and Davis didn't move. The president stared at him and again raised his eyebrow, this time further. Davis relented and did as told.

"Thank you, Mr. Davis."

The president continued outlining his guidance. "What transpires in this room remains here. You may speak freely but in confidence. Do not test my will with any leaks."

The president became silent and once more took a visual inventory of the participants. Satisfied that he had their attention, he asked Jackson Davis to present his issues.

Davis began, stumbling at first, but built his comments into a rant about Darren's attempts to stop his pipeline. He expressed his anger at Tracey for voting against WSP's project during the commission's work. His final words were directed to the former president himself. "You're trying to undermine my company's ability to succeed and be profitable."

The president replied in a calm voice, "Mr. Davis, you are suffering from several misunderstandings. We'll get to the others later, but I want to correct one of them now. Mrs. Stewart did not vote against your project, she *abstained*. But her discussion about its merits swayed several of the commission members to vote aye. The first ballot resulted in a tie. It was I who cast the deciding vote—a vote *against* your company. You may be angry with me, but not Mrs. Stewart. Were I you, however, I would hold that anger in check until this meeting concludes. You do not want to make an enemy of me."

The president shifted his gaze to Warren. "Warren, it is my understanding that the Navajo Nation granted permission for Western Slope Pipeline to cross its land. Is that right?"

"Yes, Sir. I was at the tribal council meeting that agreed to do that."

"That is all well and good, but yesterday I asked my staff to review the route of the right-of-way, and they came back with something very interesting. Seems like the pipeline is on Navajo land up to a point a few miles west of here. Then, it becomes U.S. territory again, and WSP has the legal right-of-way in the area in question. Isn't that correct?"

A smirk crossed Jackson's face, but he quickly erased it.

"The Navajo don't own land Sir; that's a white man's concept. We are the Diné—the people—and this is the Diné tah—the land of the people. We are a part of the land. We do not own it. This work which mars the land is a crime against us," Warren answered.

"Well said, Warren. But the fact remains that by U.S. laws that have been in place over 100 years, WSP is entitled to use this strip of land."

"The Navajo settled this land more than 500 years before the U.S. laws."

"I respect that, Sir. Nevertheless, I must abide by the U.S. laws in this session."

"Now, Aaron, you are a descendent of the Anasazi."

"The *Ancient Ones*, Sir."

"Sorry."

"Yes, Sir, I am. My ancestors were here 1,000 years before the Navajo." Aaron couldn't resist.

"I see. And you believe there's an ancient craft buried here that at one time carried your ancestors to this land?"

"Such a craft exists in our legends. As to it being here, I don't know. That's something Dr. Stewart believes."

The president smiled. The discussion had now reached the main point of contention. He looked at Darren. "Dr. Stewart, please tell me why you are so adamant about protecting this hill from demolition."

"I don't care about the hill. But Mr. Myers ... uh, Skeeter and I are certain the craft is buried here."

"'Certain' is a strong word, Dr. Stewart."

Darren recounted the search he and Skeeter had undertaken and the evidence that made him believe they had discovered the site.

"All I want is the time to do a few test excavations. If we find nothing, WSP can go ahead without any complaint from me. But if we do find something, then I want this site protected until we unearth the craft."

The president looked from one end of the table to another. "Sounds fair enough to me. Yet the two of you got into a brawl yesterday like a couple of grade school boys."

"He nearly cost my son his life, Sir," Darren said.

"The FBI is investigating that crime. Until they are finished with their work, I won't make any judgment about who's responsible."

Darren thought about bringing up the incident between Jackson and Tracey, but a subtle shake of her head warned him to remain silent.

Hearing no further comments, the president spoke. "I think I've got the essence of the issue before us. Thank you for your cooperation. I suggest you all take a break and go outside for some air while I work through the details. I'll call you back when I'm ready."

Chairs scooted and the participants rose and quietly left the room. Once outside, Jackson Davis headed to his lawyers, seated in their cars, engines running. Darren and Tracey walked alongside Warren and Aaron to rejoin the others.

The news crew tried to get an interview from Darren, but he declined as did Jackson Davis.

President Earlman's chopper pilot received a radio transmission from the White House. He jotted down notes on a knee pad and tore off the sheet of paper. "Start her up and be ready to leave," he commanded his co-pilot. He jumped out of the chopper and hurried to the construction shack. He knocked on the door and entered when the former president acknowledged his knock.

The news crew abruptly stopped its unsuccessful attempts at filming interviews and rushed to their helicopter. Darren observed the activity and shouted, "Hey, where are you going?" The reporter yelled back an answer over the whine of the rotor, "Texas—breaking news."

CHAPTER TWENTY

MOVING
BEYOND

President Earlman opened the door to the shack and motioned for the group to reassemble. Once everyone got back inside, he shut the door but remained standing there with his hand on the knob, gathering his thoughts. He took off his glasses and wiped them with his handkerchief. Replacing them, he glanced at the scrap of paper containing his pilot's notes, then spoke.

"I received a message from President Mitchell. There were major skirmishes along the Texas border last night. Seventeen fatalities. Also, a conflict at Wyoming's border. Two dead. At the top of the hour, the president is announcing plans to send federal troops to both states to maintain order. The governor of Texas is on record warning that such an action is unconstitutional and that he would protect his state's rights with his National Guard. The president has requested my return to D.C. and wants my report on the commission's recommendations so he can put in

193

place, on an emergency basis, actions that will help alleviate the water shortage and the resulting disorder."

The president folded the scrap of paper and placed it into his pocket. He waved everyone to their chairs.

"Here's my proposal for the reconciliation of the issue in front of us. First, Mr. Davis, I plan to change my vote to 'aye', allowing your company to receive federal funds for your project."

The tension flowed out of Jackson's body. He leaned back in his chair, faced Darren at the other end of the table and smiled at him, an expression too exaggerated to be genuine.

"And, Mr. Davis, the commission will see that your company receives an additional 50 million dollars to expedite your pipeline and help Dr. Stewart with any resources needed to excavate and remove any antique relic buried within that knoll outside."

Jackson stiffened, a scowl returning to his face. But before he could respond, the president continued, "Warren, as to the question of the access rights to the land, the commission will work with the governor of New Mexico to cede the land required between here and Santa Fe for the pipeline right-of-way to the Navajo. You will be paid a royalty for every gallon of water pumped through the line which will provide millions of dollars per year in revenue. In return, your tribal council will have the responsibility to provide the labor for the maintenance of that section of line, and your workers will be paid a competitive wage for such efforts."

Warren's face showed no reaction, but a slight nod of his head showed acceptance.

"Aaron, the relic, if it is found, will become the property of the Hopi. I recommend you offer it to the Project TIME museum in Alamogordo—at a price to be determined by your people."

Finally the president spoke to Darren. "Dr. Stewart, you will direct the excavation efforts, taking care to preserve any historical artifact. If a ship is found, you will see that it is removed from the pathway of the pipeline in an expeditious manner—no longer than a month."

"But, Mr. President—"

"No 'buts', Dr. Stewart. You'll figure something."

"Sir, if we find the ship, we know its size will be enormous. Moving it will be a major undertaking, certainly requiring more than a month."

"We don't have the luxury of giving you more time. U.S. citizens are being killed over water. We face the very real risk of military conflict between our own forces. We must do everything possible to mitigate the problem, even if it means losing some history. If that ship is found and is not out of the way in a month from this very minute, Mr. Davis has the full permission of this commission to proceed with the demolition of the obstruction. Am I clear?"

"Very clear, Sir."

"Now, there remains one detail," the president said. "For this work to go forward successfully, Mr. Davis and Dr. Stewart must put aside their differences and work together. For that to be possible, I ask that you apologize to each other and agree to move forward."

Neither man jumped to his feet. A tense silence prevailed while each waited for the other to move. The president unfolded his hands and placed them on the table. Scooting his chair backward, he rose. He looked back and forth at each man. Still no move from either. The president turned his palms upward and gestured for each to rise.

"Come on," he said.

Darren drew his feet underneath him to rise and at the same time Jackson Davis stood. The men walked toward each other on the president's side of the table and paused in front of him, facing each other. The president placed a hand on each man's shoulder. Finally, they gave a subtle nod and briefly shook hands.

"I guess that'll do," the president said. "Now, I've laid out a proposal which I am prepared to stand behind. I want a gentlemen's agreement that you all will accept these terms. Otherwise, you'll have nothing."

Warren, Aaron and Tracey joined the others in standing. All shook hands with each other. Tracey gave Darren a stiff hug. The president waved goodbye and said, "I'm off to the White House. Say a prayer for our nation."

* * *

Two days later, Jackson Davis and Darren worked side by side, reviewing prints spread out on the table. Two enormous, parallel rail trestles were being constructed from the base of the mound to the center of the canyon. One thousand feet in length, each rail was designed to hold a series of heavy, iron cradles on trunions. The cradles would hold mega-tons of weight, yet roll with precision smoothness when towed by a powerful winch.

A modular power plant complete with a steam-driven generator was en route and scheduled to be on-line in 10 days. The electricity from the plant would provide power for the whole area.

An army of Navajo men, soon to be joined by Hopis, were hand-excavating the northern face of the knoll, taking care to avoid damaging anything that might lie inside.

Jackson looked out the window. "All this based on little more than a premonition," he said.

"Look, I don't like this working relationship any more than you do," Darren replied. "When we're done, I don't plan to ever see you again. But for now, we have a common goal. You and I better pull this off or Earlman will have both our asses."

A radio inside the shack kept both men abreast of the news. No shots had yet been exchanged on either of the Wyoming or Texas borders, thanks to the discipline of the troops and their commanders, but the stand-off continued. The White House and the two governors were scrambling to prevail over each other, using an armada of attorneys and the public media. A Supreme Court panel of Justices had agreed for the court to hear the case.

"Makes our differences seem petty," Darren said.

Aaron burst through the door and ran into the room. "It's there! We've uncovered a part of the ship! Come see!"

All three rushed to the site. Darren scampered down into the excavation, Jackson following. Warren stood aside for the men. A four-foot area of the ship's exterior had been exposed. The surface consisted of a slate-gray material with a matte finish, untarnished by years of being buried.

Darren rubbed it with his hands, amazed by its texture. Jackson traced his fingertips along the surface. "You go get word to President Earlman," he said to Darren. "I'll tend to the job here."

Darren ran back to the shack and placed a call to the former president.

"Earlman here, Dr. Stewart. What do you need?"

"We found the ship, Sir! It's there!"

"Okay, get it out, now. We need that pipeline. We're sitting on a powder keg, a big one."

"Yes, Sir, we're getting it uncovered."

* * *

The pace of the excavation accelerated. Darren remained in the hole and supervised the removal of dirt and rocks from the exposed wall of the ship, taking extreme care not to damage the surface. Bucket brigades of Navajo workers removed heavy rocks, one at a time, from the top. Jackson Davis provided oversight for the assembly of the power plant and construction of the rails and trunions. He had also brought together a small city of construction trailers to be used as offices and residences.

About a hundred yards of the ship's perimeter had been cleared of its cover. The surface, with as of yet no seam, opening, antenna or other device in sight, yielded no clue of the ship's orientation. Based on measurements taken from the curvature now visible, Darren estimated the ship's diameter to be in the range of 300 feet and its height to be 75 feet or so. He roughed out some additional numbers, based on his knowledge of aircraft sizes and weights, and shook his head at the results.

Three million pounds. Fifteen hundred tons. This thing's a monster. Six times the empty weight of a Boeing 747 and about the same as that of a WWII naval destroyer. Darren studied the rail structure now beginning to take shape. *We're right at the design limit, and my numbers at best are only guesses.*

His mental calculations were interrupted by a yell from Aaron. Darren stared in the direction of his shout and saw him studying some kind of inscription that had become exposed. Darren scrambled to the spot. He knew name of the ship in the museum—*The Spirit of the Ages*—was positioned above the viewing ports and to the left of the main entry. Darren called several men to come join the work in the area of the letters becoming visible. Within a few minutes of frantic effort, the full name could be seen.

"What does it say, Dr. Stewart?" Aaron asked.

"I have no idea. I believe it's in the Pangaean language. I'll need to get Tracey to help translate it. She's fluent in Pangaean, but I'm not sure even she can decipher written text."

Darren flipped his phone open and called Tracey, who was in Gallup picking up some needed supplies. The news excited her. "I'll be there in about three hours. Keep the news crews away. We don't want to let them scoop President Earlman."

* * *

Jenna walked down the rows of trailers, searching for Dwy's temporary residence. She brought with her a basket filled with food, drinks and dessert. She knocked on his door and heard the clump-thump, clump-thump of his walking cast and crutches as he approached from the other side. He opened the door and waved her in. She placed the food on the table, arranged the tableware and invited him to sit. Dwy touched her shoulders from behind and turned her toward him. She put her arms around him. He dropped his crutches with a clatter, pulled her to him and gave her a sensual kiss, one that led to a full-bodied embrace.

She broke away, taking deep breaths in between her words. "Uh ... don't you think we should ... eat first?"

"No."

"But your cast. Won't it be awkward?"

"It comes off."

Dwy led her to his bedroom, arm around her shoulders to steady himself as he walked beside her. Once there, he sat her on the bed and began to remove her blouse. She resisted for a moment then pulled his shirt over his head.

"Are you sure about this?" she asked.

"Yes."

"Me, too!"

CHAPTER TWENTY-ONE

A MYTH UNRAVELED

By the time Tracey got to the excavation, the shadows were lengthening. In the dimming light she studied the enigmatic characters etched in the ship's wall. Their clarity and intensity varied, making the process of translation difficult. Tracey frowned; two of the letters had been eroded by something, perhaps the scouring action of the desert sand during the landing. They were indistinct and nearly unreadable. She counted the letters—six, or maybe even seven—and concluded the name might consist of one or two words. It had been years since she had worked with the written form of the Pangaean language. She pursed her lips and exhaled while she racked her brain to remember the letters. Darren knew better than to press her by asking any questions.

"Their alphabet contained seventeen letters, but their language was tonal, meaning any single letter could represent several different ones, depending upon the pitch used when pronouncing it."

"I don't understand," Darren said.

"Take our letter 'A'. It is a single letter. But if it were like the Pangaean 'A', it could represent an 'A$_1$' or an 'A$_2$' or maybe even an 'A$_3$' depending on the pitch used when it is spoken. So when it's written, the pitch is lost, and you have to determine whether it is an A$_1$, A$_2$ or A$_3$ by its context."

"Sounds difficult."

"It is, but we have some examples in English. Does the written word 'lead' mean a heavy metal or does it mean to provide direction? You can't tell from the word itself, you have to read it in context. Even then, with some words the meaning can be ambiguous and confusing. That's why it is easier to understand spoken language rather than read it."

"Can I help?"

"I'm afraid not. Let me work with this a bit more, and then I may bounce some ideas off of you."

"I know what it says," Darren said.

"No you don't."

"Yes I do. The name contains two words and totals seven letters."

"You don't."

"Try me."

"Okay, what is the name?"

"Big Ship!"

"Get out of here and leave me alone," Tracey said with a child's giggle, one that Darren had missed for a long time. "Better yet, go to my trailer and bring me my camera. I want pictures of this."

* * *

Spencer arrived at the site the next morning at Darren's request. Spencer's experience in the relocation and mounting of the smaller time-ship at the museum would be invaluable. After walking the area and reviewing the construction plans, Spencer met with Darren and Jackson.

"Damn, that thing's huge," Spencer said. "Looks to be twice the size of ours in the museum."

"Once we have it released from the ground, we're going to pull it along those rails to this docking platform," Darren said, pointing to an area on the blueprint. "The rails have a three-degree negative slope to provide a little assistance from gravity. The ship will end up on a platform centered in Kutz Canyon, about 75 feet above its floor."

"You better have some pretty massive buffer stops at the end of the rails in case that bastard gets away from you and starts to coast."

"We couldn't build them big enough. We're going to have to rely on the brakes on the trunion rollers to keep it under control."

"Just the same, I wouldn't want to be stationed at the end of the rails. Who's going to supervise the move?"

"You."

"Who do I quit to?" Spence asked, only partially in jest.

* * *

Tracey downloaded the pictures she had taken. She processed the photographs with top-of-the-line photo software left over from her press secretary days. Adjusting the exposure, contrast, brightness and other properties, she improved the readability of most of the letters. A couple remained illegible, and her efforts to decipher them fell short. She used the printer in the construction office to produce full-size pictures. She taped copies to the office wall in the proper order with the unreadable symbols designated by question marks:

Like trying to solve a troublesome crossword puzzle, she tried to think of Pangaean words that would result from various combinations of letters substituted for the question marks. She jotted words down on a scratch pad as soon as they came to mind. Some made no sense at all as a ship's name. Others were close but didn't seem right, either.

Frustrated, Tracey paced the floor, rubbing her aching temples. Then a word burst through her subconscious. She turned the sheets of paper over that had the question marks on them and used a marker to scribble the missing letters:

PORTAL! she thought. *The ship's name is "PORTAL." They named it for its ability to travel through time.*

Tracey got her phone and screamed for Darren. "I've got it! I know the name!"

In a few minutes Darren broke through the door, out of breath from running from the excavation site. Once inside, he froze in awe, looking at the papers Tracey had pinned to the wall.

"PORTAL," Tracey said. "It's named after a time portal."

"Yeah, but I still can't make out the letters."

"They're Pangaean," Tracey said.

"Pronounce the word."

"I haven't tried, yet. Let me talk you through the letters before we try the word." Tracey walked to the posted papers. "The first is the Pangaean soft 'C', like in 'Cicero.' The second one is a short 'I'. The next two letters must be combined through tonality into 'pah.' And the last two also must be combined into—"

"—pooh," Darren completed her sentence. A sense of wonder overcame him and he sat on one of the stools by a drawing board. "Cih-pah-pooh."

"Right," Tracey said. "It stands for portal."

"It's much more than that," Darren said, now fully comprehending the significance of the name. "Cih-pah-pooh is a word in the emergence myth of the Anasazi: they believe they came to the surface of the earth through an opening called a sipapu. Not an opening in the *ground*, but an ancient ship that traveled through an opening in *time*—a time portal. A ship that came from an advanced civilization that lived underground with no illness or strife. The Pangaeans were that civilization. They lived 200 million years ago in Antarctica in the southern hemisphere—'down under' as the Australians refer to it—or underground as indigenous cultures knew it."

"So the myth is true?" Tracey asked.

"True, but not in the sense we've always imagined; even more sacred. The Pangaeans who crash-landed here left the ship and journeyed south until they found a suitable place to live: Chaco Canyon. The path they traveled became a spiritual route, The Great North Road. The ship became a sacred shrine, the *sipapu*. Centuries passed and the Pangaeans, stripped of their technological infrastructure, became the Anasazi—The Ancient Ones. Out of reverence they enhanced and built up the road that led to their point of origin. That's why it seems over-designed. It had not been constructed for traffic; it commemorated their *origins*. To protect their ship from discovery by their enemies, the Anasazi covered it stone by stone, using brigades of men, women and children in the reverse manner we're employing to unearth it today.

Symbolically, once buried in stones, the Anasazi knew they could never use the ship to return to Pangaea but must instead adapt to their severe surroundings to survive. It wasn't a coyote that covered the opening and forced a change in their culture; the Anasazi did it themselves." Darren paused a few moments, letting it all sink in. "I can't wait to talk with Aaron about this. He'll give up his Aaron identity and become Eagle permanently."

"Eagle? Not Eagle-To-The-Clouds?"

"Eagle and I came to an understanding. I'll tell you about it sometime soon."

CHAPTER TWENTY-TWO

RELOCATION

Two weeks later, as a result of 24-hour shifts of work under construction lights and using energy from the modular power plant, the ship had been fully excavated. The rail trestle and the winch system were ready for use. The cradles underneath the ship were being raised by hydraulic jacks. Spence had taken the primary role in preparing the ship for its relocation, leaving Jackson to focus on resuming pipeline work, once the ship had been moved safely out of the way. Load cells on each cradle transmitted data to a central control station, and the total load had to remain below the design limit on the rail system.

Darren popped a stick of gum in his mouth, worried that the ship would prove to be too heavy to move.

"We're already above our estimate of 1,500 tons and this monster hasn't budged. Take it easy. We're getting close to the limit."

Spence, stationed beneath the ship, nodded his head. He gave continuous hand signals to the operator of the jacking system, a fingertip in the air, circling, now slower than before. The sound began as a loud rumble, more felt than heard. Creaks and metallic screeches followed, punctuated by a series of ear-splitting cracks. Spence gave a cut-off signal with his hand.

"Stop," he screamed. He walked the length of the ship between the rails, looking up at the hull for problems. The noise subsided, and quiet returned. Spence waited a few minutes and became satisfied that the sounds were normal. He gave a go-ahead signal. Darren called out readings as the load on the jacks approached the limit. The groans and shrieks began again, sounding like whales calling each other—except at an octave or two lower. The sound waves exerted a physical pressure on the people around the ship. The noise grew to a deafening level, forcing Spence to cover his ears. A horrendous boom caused everyone to jump. Two others quickly followed. After the booms, the load readings ceased climbing and held constant as the jacks continued to rise. "Darren, I think she just popped free. We'll stop here and let things stabilize while we take a final look."

Darren joined Spence under the ship. He saw a huge, ragged gouge in the hull that began at the ship's front and continued along most of the underside, leaving a streak of black.

"That's where she must have hit Shiprock Peak. Look at the damage."

"Pretty bad," Spence said, "but the hull retained its integrity. I don't see any seams opened up or any splits or cracks. I can't wait to open the hatch and get inside."

"Not until we get the ship out of the way, and then only after we build an air lock to enter. Can't take a chance of contaminating anything in the interior. We'll have to wear filtered air masks, too. Remember what happened to the explorers who entered the tomb of King Tut without any protection? They were exposed to killer viruses. Any micro-organisms inside this thing have had a thousand years to fester into something nasty."

Darren and Spence walked the short distance to the control station and made a quick review of the data being transmitted.

"Looks good, Darren." Staring at the ship, Spence was impressed by how well it had held up in the desert air, protected by its stone casing. "You know, if we could find what problem brought this ship down and get it fixed, I'll bet it would still fly."

"I intend to give you that chance, Spence, but not a word to anyone."

Spence's face turned into an expression of pure shock. He had only been kidding about flying, but he knew Darren wasn't.

* * *

Exhausted from the day's work, Darren entered Tracey's trailer. "Anybody home?"

"In the bedroom."

Darren walked to her, and she greeted him with a hug. Over her shoulder, he saw her laptop and carry-on bag packed and lying on the bed.

"Traveling?" he asked.

"Earlman called earlier this evening. He's requesting an emergency meeting of the commission in D.C. to brief President Mitchell on possible options for defusing some of the tensions at the center of the standoff."

"You should have some good news for him. Looks like the pipeline project will be able to get back on schedule. We'll start moving the ship tomorrow. If all goes well, we should be finished before you get back."

Tracey backed away from her embrace, an expression of chagrin crossing her face. "Good news, yes, but it's not enough. The commission's recommendations won't get the job done, even if every one of our projects is a success. We don't have a good answer for President Mitchell."

"You know it doesn't make sense to shore up L.A. and the rest of the Western Slope with a bundle of costly, bureaucratic projects that will only make the failure bigger when it occurs."

"I've tried to make that case with Earlman, but ... although he listens ... he refuses to buy it."

"Then tell him that after you get back, you and I are going to take a little journey to help him with his decision."

Tracey stared at Darren. She had been married to him too long to believe he meant anything other than exactly what he said.

"Where are we going?"

"Chaco."

"But we've been there."

"Not really."

Darren took her hand and said, "Before you go, we need to talk."

"Yes, we do."

"I made a mistake. A big one."

"Yes, you did."

"There are only two people I love in the world. You and our son. In trying to respect Dwy's wishes, I betrayed your trust."

"I lost my confidence in you, and we almost lost our son."

Darren lowered his head. Her words hurt.

"I'm sorry," he said.

"But you found him when no one else could. You saved his life. Then you risked your own confronting a man we both hate. When I saw you on TV out there on top of that hill laced with explosives, I realized I had played a role in this whole situation, too. I didn't handle Davis very well, either. I'm sorry, too."

Darren pulled her to him and kissed her. He held her close for a moment. "Okay, Trace, there will be no more talk of mountains. We've faced more than our share, and we're going to come out fine."

* * *

Late that evening, Skeeter picked his way through the rubble surrounding the ship. Using a hammer and chisel borrowed from WSP, he plinked and chinked away at the stones. Soon, he began humming. He labeled the samples and crammed them into a tool pouch that soon took on the over-extended shape of a squirrel's cheeks, stuffed with nuts. When Skeeter reached the ship's main entry, he rested a moment on a boulder. Something on the ground beneath the door caught his eye, a partially exposed slab with strange lines on it. He walked to it and knelt to examine it closer. He brushed the sand away like an umpire clearing home plate. *I'll be damned—a petroglyph. Looks like a marker of some kind. Been buried all these years.* Skeeter cocked his head from one side to another, trying to make out the faint figures carved in the slab. *I'll get Aaron. He'll know what it means.*

* * *

At sunrise the next morning, Spence positioned himself between the front cradles underneath the ship. From his vantage point, when he looked down the rails, he could see their lines converging on the platform 1,000 feet away and 30 feet lower that was to be the ship's destination. Two three-inch diameter, high-strength, braided steel cables connected each of the front cradles to a winch located at the far end of the rails.

Spence viewed the panorama around him. In the distance he could see the control station, where Darren was monitoring the move. Both men were in contact by radio.

A scattering of spectators stood outside the perimeter fence, and the news chopper, back from Texas, circled overhead. Spence took in a deep breath.

"Okay, Darren, let's take up the strain on the cables. Do it easy, man."

Spence fingered a flare gun, holstered on his waist, assuring himself he could draw it and fire it if necessary. The flare gun represented a last-ditch, emergency shut-down signal in case radio communications failed for some reason. Spence eyed the bail-out path he had chosen. *If I have to fire that flare, I'll do it in mid-air on my way out of here.*

Spence could see heavy black smoke from the engine on the winch. The cables tightened until they became snug.

"Whoa!" Spence radioed.

He stepped to the side of the cradle and pressed his ear and cheek against the support housing. Making certain his body was clear of any of the moving mechanism, he gave the go-ahead.

Again he saw the plume of black smoke; the noise from the motor's acceleration reached him a second later. The cables tightened, making a sound like a humongous guitar string being plucked and tightened with the tuning key. The engine reached its maximum torque, placing an enormous strain on the cables.

"Keep pulling!" Spence called. He could detect no movement and began to worry that the machine didn't have enough pulling power. Then, a slight shudder. His ear picked up a squeal like a rail car's brakes. Another shudder. Then motion!

"It's moving. Back off the torque!" Spence yelled. Now that the ship had broken loose, the trick was to keep it from accelerating and sliding out of control down the slight grade.

"Remember, no more than a foot a minute. Anything more and we will have to jam on the brakes."

Spence didn't want to resort to that. The cradles didn't have any brakes in the normal sense. The braking was sacrificial. Huge, hydraulic-driven clamps, when activated, would grip the rails and lock closed. Once applied, the brakes could not be released. Worse, their application would most likely damage the trunion rollers beyond repair.

Spence listened to Darren on the radio, calling out the velocity numbers.

"Five inches per minute ... six ... six ... seven ..."

"That's too much. Keep reducing the pull. She's beginning to coast downhill," Spence screamed.

The smoke from the exhaust stack changed to white, signifying the engine had been shifted into neutral.

"Seven inches per minute ... eight ... nine," Darren called.

"Darren, get ready to brake. Don't let the speed get above twelve."

Darren flipped open the hinged cover over the brake button. "I won't let that happen," he said, his hand trembling. "Ten ... eleven ... eleven ... looks like it's going to max out at eleven inches per minute, Spence."

Spence exhaled. He touched the cradle housing and felt no unusual vibration. *Seems pretty smooth.* "Let her slow to six inches per minute, Darren, then apply minimum torque. Try to stabilize the speed around eight. Things look fine here. I've got a crew of men walking along each cradle watching and listening for any trouble. I'm coming in to join you."

A few minutes later, Spence joined Darren in the control station and anxiously scanned the computer monitors. Things looked fine. One of the two TV screens on the main console showed a wide-angle view of the ship's journey. The other screen provided close-up pictures of each cradle, rotating through each of the eight stations in succession.

Darren glanced at his watch. "If all goes well, we should travel the 1,000 feet in about 12 hours. Not a bad speed for a ship that once took 200 million years to get here from Pangaea, eh, Spence?"

"If all goes well."

* * *

En route to D.C. and awaiting her connection in Denver, Tracey elbowed her way through the crowd surrounding the TV screen until she could see the image being projected. In the aerial view taken from the helicopter, the time-ship seemed to be motionless, midway along its route. But the announcer assured the television audience it was moving. She watched the drama in fascination. *I hope President Earlman's seeing this. He took a big risk to help me. This wouldn't be happening without his intervention.*

She boarded her flight and settled in her seat, mentally sifting through the points she planned to make with President Earlman. Once in the air, she watched the monitor on the partition in front of the cabin as it gave updates about the time-ship's relocation.

Tracey smiled. Any good news would provide a welcome distraction from the tense situation at the Texas border, a stand-off that had the potential to escalate into military action at any moment.

You go, Darren. You keep making this woman proud of you—and deliriously in love with you. You just wait until I get back.

* * *

Skeeter caught up with Aaron. With the time-ship safely away from the area, he led Aaron to his discovery. Pointing to the slab of rock, he watched Aaron study its surface.

"See, Aaron. It's like I told you. What does it mean?"

Aaron looked at the figures carved into the rock. He rose to a standing position and turned to the north, lifting his face toward the sky. Skeeter remained silent, waiting for Aaron to speak.

"It's a memorial. It gives thanks to the heavens for those who survived and commemorates those who did not. This is a most sacred place. Respected Spirits are all around me. I am empowered by their collective will. This is the point of my origin. It is here my ancestors first stepped to the ground. I am grateful to them."

Aaron motioned for Skeeter to stand next to him. He explained that the figures carved into the slab above the horizontal line represented those who had survived. Those below the line had not. A small circle at the center of the line represented the portal they came through. Tears streamed down Aaron's cheeks.

"This stone must never be moved. It is hallowed ground."

* * *

Late in the afternoon, Darren and Spence slowed the time-ship's progress as it closed the distance to its final docking point. With inches to go, they reduced the torque on the winch to zero. The cradles reached the stops at the end of the rails, and the ship's momentum caused it to sway forward a few degrees before it finally rocked back and halted.

"Lock her down!" Darren shouted.

Crews scrambled to each cradle and bolted huge chocks in place, securing the ship. Once they were done, Darren and Spence watched the monitors in silence, on alert for any motion. None seen, they turned to each other and for the first time that day, showed their emotions.

"It's finished!" Darren shook Spence's hand, pounding him on the back with his other hand. "You did it! Way to go!"

Spence, caught off guard by Darren's excitement, responded by clapping his boss on his shoulder and shouting with joy. After a minute or two, they both calmed down, a little embarrassed by their display in front of the others in the room.

"Okay, everybody," Darren said, "back to business. Set up the security perimeter around the ship. No one gets close without my authorization."

* * *

President Mitchell addressed the Earlman Commission with a stern face. The members knew without being told that he was not pleased.

"You've taken six months, studied this situation to death, put together a list of projects that would make FDR's programs seem minuscule, and you tell me you can't provide sufficient water to L.A. to keep it viable?"

"No, Sir," former President Earlman responded.

"There's a war brewing along the Texas border. American citizens are being killed. Other states are threatening to join with Texas in a blockade against westerners returning across the divide—and this is the best you can do?"

President Earlman nodded, his gaze shifting away from the president. "I'd go stand on the border myself, Sir, as would all the commission members. I'd stand with you anywhere, but I won't lie to you. There's not enough water, Sir. It may be time for you to accept that premise. It took me way too long, myself."

No one spoke. President Mitchell rested his chin in his hands. "What about the WSP project?"

"It should be pumping water within a week, 10 days at the most. They are installing the last section of line now. But it won't be enough."

"What do you recommend?"

"My commission needs a new objective. How do we shift our population away from the areas that don't have sufficient water? We're not the first civilization that has been in this position."

Tracey listened in amazement. Had he really reached that conclusion?

"No other alternative, as far as you're concerned?" President Mitchell asked.

"Pray that the drought is ended. At least that would buy us some time."

President Mitchell clenched his jaw and drummed the fingertips of one hand on his desk, leafing through the commission's report with the other. He shook his head, slammed the report on his desk, and stood.

"I will not accept this report, President Earlman," President Mitchell said. "You have six weeks to bring me back recommendations that will work. If you can't do that, I will disband this commission and appoint one that can."

CHAPTER TWENTY-THREE

REFITTING THE PORTAL

A few weeks later, Darren and Spence stood inside the air-lock at the main entrance to the time-ship. Clad in full biological suits, complete with self-contained breathing equipment, they waited until the pressure inside the air-lock became slightly negative. Spence had a tool pouch filled with pry bars and other items that might be necessary to break open the hatch. In addition to the video camera strapped around his neck, Darren carried a bucket full of sample bottles. Both men turned on their flashlights.

"Ready?" Darren asked Spence.

"Let's do it."

"We're going in," Darren spoke into the transmitter inside his helmet.

Spence raised the cover over the latch and grabbed the handle of the locking mechanism. He gave it a tug, expecting it to be frozen. To his surprise, it moved with little resistance, and clicked into the "open" position. Spence stepped back from the hatch. Nothing happened.

"No juice," Darren said. "Couldn't expect the ship's energy cells to store electricity for a thousand years. Try the hand-crank."

Spence turned the wheel next to the latch. Darren saw the hatch begin to open inward. A rush of air gushed from the ship's interior, drawn by the lower pressure in the air-lock.

"That's it," Darren said. "It's coming. Keep it up."

Spence cranked until the hatch completely opened. Both men peered inside. Darren probed the darkness with his flashlight. He saw the ship's control console. Holding the light alongside the camera, Darren videoed the interior. All appeared to be pristine.

Using sampling tubes to test the atmosphere, Darren checked the oxygen level and verified the absence of common toxic chemicals.

"Seems okay, but keep your mask on. You follow me."

The two men stepped inside, leery of possible surprises. Spence approached the control panel, sweeping the instruments and controls with his light.

"About the same as ours at the museum. Some differences, but not many."

Spence sat in the commander's chair and stared toward the view ports, their electro-chromic glass now opaque due to a lack of applied voltage.

"Get some power to this thing, and it'll fly. More fun than that simulator back at the museum," he said.

"Remember, something brought them down. From the way they left things, it looks like they thought they could make repairs and continue their journey. For some reason, they didn't."

The alarm sounded on Darren's air tank, signaling he had approximately 20 minutes of air remaining.

"Time to go, Spence. Enough for today. Next time, we'll have power."

The men left the ship and closed the hatch behind them. Once the access elevator reached the ground, they stepped out into the desert sun, temporarily blinded by its brilliance.

* * *

Illuminated by banks of high-intensity construction lights, the time-ship's imposing image became surreal after dark as crews of technicians, under Spence's direction, checked out its systems. Auxiliary power surged through the ship, provided by an umbilical cord of electrical cable. Weary and frustrated after months of work, Spence, spoke with the engineers. His original theory about a quick fix of the problem that brought the ship to a crash landing had proven to be wrong. Spence approached Darren to brief him on the situation.

"Darren, the rotor in the inertial compensation system failed, and the whole unit disintegrated. That's what brought them down. We might be able to reconstruct those mechanical components, but shrapnel took out three banks of computer-driven electronic controls. The inertial system's computers are fried, and we have no prints or even the design basis for the controls. We don't have sufficient knowledge of the technology to make repairs. We've been trying, but we're like cavemen rebuilding an airliner's instrument console. It's not going to happen."

Darren knew the impact of Spence's report. Without the inertial system, the ship would never get off the ground. It might take a decade or more to develop the capability to make repairs. His dream of flying the ship had been dashed.

"How's everything else?" he asked.

"Showroom condition," Spence said. "They knew how to build things to last."

Darren walked to the row of view ports, now transparent because of a voltage applied, and stared outside. He could see the pipeline in the distance and knew that water now coursed through it on its way to L.A. The thought of Jackson Davis successfully completing the project angered Darren. *I took a stand on principle, risked everything, and for what? This bird that won't fly ... a complex mechanical behemoth that is as earthbound as some stupid ostrich?*

Darren turned back to Spence. "Okay, isolate the inertial system from everything else. We don't want any cross-connections that would interfere or cause further damage. We'll put a team of scientists together and begin working on the solution. Come on, let's call it a day."

"Not so fast, Darren, there's something else you need to see."

Spence led Darren to a screen in the navigation portion of the ship's instrument panel. He brought it to life by tapping it with his finger tip. He whizzed through data entry, responding to requests for information as each new screen popped up. After a few moments, he paused, satisfied with the result. "Look at this," he said.

Darren studied the monitor. The screen displayed a myriad of white dots of differing sizes and intensities. A dot at the very center was surrounded by an orange, logarithmic spiral that extended to the edge of the display. A green line at an angle to the horizon intersected the dot. One of the smaller dots in the lower right portion of the screen was surrounded by a small, blue ellipse. He could understand some of the graphics, but not any of the captions, since they were in the Pangaean language. "Is it a star map?" he asked.

"Watch," Spence said. He tapped in a few commands and the display became animated. The dot in the center progressed along the band of the spiral. The green line slowly rotated around the dot as it moved. The ellipse spun around the smaller dot at a rate that made it almost a blur. The millions of other dots slowly changed their positions with respect to each other. The motion was hypnotic.

"A star map used for navigation?" Darren asked.

"You're close. Add the fourth dimension."

The realization hit Darren, stunning him. His heart rate rose, and he inhaled several times to catch his breath. He now knew what his old friend Dwyer meant when referring to the lost time-ship. He said, "Find it and you will discover the secret of our origins."

"It's a map used for navigation with a galactic clock to measure elapsed time during time travel," Darren said.

"Tell me more, so I'll know that wasn't just a good guess."

Darren explained that the dots were indeed stars. As the ship traveled through time, the stellar positions changed. The dot on the spiral represented the exact center of the Milky Way, with the green line being the axis of the galaxy. The ellipse represented the solar system, the dot at its center being the sun. The ellipse rotated some 26,000 times for each revolution of the galaxy's axis.

"It's like a stellar GPS. They used navigational fixes from stars instead of from satellites to determine their position. But they added the fourth dimension. Instead of a watch or calendar to tell time, they tracked galactic alignments, each one representing a span of 26,000 years."

Darren's mind raced on. *Our watches use a quartz crystal to establish a constant frequency. The Anasazi used the precession of the earth's axis as the basis for their measurement of elapsed time.* Darren remembered Aaron's comment about the fire-ship legend and how it "traveled through the skies as the stars changed overhead." *That's what he meant. The ship was a time traveler.* Darren recognized that the dot's position on the spiral represented the cumulative time that had passed so the travelers could always tell their exact position in time.

"Wait a minute," Darren said. "I think this answers the clue Dwyer left for us. The spiral originates at the center of the galaxy. The last thing he told me was that the Pangaeans believed they came from the stars. Not from the Pleiades star cluster—they're too young—but instead from a star in the very center of our galaxy, an undiscovered star that's obscured in the blackness of the Dark Rift."

"I think you're right," Spence said.

But Darren hadn't finished his thought yet. *The Gate of the Spirits glyph had a spiral carved around the hole at the center that aligned with the winter solstice sun. The spiral in petroglyphs is known to represent a migration or ...*

"My God," Darren said, "the Anasazi used this navigation equipment for their time travel, but when the batteries on the ship drained, the system became useless. That's why they created the Gate of the Spirits glyph. The spiral on that glyph represents their origins. They could predict when the next galactic alignment would take place, and how far in time they were away from it. Hoping for rescue, they were prepared to tell their rescuers exactly where they could be found in time."

"Do you think they were rescued?" Spence asked. "Is that why they vanished without a trace of where they went?"

"Perhaps, but the only way to know for sure would be to have been there when they disappeared. They knew years in advance that something was going to happen. They bricked their pueblo closed as if to preserve it for the ages after they left."

"Well, since we weren't there, I guess we'll never know for sure," Spence said.

Spence's comment caused Darren's mind to swirl, thoughts cascading through his head about possible solutions to the enigma about the fate of the Anasazi.

* * *

Darren lay awake that night with Tracey snuggled against him and asleep in his arms. Tortured by conflicting emotions, he couldn't sleep. Disappointment from the ship's inability to fly overwhelmed him. Forced to leave the ship in place, he could try to make it a scientific attraction, but that didn't excite him, either. *Too remote. Few people would ever see it and marvel at the civilization that built it and even more important, appreciate the colonists who flew it and the culture they spawned.*

Offsetting his disappointment were enticing thoughts about being close to unraveling the mystery about the disappearance of the Anasazi. Darren knew that Eagle and Jane Bowen—his professor friend in the field of archeo-astronomy—would share his enthusiasm about the prospects of filling in a gap in the history of the Chaco culture.

Darren worried that Tracey might be devastated by the commission's demise. She hadn't said much about it, but her mood had been somber ever since she returned from D.C. Darren stroked her hair, not waking her, but feeling the closeness that had been missing from both their lives. His mind returned to Pangaea and reflections of the trip he and she had taken together.

Then the idea came to him, startling in its simplicity, yet offering the possibility of an enormous impact. Before he could process it further, he fell into the abyss of a deep sleep.

CHAPTER TWENTY-FOUR

THE JOURNEY HOME

Darren awoke at sunrise the next morning and rustled Tracey out of bed. Over coffee he told her about his idea. His enthusiasm caught on with her, and they talked about the steps necessary to develop a plan.

"I've got people to get lined up," Darren said. "I'll go to Chaco today and see if Jane will come with us. I think she'll jump at the opportunity. Then there's Eagle … and Spence."

"I'll call Earlman. He'll want to know. The least I can do is fill him in."

Then a look of concern crossed Tracey's face. "Darren, I'm not sure I can go through the effects of being a passenger in a time-ship again. I came close to losing it the last time I rode in one."

"Don't worry. Your disorientation and nausea came from the inertial system that's required to eliminate the ship's mass and let it fly. The ship can't fly because that system is out of commission, so it won't bother you."

Tracey looked relieved. She offered Darren another thought.

"If the ship will be staying on the ground, it should make it easier for Aaron ... uh, Eagle to get on board."

"I hadn't thought of that, but you're right."

Darren tore a page from a tablet he had been making notes on.

"Here's a list of groceries and supplies we need to take with us. I should be back by this evening. I'll make all my contacts and assemble the crew. We'll board tonight."

"Darren, what do we tell Dwy and Jenna?"

"We'll both talk to them in the morning—and Skeeter, too. Now hurry, we've got a lot to do."

* * *

The aide stationed at the president's door waved former President Earlman into the Oval Office. He greeted President Mitchell and sat on the couch across from him.

"Matt, I've been a long-time supporter of yours," President Earlman said. "I'm going to be straight with you. No one will know of this conversation but you and me, so get ready to hear from your uncle."

"I wouldn't have expected anything less, Richard," President Mitchell said with a smile. "Go on."

"The commission is named after me. When you rejected our report, it humiliated me."

President Mitchell shifted his position, seeking words to soften the personal impact on the man he most respected. But before he could respond, Earlman continued.

"But it was the right thing to do. I should have seen it coming."

Perplexed, President Mitchell listened to Earlman's words.

"My advice, Matt, is to allow attrition to take its natural course. It won't be popular. It might even cost you an election. But, it's the right thing to do. It will save the most lives in the long run. We shouldn't continue to build an infrastructure we can't sustain. You can even use my failed commission's work as political cover."

President Earlman sat back and crossed his legs, watching for a reaction. The most powerful man in the world and that man's predecessor and mentor stared at each other in silence, each mindful of the awesome responsibilities of the office.

"Would you have done it, Richard?" President Mitchell asked.

"I don't know if I could have," Earlman replied, "and I'm thankful for once that the decision is not mine to make." President Earlman stood and turned to leave. "It's yours. Good luck, my friend. I'll stand by you—whatever you do."

* * *

At sunrise, Spence began the complex process to bring the time-ship to life. His practiced hands touched the keyboard and flipped switches in a sequence he had performed on the simulator at the museum hundreds of times. Under his breath, he called out the checklist items as if there were a co-pilot to respond. He looked at the vacant seat next to him and swore to be extra careful, since he had no one to catch a mistake.

Darren had recruited both Jane and Aaron. Each walked around the cabin, Jane in awe and Aaron with concern, trying to stay out of the way. Aaron carried his duffle bag filled with shaman's clothing and the objects he needed for his rituals. Jane clutched a portfolio containing photographs of the major buildings at Chaco and of the petroglyphs found throughout the site.

Darren and Tracey gathered with Dwy and Jenna at the rear of the cabin for privacy.

"Promise me you'll return," Dwy said. "I couldn't stand the thought of losing either of you."

Dwy and his dad embraced. "Dad, come back."

Darren rested his hand on Dwy's shoulder. "Dwy, I learned that to truly love someone, you have to be able to let them go. They'll return and be stronger for it. It happened with you, although you gave us the fright of our lives, and it happened with your mother and me. I promise we'll come back, but if we don't—"

"—don't even say it, Dad. Don't go there. Just come back."

"Sorry, I'm going to say it. If we don't come back, you live out your life knowing that both your mother *and* your dad loved you. The best way for you to return that love would be to do something worthwhile—something you have a passion for. But in the meantime, Eagle has promised me he'll use his powers to somehow let you know we're all right."

"What can he do? There's no way to communicate across time."

"I don't know, but he's certain he can."

Tracey stood next to the men and put her arms around them. Dwy broke away.

"Mom, Jenna's coming to Sedona."

"Wonderful. She'll love her visit."

"No, Mom, you don't understand. Jenna's coming to Sedona—with me."

It took a moment, but Tracey realized the significance. She reached for Jenna and with her arm, pulled her into the group.

"Wonderful," she said.

* * *

Skeeter stood at the base of the elevator, awaiting Dwy and Jenna. When they appeared, he led them along the catwalk on the trestle back to level ground. They turned and watched the ship.

Within minutes, its color shifted to lighter and lighter tones of gray followed by translucence. In an instant, the ship disappeared, leaving behind a hot metallic odor immediately recognized by Skeeter.

"They're on their way," he said. "Say a prayer for their return."

A drop of something splashed against Skeeter's forehead. He held out his hand, palm upward. Another drop, then several more.

"Rain," he said in amazement. "Rain in Chaco, of all places. It's not rained here for years."

"Do you think the ship caused it?" Dwy asked.

"No," Skeeter replied, staring at rain bands on the horizon, "It may be a tease, or … or a tipping point. We'll have to see."

* * *

The journey didn't take long. For those inside the ship, only a few moments passed. A slight lurch was the only indication that anything at all had happened. Spence began shutting down the systems to leave the ship in a safe condition. Once satisfied his work had been completed, he rose from his chair and led the group to the door.

"Okay, everyone, stay together," Darren said.

"Where's Aaron?" Tracey asked, noticing his absence.

In a moment, Aaron came from behind a partition, clad in his shaman's regalia and his face painted.

"Eagle-To-The-Clouds!" Tracey shouted.

"No, Mrs. Stewart, please call me 'Eagle.' It's simpler," he said with a wink.

Spence opened the hatch, and as it rose, they all stooped to catch the first sight of their surroundings. The terrain looked the same, but with two obvious differences. Kutz Canyon had disappeared and the knoll had returned. Darren led the group out the hatch and onto the surface of the ground. They walked toward the knoll.

"Don't get any closer," Darren said. "The original ship's still buried there." He looked over his shoulder to the time-ship that had brought them back to Chaco. "After we excavated the ship and moved it to the center of the canyon, I realized we could use it to return here without occupying the same space as the ship underneath the rocks. Time travel physics don't allow that to happen without catastrophic consequences."

"What's the problem with us getting any closer?" Tracey asked.

"I can't be sure that no one has anything from the ship in their pocket—a scrap of paper, some object or other piece of equipment. You may not even be aware of it yourself, but the physics would know. BOOM!" Darren said.

"Give me a few minutes while you look around," Eagle said, drawing some tools from his duffle bag. "I've got something to do."

"Just don't get too close," Darren said.

"I won't."

Darren pointed out the Great North Road to Jane. Untouched by centuries of erosion, its features were more distinct than she had ever seen. Darren heard Eagle hammering and chiseling a rock. He began to chant, his words punctuated by the clinking of the tools.

Just like Skeeter, Darren thought.

Eagle returned and rejoined them as they began walking on the road, heading south. In a few hours, they approached the edge of the sandstone cliffs above Chaco Canyon. White smoke rose from the kivas at Pueblo Bonito, in its full five-story glory. Stone cutters labored along the pueblo's walls, chipping rocks and shaping them to fit.

"They're closing up the windows. They're in the process of preparing to leave. We can finally talk to them and solve the mystery of their departure," Jane said.

"—and we can find out if the lack of water drove them to it," Tracey added.

Children played in groups around the pueblo, chasing each other through the openings and scaling the walls.

Eagle stepped to the very edge of the cliff and stood—prayer sticks outstretched—facing the people below. He began a chant that echoed across the canyon. One of the young boys below spotted him and yelled to the others, pointing out the apparition above. The men dropped their work, picked up their weapons and raced up the trail toward the top.

"Eagle, our lives are in your hands," Darren said, gathering the members of the group in a cluster. "Hopefully, the Anasazi will understand enough of your native language to regard us as friends."

"What should I say to them?"

The men topped the canyon's rim and raced toward them. Eagle began speaking in his native Hopi language. Vimmy wagged his tail, panting in excitement. The men stopped short of the group, and an impromptu standoff followed, an ancient culture encountering a modern one. One of the Anasazi spoke to Eagle. The others remained silent.

Eagle turned to Darren. "I think he understands a few words. Not many, but a few."

"Keep saying 'friend,'" Darren said.

Eagle turned back toward the men and spoke again, repeating the Hopi word for friend. Eagle laid his prayer sticks on the ground and walked toward the leader, who in turn, sheathed his knife. The two approached each other. Eagle smiled and said, "We are friends. We've come to learn. We need your help."

Vimmy could stand it no longer. He bounded toward the two men and danced around them with puppy-like abandon, barking and jumping and swishing his tail. Darren led Tracey by the hand to the Anasazi.

"Tell them," he said.

Tracey smiled and spoke in Pangaean to the Anasazi. "We are your children, and you are our ancestors."

The expressions on the faces of the Anasazi men broke into smiles of understanding.

"Welcome," the man facing Eagle said.

* * *

Skeeter led Dwy and Jenna to the petroglyph at the ship's door. He knelt and brushed the sand from the stone.

"Aaron told me to look here," he said, "And if they made it safely, he would tell us."

Dwy saw it first, then Jenna, who covered her mouth in surprise. Skeeter sat back on his haunches and said, "Well, I'll be damned."

On the stone was a carving that had not been there before. It depicted a man, a woman and a dog in front of the protection of an eagle's wings. All the figures were carved above the line.

"They made it."

MEMORIAL FLIGHT

Dwy and Jenna met Skeeter and Sandy in Gallup on the second anniversary of Darren and Tracey's departure.

"Morning, Mayor," Dwy said as he greeted Skeeter. "How's the new leader of Alamogordo doing?"

"Dwy, some days I wish I could go back to rocks. They're not as demanding," Skeeter replied. "And how about your little one?"

"Mr. Darren Tracy Stewart is doing just fine, thank you, even though he's keeping us both up at night. He's staying with a friend while we are here."

"It was nice of you to find a way to name him after both of your parents."

"With one little twist. We took the "e" out of mom's name. More appropriate for a guy—and also honors my granddad, Tracy."

"Well, your parents will both be overjoyed to see their grandson when they get back."

Dwy's expression turned somber. Jenna squeezed his hand. "Yeah, when they get back," he said.

Dwy suggested they all should have a cup of coffee while his plane was being fueled. Sandy and Jenna chatted about the new baby. Dwy scanned the cloudless sky. "The rainy times didn't last long, did they, Skeeter?"

Skeeter shook his head. "Above normal for just one season. At least long enough that President Mitchell convinced Texas and the other states to withdraw their troops and re-open their borders. Too bad he lost his bid for re-election, though."

"That guy we've got in there now, who won by promising everyone living on the Western Slope all the water they wanted without raising taxes or increasing the debt? Just shows we can't focus on long-term solutions with our cultural attention deficit disorder," Dwy said. "That's why I sold my business and Jenna and I are involved in a national water conservation movement."

"Your parents would be proud of your efforts."

"At least the rainfall gave us enough of a respite to reduce the amount water pumped through WSP's pipeline," Dwy smiled. "Speaking of that, did you hear the news last month about the mess Jackson Davis got himself into?"

"I did. I was afraid that sleazebag was going to get himself elected California's governor. Would have, too. He had a pretty good lead just before he got caught in that campaign funds scandal. Now the only term he's got to look forward to is a jail term." Jenna broke into the conversation. "Dwy, tell them about the letter you got from President Earlman yesterday."

"He sent me some words of encouragement about my parents. Said he was enjoying being out of politics and being a real uncle to all his nieces and nephews. Wanted to let us know to call him if we ever needed him."

Dwy picked up the tab for the coffee and suggested they head for his plane. In a few minutes they were all aboard and en route to Kutz Canyon. On the way, Dwy talked to Skeeter about

Warren being elected speaker for the Navajo Tribal Council and about the success he was having improving the educational and medical facilities on the reservation with the funds generated by the pipeline.

That triggered a thought with Skeeter. "Can you believe Aaron managed to sign a deal selling that ship to NASA for a hundred million dollars just before he left in it with your folks? The Hopi Nation has already started receiving payments—and NASA has no ship."

"NASA will get their ship back someday," Dwy said. *Promise me they will, Dad.*

When they reached the site of the ship's departure, Dwy flew over the launch pad and waggled the plane's wings in a salute to his dad. He blew a kiss to his mom. "Thanks for conceiving the idea for the memorial, Skeeter, especially the ship's name, *The Lost Portal*. It's the only thing that gives me hope. I come here sometimes and stand before it. I talk to both Mom and Dad—and Aaron and the others, too."

Skeeter put one of his big hands on Dwy's shoulder. "Let's go home, son. Your parents are there, just in a different time, that's all. One day that ship will pop back in sight, they'll get out and have a real adventure to tell us all. You're not going to want to miss it."

THE LOST PORTAL

—We await the safe return of these travelers—

Dr. Darren Stewart • Tracey Stewart • Aaron Eaglecloud
Professor Jane Bowen • Richard Spencer
and "Vimmy"

CPSIA information can be obtained at www.ICGtesting.com
Printed in the USA
LVOW041305030412

275935LV00001B/23/P